The Battle of Dorking &
When William Came

George Tomkyns Chesney (1830–95), born into a distinguished military family, entered the Bengal Engineers as a second lieutenant in 1848. After outstanding service in India he was recalled to England in 1870 and charged with the founding of the Royal Indian Civil Engineering College at Staines in Middlesex. In February 1871 he sent John Blackwood an outline for a short story. This became *The Battle of Dorking: Reminiscences of a Volunteer* which appeared anonymously in the May number of *Blackwood's Edinburgh Magazine* in 1871.

Recalled to India in 1881, he served with great distinction and became Military Member of the Governor-General's Council in 1886. He finally left India as General Sir George Tomkyns Chesney in 1892, and in that year he was elected Member of Parliament (Conservative) for Oxford. He is remembered to this day in the award of the Sir George Chesney Gold Medal. The first award went to Captain A. T. Mahan USN, May 1900.

Hector Hugh Munro ('Saki') was born in Akyab, Burma, 18 December 1870, and was killed in action during the assault on Beaumont Hamel, 14 November 1916. He had considerable experience as a foreign correspondent for the *Morning Post* (Balkan War of 1902–3: Warsaw, St Petersburg, Paris from 1904 to 1906). He was one of the more original writers of his time, with a gift for the witty, ingenious, and satirical stories found in *The Chronicles of Clovis* (1911), *Beasts and Super-Beasts* (1914). His two full-length narratives, *The Unbearable Bassington* (1912) and *When William Came* (1913), are characteristic of Saki's search for his own true self in Murrey Yeovil and in Comus Bassington.

I. F. Clarke ended a varied teaching career as the Foundation Professor of English Studies in the University of Strathclyde (1958–81). He pioneered the study of future-war fiction with his book *Voices Prophesying War: 1644–1984* (2nd edn., 1992). His anthology, *The Tale of the Next Great War: 1871–1914* (1995), is the first in the five-volume series *Future-war Fiction: 1763–2001*.

The Battle of Dorking

George Tomkyns Chesney

— *&* —

When William Came

Saki

Introduced by

I. F. Clarke

Oxford   New York

OXFORD UNIVERSITY PRESS

1997

Oxford University Press, Great Clarendon Street, Oxford OX2 6DP

Oxford New York
Athens Auckland Bangkok Bogota Bombay
Buenos Aires Calcutta Cape Town Dar es Salaam
Delhi Florence Hong Kong Istanbul
Karachi Kuala Lumpur Madras Madrid
Melbourne Mexico City Nairobi Paris
Singapore Taipei Tokyo Toronto

and associated companies in
Berlin Ibadan

Oxford is a trade mark of Oxford University Press

First Published as an Oxford Paperback 1997

British Library Cataloguing in Publication Data
Data available

Library of Congress Cataloging in Publication Data
Data available

ISBN 0–19–283285–9 (Pbk.)

1 3 5 7 9 10 8 6 4 2

Typeset by Best-set Typesetter Ltd., Hong Kong
Printed in Great Britain by
Mackays Ltd.
Chatham, Kent

OXFORD POPULAR FICTION

General Editor   Professor David Trotter
Associate Editor   Professor John Sutherland
Department of English, University College London

Amongst the many works of fiction that have become bestsellers and have then sunk into oblivion a significant number live on in popular consciousness, achieving almost folkloric status. Such books possess, as George Orwell observed, 'native grace' and have often articulated the collective aspirations and anxieties of their time more directly than so-called serious literature.

The aim of the Oxford Popular Fiction series is to introduce, or re-introduce, some of the most influential literary myth-makers of the last 150 years—bestselling works of British and American fiction that have helped define a new style or genre and that continue to resonate in popular memory. From crime and historical fiction to romance, adventure, and social comedy, the series will build up into a library of books that lie at the heart of British and American popular culture.

CONTENTS

INTRODUCTION

'You ask me to tell you, my grandchildren, something about my own share in the great events that happened fifty years ago. 'Tis sad work turning back to that bitter page in our history, but you may perhaps take profit in your new homes from the lesson it teaches. For us in England it came too late.'

Too late! Too late! Those melancholy words once spoke sorrow to a nation. The lamentations and the gloomy foreboding prepared millions of readers for the coming conquest of the United Kingdom foretold in *The Battle of Dorking: Reminiscences of a Volunteer*. That admonitory tale of German victories and British subjugation was an unknown soldier's response to the Franco-German War of 1870 and his unique contribution to the great debate then going on about the future of the British Army. His story proved to be the sensation of the century, long remembered for the many furious counter-attacks that followed after it first appeared in the May number of *Blackwood's Edinburgh Magazine* in 1871. In some 22,000 words an author, not practised in writing fiction, sounded a Last Post for the British Empire that alarmed the nation, angered the prime minister, astonished all Europe, and taught anxious patriots everywhere how to tell the tale of 'The Next Great War'. More than that—it was the first short story to have an instant response throughout the world. By the end of 1871 there had been overseas printings in New York and Philadelphia; Toronto (2 editions); Melbourne and Dunedin; and within months there were immediate translations into French, German, Danish, Dutch, Italian, Portuguese.

The anonymous author was Lieut.-Col. Chesney, late Bengal Engineers and later General Sir George Tomkyns Chesney, Member of Parliament for Oxford. He was the first of the paper warriors: his *Battle of Dorking* made him the founding father of a most purposive and, at times, highly effective form of fiction that has not yet ceased to describe the shape of wars-to-come—witness the two million copies and ten translations of General Sir John Hackett's *The Third World War* (1978). Chesney's story had its origin in the shock reaction to the swift, unexpected German victories in the War of Surprises in 1870.

Like most of his contemporaries he had shared Matthew Arnold's expectation of 'the French always beating any number of Germans who come into the field against them'.[1] By the end of 1870, however, the stunning German victories and the new means of warfare—the electric telegraph, breech-loading artillery, and the use of railway transportation—cast ominous shadows on the decades ahead. The *Annual Register* faithfully recorded the general sense of stupefaction: 'Only by becoming, in imagination, the readers of some historical work . . . can we form an idea of the place that must be found in the world's annals for the catastrophe of Sedan and the siege of Paris.'

In January 1871, as the German kings, princes, and grand dukes gathered at Versailles for the inauguration of the First Reich in the Galerie des Glaces, the future—of Europe, of the armed forces, and of the United Kingdom—engaged the attention of the British newspapers and journals. Ever since Edward Cardwell, one of the great military reformers, became Secretary of State for War in 1868, his plans for the reorganization of the Army had provoked intense opposition. He abolished the purchase of commissions, instituted a short service system which increased the reserve, introduced the fusion of regular, auxiliary, and reserve forces, and by these measures laid the foundations of the modern British Army.[2] The arguments about his reforms coincided with, and added to, the great debate about the future of Europe that began soon after the German Third and Fourth Armies had established their headquarters at Versailles. The nervous pointed to the well-armed and highly trained German armies. They would be more than a match for a far smaller British force, if they were ever to establish a bridgehead in the United Kingdom. Those in search of total security saw salvation in a conscript army. For them the undoubted fact of British naval superiority foundered on the ingenious supposition of 'the absence of the Fleet'. That gave Chesney a frightening opener for his tale of terror: 'the fleet was scattered abroad—some ships to guard the West Indies, others to check privateering in the China Seas, and a large part to try and protect our colonies on the Northern Pacific shore of America'.

[1] *Letters of Matthew Arnold*, ed. George W. E. Russell (London: Macmillan, 1895), i. 96.
[2] Edward Spiers, 'The Late Victorian Army: 1868–1914', in David Chandler and Ian Beckett, *The Oxford Illustrated History of the British Army* (Oxford University Press, 1994), 189–214.

On 3 January *The Times*'s military correspondent (HQ German Army of the Loire) reported that the invasion of England was 'a rather favourite topic of conversation' with German officers. Some were talking of 'a bridge of boats from Calais to Dover or thereabouts; not, of course, as the means for a first landing, but to pass over the reinforcements to a small army landed first and protected by field works'. On 9 January another writer, in the *Pall Mall Gazette*, gave his reasons for thinking that the defence forces were 'not sufficiently large or sufficiently organized to make invasion virtually impossible'. Did Chesney read those reports? He undoubtedly had the defence of the nation on his mind on 7 February, when he sent John Blackwood the outline for a short story, 'describing a successful invasion of England, and the collapse of our power and commerce in consequence'.

Ten weeks later the compositors started work on Chesney's *The Battle of Dorking*, the first entry for No. 667 of *Blackwood's Magazine*.[3] By the end of the first week in May the colonel's story had set off a series of major explosions that lasted for some four months. First, on 8 May *The Times* reacted testily with a leading article, deriding *The Battle of Dorking* and complaining it was 'really hard that the key-note of a new panic should be struck at the very moment we are doing our best, at no small cost of money and controversy, to put an end to old ones'. It was the opening round in a new kind of Press warfare, and *The Times* led the counter-attack with what was quite unusual for the old Thunderer—a short story on the topic of the day. The anonymous account of a final British victory in *The Second Armada* was a sign of vehement disapproval from *The Times*; and it was heavy gunfire from Abraham Hayward—wit, celebrated connoisseur, and a writer with a sharp pen. On 22 June a leader in *The Times* begged 'to present our readers with a sketch of an Invasion of England which, though less elaborate in description than *The Battle of Dorking*, has quite as much claim to be considered a just view of the event of such an enterprise'. It was the beginning of the counterblasts and of a very busy time for the Blackwood presses at George Street in Edinburgh. By the end of May they had gone through six reprintings of the May number; and then John Blackwood struck gold, when they began to turn out a

---

[3] There were literal errors in the first printing. The text in the present edition is reproduced (by the kind permission of Liverpool University Press) from the revised version, based on the corrected pamphlet editions, presented in I. F. Clarke, *The Tale of the Next Great War: 1871–1914* (1995).

sixpenny edition at the rate of 80,000 copies a month. From May to
October Chesney's tale of the war-to-come held the attention of the
nation and of the world.

Chesney and Blackwood deserved their good luck. The publisher
and the colonel had read the signs of the times accurately. They knew
that by the January of 1871 the new political factors and the contemporary military considerations were approaching the temperature of
fusion. On 25 April, as the printers were at work in Edinburgh, the
members of the Bridgnorth Literary and Scientific Institution heard
Lord Acton discourse on the uncertainty factor. The man who knew
everything about history announced that the German victories had
destroyed the old map of the future: 'To exhibit a coherent chain of
causes in the revolution of the last nine months, which has shifted the
landmarks of European politics, and has given new leaders to the
world, is still an impossible task.'[4] A week later another eminent
historian, Edward Augustus Freeman, told the readers of *Macmillan's
Magazine* that the manifest lack of phlegm was yet another case of
British alarmism. The nation was going through 'one of those curious
fits of panic which seem ever and anon to seize upon the English
nation, and which, after exciting everybody for a while, die away and
are forgotten'.[5]

The *Battle of Dorking* episode, however, was not forgotten. One
reason was the flood of short stories, some eighteen in all, that attacked the Chesney story with their own very different accounts of
the German invasion: *After the Battle of Dorking, The Battle of Dorking a
Myth, The Other Side at the Battle of Dorking, The Siege of London*, and so
on to the last of them in 1885, *The Invasion of 1883*. Chesney led and
the rest had no choice but to follow, because the narrative mode of
The Battle of Dorking had proved so successful. The Volunteer has a
double role: as the fictional equivalent of the contemporary volunteer, he stands for the national failure to create an effective defence
force; and as the narrator he tells all and explains all. The expository
style sets out the reasons for the great disaster, when the narrator
notes the unmistakable signs of too little and too late: 'The rich were
idle and luxurious; the poor grudged the cost of defence. Politics had

    [4] Lord Acton, 'The War of 1870: A Lecture delivered . . . on the 25th of April,
1871' (London: Longmans, 1871), 3.
    [5] Edward A. Freeman, 'The Panic and its Lessons', *Macmillan's Magazine* (May
1871), 1–14.

become a mere bidding for radical votes . . . Truly the nation was ripe
for a fall.' This was myth-making for the new age of breech-loading
artillery and railway transport battalions. Prepare for the future or
perish—that was the lesson Chesney sought to spread.

The events of 1870 serve as the ominous prelude to his retro-
spective history. The projected German conquest of the United Kingdom was far too close to the French disaster for comfort. Had not
Blackwood's readers already seen how 'the same Power, only a few
months before, moved down half a million men on a few days' notice,
to conquer the greatest military power in Europe'? History could
repeat itself: 'There, across the narrow Straits,' Chesney warned, 'was
the writing on the wall, but we would not choose to read it. The
warnings of the few were drowned in the voice of the multitude.'
Chesney began with a leap into the new time-dimension of techno-
logical warfare—'the fatal engines which sent our ships, one after the
other, to the bottom'. His variant on the old-style floating torpedo
marks the appearance of the secret weapon, which would become
a favoured device in future-war stories and, as Chesney demons
trated, a most convenient means of removing the Royal Navy from the
action.

Chesney wrote from exceptional military experience. He had distinguished himself as Brigade Major of Engineers during the siege of
Delhi; and, thanks to the realistic techniques he had learnt from the
fiction of Erckmann-Chatrian, the plain prose of a military appreciation developed into a vigorous, first-person narration. The Volunteer's *post bellum* report from the year 1921—an old man writing to his
grandchildren—was a clever move: the feelings concealed the propa-
ganda. And so, as the enemy advance on London from Guildford and
Dorking, the mood changes in perfect synchrony with the story,
moving from initial anxiety to growing dismay and final despair.
There is a comparable movement on the enemy side. They enter as
an irresistible force—the source of mounting alarm, of false rumours
and inaccurate reports. Chesney is most careful to show how the
invasion affects the nation at every level. We join in the last days of
Old England when the Volunteer leaves home; and we experience
the calamity that strikes Travers and his family. The main attention
concentrates on the British forces, on named regiments and on members of the Volunteer's unit who compose a microcosm of the feck-
less, ill-prepared nation they have to defend. In a series of brilliant

episodes Chesney contrasts British incompetence with the careful training and military experience of the enemy. The British are a confused mass, 'retreating, firing as they went, followed by the advancing line of the enemy'. The Germans appear with great effect on two occasions: first, the unit billeted in the Travers's house are front-line soldiers who sum up the British as good, but not good enough; second, the *Hauptmann*—'a fine soldier-like man, but nothing could exceed the insolence of his manner'—who represents the immeasurable superiority of the enemy.

By October 1871 the end of the *Dorking* incident was in sight. The timid had recovered their nerve and were bold enough to ask anyone with a trifling injury, 'Weren't you wounded at the Battle of Dorking?' Many, however, continued to take Chesney's example with great seriousness. American, British, French, and German writers learnt from the English colonel how to deliver a forceful lesson on naval armaments or on the dangers of military unpreparedness. In 1887, for example, the anonymous author of a fiercely anti-British story, *Plus d'Angleterre*, was gentleman enough to acknowledge his debt to 'that ingenious fiction called *The Battle of Dorking*'; and as late as 1900 a most enterprising publisher, Grant Richards, calculated that the folk memory of Chesney's story was still strong enough to warrant an action-replay of the original. He commissioned a distinguished soldier, Colonel Maude, to write a book about a successful French invasion; and he gave it the title *The New Battle of Dorking* 'in the hope that it might have the same kind of success that its predecessor had three decades earlier'.

Chesney was the great precursor. After 1871 the tale of the war-to-come became a minor, and at times most profitable, publishing industry in Europe. As the level of literacy went on rising, supply increased to satisfy the immense, growing interest in tales of the war-to-come. By the 1890s the short story gave way to book-length serials in the illustrated magazines and in the new popular newspapers. When the imperialist illustrated magazine *Black and White* began in 1891, for instance, the editor judged that 'a full, vivid and interesting picture of the GREAT WAR of the Future' would be good for sales. He commissioned Admiral Sir Philip Colomb, a most eminent Victorian, and other experts to collaborate in writing *The Great War of 1892*. The results were most satisfactory: sales multiplied, special editions and translations followed, and by 1894 the German version—with an introduction from General von Bülow—had reached its fifth edition.

That success was noted by Alfred Harmsworth, then in his early days as the ablest entrepreneur in the development of the new mass press. He sent for William Le Queux who was beginning to make a name for himself as a writer of sensational fiction. Together they planned a serial, *The Poisoned Bullet*, which drew on contemporary speculations about the possible consequences of the Franco-Russian Treaty of 1893. The Le Queux look-ahead opened in *Answers* on 23 December 1893 in the most sensational way possible for the Press of that time. Banner headlines told a tale that left little to the imagination.

INVASION OF ENGLAND
War Declared by France and Austria
The Enemy Already Advancing
Manifesto by the Tzar

The serial ran every week until the victorious conclusion—'Fateful Days for the Old Flag'—on 2 June 1894. The success of the serial (a half-million sales for *Answers*) taught Harmsworth a lesson he never forgot. There was nothing like a good war—real or imaginary—to send up circulation figures.

In the following year, when Harmsworth stood as Conservative candidate for Portsmouth in the general election of 1895, he decided to open his campaign by buying the Portsmouth *Evening Mail*. The new editor was *The Times* naval correspondent and esteemed historian of the Royal Navy, William Laird Clowes; and he had orders to collaborate with one of Harmsworth's young men, Beckles Willson, in concocting *The Siege of Portsmouth*. 'Off to London tomorrow,' Beckles Willson noted in his journal, 'to see Laird Clowes and compile a thrilling serial for his newspaper.' On 10 June Laird Clowes promised readers of the *Evening Mail* 'a stirring narrative, written by distinguished naval and military authorities, dealing with the Siege of Portsmouth, and how our country was invaded by the French and Russians'.

In this way, so Harmsworth calculated, the Unionists would attract the crucial votes of the dockyard workers. They were expected to note how allegedly obsolete forts, supposedly antiquated coastal defence systems, and deficiencies in ships and supplies would cause the great disaster. The story opens in the Chesney manner with the destruction of the Channel Squadron. When the population of Portsmouth see the shattered condition of the remnants, 'thousands who lined the shore poured forth execrations against the blind policy which had seen without suspicion the ever-nearing intimacy between France and Russia which had thus exposed to destruction one of the finest divisions of the British Fleet'. Beckles Willson and Laird Clowes, however, had laboured in vain: Harmsworth was not elected.

Five years later Germany had begun to replace France as the most likely enemy in the new tales of '*The Next Great War*', and for the first time in the history of the *Zukunftskriegroman* German writers began to describe their coming struggle with the United Kingdom. The immediate cause for this change (and for the Entente with the French in 1904) was the German decision to build a great navy. Their Naval Laws of 1898 and 1900 mark the beginning of the great divide between the two nations; and the earliest manifestations of that difference can be seen in T. W. Offin's *How the Germans took London* and Karl Eisenhart's *Die Abrechnung mit England* (both 1900). From 1900 onwards, as the tales of the war-to-come with Germany flooded from the presses, British writers established a composite myth of 'The German Invasion'. Erskine Childers revealed the first stage—the naval preparations—in his classic *Riddle of the Sands*. Others followed with variations on the ridiculous 'Army in Waiting'—the thousands of Germans ostensibly in regular employment throughout the United Kingdom, but in reality all waiting for 'Der Tag'. They can be seen at work in Walter Wood's *The Enemy in our Midst* (1906): 'They formed what was known, in certain high German quarters, as the Committee of Secret Preparations. Their purpose was simple and definite—to make England ready for invasion and capture.'[6]

By 1906 the British and the Germans were already at war in fiction. As Europe advanced towards the long-expected conflict, a surge in future-war stories followed after every international crisis. The Tangier incident of 1905 led to the most scandalous and sensational event of 1906—the serialization of William Le Queux's notorious *Invasion of 1910* in the *Daily Mail*. 'Never before has this rabble-rousing propa-

---

[6] See the excellent account in Charles Lowe, 'About German Spies', *Contemporary Review*, 529 (1910), 42–56.

ganda against Germany had so widespread and so unsettling an effect on the country.' That was the reasonable verdict of one German observer in a serious and restrained report on the British and their future-war stories.[7] Had he known the full story, he could have written at length about patriotism and profit. That traffic began in 1905, when Harmsworth (Baron Northcliffe by then) commissioned William Le Queux to write a full-length tale of the German invasion. Le Queux went to the source of military knowledge, Field Marshal Lord Roberts, formerly Commander-in-Chief of the British Army; and with the best of advice he began his story in the right military manner—German landings on the south coast and a pincer movement on London. Northcliffe was not impressed. The Germans had to go into every town and village where the *Daily Mail* was read. No one knows what Lord Roberts said; but Le Queux's revised version had German troops storming ashore at Lowestoft and savage Uhlans galloping through places as far apart as Preston and Chelmsford. The story did wonders for the sales of the *Daily Mail*. When the serial was published as a book, it sold over a million copies and there were translations into twenty-seven languages, including Arabic, Syrian, and Chinese.

Three years later eighteen future-war stories followed on the Austrian annexation of Bosnia-Herzegovina in 1908. Their titles all spoke of war: *How England Was Saved*, *Die Engländer kommen*, *The War Inevitable*, *Deutschlands Flotte im Kampf*, *The Great Raid*. One or them was a delightful exception to the standard tale of victory or defeat: *The Swoop! or, How Clarence Saved England: A Tale of the Great Invasion* (1909). The author was P. G. Wodehouse, then in his apprentice days before he discovered his true form. In the manner of the later master, however, he used derision and ridicule to make fun of the 'German Invasion' stories. The hero who saves the nation is Clarence MacAndrew Chugwater, 'one of General Baden-Powell's Boy Scouts'. He defeats the combined forces of Germany, Russia, China, Monaco, the Mad Mullah, and the Swiss Navy plus detachments of Young Turks and Moroccan brigands.

Although the ritual appearance of the German commander-in-chief had signalled the end in stories like Le Queux's *Invasion of 1910*, the

---

[7] v. R., 'Die Invasion Englands in englischer Beleuchtung', *Marine-Rundschau* (Nov. 1908), 1246–58.

long dark night of the German Occupation had to wait until 1913 for
Saki to write the life and times of Wilhelm the Conqueror. His most
original account of the Hohenzollern occupation in *When William
Came* added a new dimension to the myth of the German Invasion. In
a most satisfying way it completed the great cycle of these stories
which ran from *The Riddle of the Sands* through many victories and
defeats—*How England was Saved, The Invasion that did not Come Off,
Lord Roastem's Campaign in North-Eastern France, Great Was the Fall*—
to the climactic moment when 'in the pleasant May sunshine the
Eagle standard floated and flapped, the black and yellow pennons
shifted restlessly, Emperor and Princes, Generals and guards, sat
stiffly in their saddles, and waited'.

In his way Saki was as original and as well suited for his task as
Chesney had been for *The Battle of Dorking*. Where the soldier had
pointed to the lack of will that led to national failure, the satirist
explored the materialism and self-interest that eats at the moral fibre.
When Saki came to write *When William Came*, he was already an
experienced journalist who had done well in the Balkans, Russia, and
France. He had become a successful writer with a well-deserved
reputation for his wit and epigrams, his ingenious fiction, and for the
constant entertainment he provided. At heart he was a moralist who
wanted all his fellows to live up to his highest ideals. Courage, right
principles, and a selfless patriotism—these were the measures by
which he judged the world. The case of Saki *v.* The People opens
with his sketch of Cicely Yeovil who 'felt that she was the best person
to pursue her own ends and cater for her own wants'. Then Murrey
Yeovil appears, the traveller back from distant parts, who has to find
his way through the brave new world of the Hohenzollerns. It is a
voyage of rediscovery, a search for the known contours of a lost land
presented as a journey through a dark world of fallen angels and
active demons. The war is over, the Hohenzollerns rule their new
Reichsland from the old palace in London, and Saki delivers a last
judgement upon a conquered nation. He points to the life-destroying
failure of conscience and, therefore, of will that must always lead to
false choices. He echoes Chesney with Dr Holham's account of too
little and too late: 'The enemy were a nation apprenticed in arms, we
were not even the idle apprentice; we had not deemed apprenticeship worth our while.' His touchstone recalls the lines of another
contemporary patriot, Arthur Cecil Spring-Rice:

> I vow to thee, my country—all earthly things above—
> Entire and whole and perfect, the service of my love.

As Yeovil learns how the self-regarding activities of the many are still as vigorous as ever, the reader is shown how the nation has accepted 'the necessity of the life of the country going on as if nothing had happened'. The heart of the matter, as Saki shows, lies interred in the past. He follows the way back to first things in his elegiac account of the English countryside seen from the train on Yeovil's visit to Torywood. The British merited their military disaster, says the Hungarian on the train, because they 'grew soft and accommodating in all things'. They would not live up to their beliefs. At this point, thirty years before Captain Charles Ryder began his account of life in the Arcadia of *Brideshead Revisited*, Saki reveals what Ryder was to discover—the intimate connection between belief and duty. As the unsparing Hungarian critic tells Yeovil, the ultimate failure came 'when they had emptied all the divine mystery and wonder out of their faith, naturally they grew tired of it, oh, but dreadfully tired of it'. The narrative dissolves to show what Old England was and what it prized most. The setting is the old house at Torywood. There at the centre, still fighting the good fight with all her might is an indomitable old woman—Eleanor, Dowager Lady Greymarten. 'I would stir up a longing,' she says, 'a determination for the future that we must win back. I would be a counter-agent to the agents of the *fait accompli*.' The words are a summons to the Happy Warrior who 'makes his moral being his prime care'. He is the man, in Wordsworth's 'Character of the Happy Warrior' (1807):

> Who comprehends his trust, and to the same
> Keeps faithful with a singleness of aim;
> And therefore does not stoop, nor lie in wait
> For wealth, or honours, or for worldly state.

The summons sounds in vain for Yeovil. His fever, the consequent lassitude of spirit and sluggishness of blood—these are symptomatic of the national torpor and indolence that had led to unconditional surrender. Yeovil fails the test, because he is not man enough to choose the hard way. Saki ends by testing the reader. There is the young man who 'had given up the fight and joined the ranks of the hopelessly subservient' and there were the 'young hearts that had not forgotten, had not compounded, would not yield'. What is the choice to be? What must a man do? 'Under which king, Bezonian? speak, or die' (*2 Henry IV*).

Less than a year after the publication of *When William Came* in 1913 two Bosnian Serbs had fired the fatal shots at Sarajevo, and the chain reaction of European alliances had led to the First World War. That European conflict had been prefigured and anticipated in more than four hundred future-war stories in the forty-three years between Chesney's *The Battle of Dorking* in 1871 and Sir Arthur Conan Doyle's remarkable anticipation of submarine warfare, *Danger!*, which had appeared in the *Strand Magazine* for July 1914. Those stories now compose a collective monument to the last age of innocence, when the happy marriage between science and society looked set to last for ever. They are a singular form of a consensus literature that once united British, French, and Germans in a set of false assumptions about the war they all expected. In the old book of the future it was written that the next great war would be like past wars—limited in scale, relatively humane in conduct, marked by fast-moving campaigns and set-piece battles in which the infantry advanced at the double and the cavalry ended the action with a thundering charge.

Those who went with songs to battle in 1914 were blind men, locked into a false dream about the future. They thought that they could have their wars and enjoy them. In those last, long years of peace, 'war still appealed to the imagination'.[8] The romance of war began in the adolescence of the tens of thousands who would die on the Somme. From George Alfred Henty and his heroic yarns and from the many books about 'The Deeds that Won the Empire' the young learnt the lessons of imperial destiny and the sure triumph of the nation. From first to last it was a male dream. Only one woman ever entered the 'men only' world of future-war fiction. She was the redoubtable Baronness Bertha von Suttner, one-time secretary to Alfred Nobel, founder of the Austrian Peace Movement in 1891, and recipient of the Nobel prize for peace in 1905. Her most famous story, *Die Waffen Nieder* (1891), told the tale of war as it really was: the pain of mothers, of wives and families, the suffering in the casualty clearing stations; and the romantic language of the war correspondents that hid the brutal realities of the battlefield.

---

[8] Herbert Read, *Annals of Innocence and Experience* (London: Faber & Faber 1946), 118.

Everything changes when tomorrow becomes today. After so many tales of the war-to-come the future turned out to be a brief sojourn in a no man's land of unknown soldiers and vast military cemeteries. If the tales of the war-to-come had foretold the battles for Verdun, would they have ended with the immense Ossuary at Douaumont? If Saki had foreseen the atrocious Battle of the Somme, would he have ended his tale with the assault on Beaumont Hamel? When the war came, Saki was no Murrey Yeovil. In 1914, at the age of 44, he enlisted, refused a commission, and as a lance-sergeant went to the Western Front in 1915. In the early hours of 14 November 1916, close to Beaumont Hamel, he was resting in a shell-hole with some of his section when he was killed instantly. His last words were: 'Put that bloody cigarette out.'

SELECT BIBLIOGRAPHY

EDITIONS

The Battle of Dorking, in I. F. Clarke, *The Tale of the Next Great War: 1870–1914* (Liverpool University Press, 1995), 27–73.
When William Came: A Story of London under the Hohenzollerns, with an Introduction by Lord Charnwood (London: John Lane, 1929).

FURTHER READING

Beckett, I. F. W., and Gooch, J. (eds.), *Politicians and Defence: Studies in the Formulation of British Defence Policy, 1845–1970* (Manchester University Press, 1981).
Chandler, D., and Beckett, I. (eds.), *The Oxford Illustrated History of the British Army* (Oxford University Press, 1994).
Clarke, I. F., *Voices Prophesying War* 2nd edn. (Oxford University Press, 1992).
—— *The Tale of the Next Great War: 1871–1914* (Liverpool University Press, 1995).
Ensor, R. C. K., *England, 1870–1914* (Oxford: Clarendon Press, 1968).
Gretton, R. H., *A Modern History of the English People* (London: Grant Richards, 1913).
Halévy, E., *A History of the English People* (London: Ernest Benn, 1934).
Liddell Hart, B. H., *History of the First World War* (London: Cassell, 1970).
Mansergh, N., *The Coming of the First World War* (London: Longman, 1949).
Marder, A. J., *From the Dreadnought to Scapa Flow*, vols. i–v (London: Oxford University Press, 1961–70).
Spiers, E. M., *The Army and Society, 1815–1914* (London: Longman, 1980).
Taylor, A. J. P., *The Course of German History* (London: Methuen, 1961).

The Battle Of Dorking

The Battle of Dorking:
Reminiscences of a Volunteer

GENERAL SIR GEORGE TOMKYNS CHESNEY

You ask me to tell you, my grandchildren, something about my own share in the great events that happened fifty years ago. 'Tis sad work turning back to that bitter page in our history, but you may perhaps take profit in your new homes from the lesson it teaches. For us in England it came too late. And yet we had plenty of warnings, if we had only made use of them. The danger did not come on us suddenly unawares. It burst on us suddenly, 'tis true, but its coming was foreshadowed plainly enough to open our eyes, if we had not been wilfully blind. We English have only ourselves to blame for the humiliation which has been brought on the land. Venerable old age! Dishonourable old age, I say, when it follows a manhood dishonoured as ours has been. I declare, even now, though fifty years have passed, I can hardly look a young man in the face when I think I am one of those in whose youth happened this degradation of Old England— one of those who betrayed the trust handed down to us unstained by our forefathers.

What a proud and happy country was this fifty years ago! Free trade had been working for more than a quarter of a century, and there seemed to be no end to the riches it was bringing us. London was growing bigger and bigger; you could not build houses fast enough for the rich people who wanted to live in them, the merchants who made the money and came from all parts of the world to settle there, and the lawyers and doctors and engineers and others, and trades-people who got their share out of the profits. The streets reached down to Croydon and Wimbledon, which my father could remember as quite country places; and people used to say that Kingston and Reigate would soon be joined to London. We thought we could go on build- ing and multiplying for ever. 'Tis true that even then there was no lack of poverty; the people who had no money went on increasing as fast as the rich, and pauperism was already beginning to be a difficulty; but if the rates were high, there was plenty of money to pay them with; and as for what were called the middle classes, there really seemed no limit to their increase and prosperity. People in those days thought it quite a matter of course to bring a dozen children into the world—or, as it used to be said, Providence sent them that number of babies; and if they couldn't always marry off all the daughters, they used to manage to provide for the sons, for there were new openings to be found in all the professions, or in the government offices, which went on steadily getting larger. Besides, in those days young men could be sent out to India, or into the army or navy; and even then emigration was not uncommon, although not the regular custom it is now. Schoolmasters, like all other professional classes, drove a capital trade. They did not teach very much, to be sure, but new schools with their four or five hundred boys were springing up all over the country.

Fools that we were! We thought that all this wealth and prosperity were sent us by Providence, and could not stop coming. In our blindness we did not see that we were merely a big workshop, making up the things which came from all parts of the world; and that if other nations stopped sending us raw goods to work up, we could not produce them ourselves. True, we had in those days an advantage in our cheap coal and iron; and had we taken care not to waste the fuel, it might have lasted us longer. But even then there were signs that coal and iron would soon become cheaper in foreign parts; while as to food and other things, England was not better off than it is now. We were so rich simply because other nations from all parts of the world were in the habit of sending their goods to us to be sold or manufactured; and we thought that this would last for ever. And so, perhaps, it might have lasted, if we had only taken proper means to keep it; but, in our folly, we were too careless even to insure our prosperity, and after the course of trade was turned away it would not come back again.

And yet, if ever a nation had a plain warning, we had. If we were the greatest trading country, our neighbours were the leading military power in Europe. They were driving a good trade, too, for this was before their foolish communism (about which you will hear when you are older) had ruined the rich without benefiting the poor, and they were in many respects the first nation in Europe; but it was on their army that they prided themselves most. And with reason. They had beaten the Russians and the Austrians, and the Prussians too, in bygone years, and they thought they were invincible. Well do I remember the great review held at Paris by the Emperor Napoleon during the great Exhibition, and how proud he looked showing off his splendid Guards to the assembled kings and princes. Yet, three years afterwards, the force so long deemed the first in Europe was ignominiously beaten, and the whole army taken prisoners. Such a defeat had never happened before in the world's history; and, with this proof before us of the folly of disbelieving in the possibility of disaster merely because it had never happened before, it might have been supposed that we should have the sense to take the lesson to heart. And the country was certainly roused for a time, and a cry was raised that the army ought to be reorganized, and our defences strengthened against the enormous power for sudden attacks which it was seen other nations were able to put forth. But our Government had come into office on a cry of retrenchment, and could not bring themselves to eat their own pledges. There was a Radical section of their party, too, whose votes had to be secured by conciliation, and which blindly demanded a reduction of armaments as the price of allegiance. This party always decried military establishments as part of a fixed policy for reducing the influence of the Crown and the aristocracy. They could not understand that the times had altogether changed, that the Crown had really no power, and that the Government merely existed at the pleasure of the House of Commons, and that even Parliament-rule was beginning to give way to mob-law. At any rate, the Ministry were only too glad of this excuse to give up all the strong points of a scheme which they were not really in earnest about. The fleet and the Channel, they said, were sufficient protection. So the army was kept down, and the militia and volunteers were left untrained as before, because to call them out for drill would 'interfere with the industry of the country'. We could have given up some of the industry of those days, forsooth, and yet be busier than we are now.

But why tell you a tale you have so often heard already? The nation, although uneasy, was misled by the false security its leaders professed to feel; the warning given by the disaster that overtook France was allowed to pass by unheeded. The French trusted in their army and its great reputation, we in our fleet; and in each case the result of this blind confidence was disaster, such as our forefathers in their hardest struggles could not have even imagined.

I need hardly tell you how the crash came about. First, the rising in India drew away a part of our small army; then came the difficulty with America, which had been threatening for years, and we sent ten thousand men to defend Canada—a handful which did not go far to strengthen the real defences of that country, but formed an irresistible temptation to the Americans to try and take them prisoners, especially as the contingent included three battalions of the Guards. Thus the regular army at home was even smaller than usual, and nearly half of it was in Ireland to check the talked-of Fenian invasion fitting out in the West. Worse still—though I do not know it would really have mattered as things turned out—the fleet was scattered abroad: some ships to guard the West Indies, others to check privateering in the China Seas, and a large part to try and protect our colonies on the Northern Pacific shore of America, where, with incredible folly, we continued to retain possessions which we could not possibly defend. America was not the great power forty years ago that it is now; but for us to try and hold territory on her shores which could only be reached by sailing round the Horn, was as absurd as if she had attempted to take the Isle of Man before the independence of Ireland. We see this plainly enough now, but were all blind then.

It was while we were in this state, with our ships all over the world, and our little bit of an army cut up into detachments, that the Secret Treaty was published, and Holland and Denmark were annexed. People say now that we might have escaped the troubles which came on us if we had at any rate kept quiet till our other difficulties were settled; but the English were always an impulsive lot: the whole country was boiling over with indignation, and the Government, egged on by the press, and going with the stream, declared war. We had always got out of our scrapes before, and we believed our old luck and pluck would somehow pull us through.

Then, of course, there was bustle and hurry all over the land. Not that the calling up of the army reserve caused much stir, for I think there were only about 5,000 altogether, and a good many of these were not to be found when the time came; but recruiting was going on all over the country, with a tremendous high bounty, 50,000 more men having been voted for the army. Then there was a Ballot Bill passed for adding 55,500 men to the militia; why a round number was not fixed on I don't know, but the Prime Minister said that this was the exact quota wanted to put the defences of the country on a sound footing. Then the shipbuilding that began! Ironclads, despatch-boats, gunboats, monitors—every building-yard in the country got its job, and they were offering ten shillings a day wages for anybody who could drive a rivet. This didn't improve the recruiting, you may suppose. I remember, too, there was a squabble in the House of Commons about whether artisans should be drawn for the ballot, as they were so much wanted, and I think they got an exemption. This sent numbers to the yards; and if we had had a couple of years to prepare instead of a couple of weeks, I daresay we should have done very well.

It was on a Monday that the declaration of war was announced, and in a few hours we got our first inkling of the sort of preparation the enemy had made for the event which they had really brought about, although the actual declaration was made by us. A pious appeal to the God of battles, whom it was said we had aroused, was telegraphed back; and from that moment all communication with the north of Europe was cut off. Our embassies and legations were packed off at an hour's notice, and it was as if we had suddenly come back to the Middle Ages. The dumb astonishment visible all over London the next morning, when the papers came out void of news, merely hinting at what had happened, was one of the most startling things in this war of surprises. But everything had been arranged beforehand; nor ought we to have been surprised, for we had seen the same power, only a few months before, move down half a million men on a few days' notice, to conquer the greatest military nation in Europe, with no more fuss than our War Office used to make over the transport of a brigade from Aldershot to Brighton—and this, too, without the allies it had now. What happened now was not a bit more wonderful in reality; but people of this country could not bring themselves to believe that what had never occurred before to England could ever possibly happen. Like our neighbours, we became wise when it was too late.

Of course the papers were not long in getting news—even the mighty organization set at work could not shut out a special correspondent; and in a very few days, although the telegraphs and railways were intercepted right across Europe, the main facts oozed out. An embargo had been laid on all shipping in every port from the Baltic to Ostend; the fleets of the two great powers had moved out, and it was supposed were assembled in the great northern harbour, and troops were hurrying on board all the steamers detained in those places, most of which were British vessels. It was clear that invasion was intended.

Even then we might have been saved, if the fleet had been ready. The forts which guarded the flotilla were perhaps too strong for shipping to attempt; but an ironclad or two, handled as British sailors knew how to use them, might have destroyed or damaged a part of the transports, and delayed the expedition, giving us what we wanted, time. But then the best part of the fleet had been decoyed down to the Dardanelles, and what remained of the Channel squadron was looking after Fenian filibusters off the west of Ireland; so it was ten days before the fleet was got together, and by that time it was plain the enemy's preparations were too far advanced to be stopped by a *coup-de-main*. Information, which came chiefly through Italy, came slowly, and was more or less vague and uncertain; but this much was known, that at least a couple of hundred thousand men were embarked or ready to be put on board ships, and that the flotilla was guarded by more ironclads than we could then muster. I suppose it was the uncertainty as to the point the enemy would aim at for landing, and the fear lest he should give us the go-by, that kept the fleet for several days in the Downs; but it was not until the Tuesday fortnight after the declaration of war that it weighed anchor and steamed away for the North Sea.

Of course you have read about the Queen's visit to the fleet the day before, and how she sailed around the ships in her yacht and went on board the flag-ship to take leave of the admiral; how, overcome with emotion, she told him that the safety of the country was committed to his keeping. You remember, too, the gallant old officer's reply, and how all the ships' yards were manned, and how lustily the tars cheered as her Majesty was rowed off. The account was of course telegraphed to London, and the high spirits of the fleet infected the whole town. I was outside the Charing Cross Station when the Queen's special train from Dover arrived, and from the cheering and shouting which greeted her as she drove away, you might have supposed we had already won a great victory. The leading journal, which had gone in strongly for the army reduction carried out during the session, and had been nervous and desponding in tone during the past fortnight, suggesting all sorts of compromises as a way of getting out of the war, came out in a very jubilant form next morning. 'Panic-

stricken inquirers', they said, 'ask now, where are the means of meeting the invasion? We reply that the invasion will never take place. A
British fleet, manned by British sailors whose courage and enthusiasm
are reflected in the people of this country, is already on the way to
meet the presumptuous foe. The issue of a contest between British
ships and those of any other country, under anything like equal odds,
can never be doubtful. England awaits with calm confidence the issue
of the impending action.'

Such were the words of the leading article, and so we all felt. It was
on Tuesday, the 10th of August, that the fleet sailed from the Downs.
It took with it a submarine cable to lay down as it advanced, so that
continuous communication was kept up, and the papers were publishing special editions every few minutes with the latest news. This
was the first time such a thing had been done, and the feat was
accepted as a good omen. Whether it is true that the Admiralty made
use of the cable to keep on sending contradictory orders, which took
the command out of the admiral's hands, I can't say; but all that the
admiral sent in return was a few messages of the briefest kind, which
neither the Admiralty nor any one else could have made any use of.
Such a ship had gone off reconnoitring; such another had rejoined—
fleet was in latitude so and so. This went on till the Thursday morning. I had just come up to town by train as usual, and was walking to
my office, when the newsboys began to cry, 'New edition—enemy's
fleet in sight!'

You may imagine the scene in London! Business still went on at
the banks, for bills matured although the independence of the country was being fought out under our own eyes, so to say; and the
speculators were active enough. But even with the people who were
making or losing their fortunes, the interest in the fleet overcame
everything else; men who went to pay in or draw out their money
stopped to show the last bulletin to the cashier. As for the street, you
could hardly get along for the crowd stopping to buy and read the
papers; while at every house or office the members sat restlessly in
the common room, as if to keep together for company, sending out
some one of their number every few minutes to get the latest edition.
At least this is what happened at our office; but to sit still was as
impossible as to do anything, and most of us went out and wandered
about among the crowd, under a sort of feeling that the news was got
quicker at in this way.

Bad as were the times coming, I think the sickening suspense of that day, and the shock which followed, was almost the worst that we underwent. It was about ten o'clock that the first telegram came; an hour later the wire announced that the admiral had signalled to form line of battle, and shortly afterwards that the order was given to bear down on the enemy and engage. At twelve came the announcement, 'Fleet opened fire about three miles to leeward of us'—that is, the ship with the cable. So far all had been expectancy; then came the first token of calamity. 'An ironclad has been blown up'—'the enemy's torpedoes are doing great damage'—'the flagship is laid aboard the enemy'—'the flagship appears to be sinking'—'the vice-admiral has signalled'—there the cable became silent, and, as you know, we heard no more till two days afterwards, when the solitary ironclad which escaped the disaster steamed into Portsmouth.

Then the whole story came out—how our sailors, gallant as ever, had tried to close with the enemy; how the latter evaded the conflict at close quarters, and, sheering off, left behind them the fatal engines which sent our ships, one after the other, to the bottom; how all this happened almost in a few minutes. The Government, it appears, had received warnings of this invention; but to the nation this stunning blow was utterly unexpected. That Thursday I had to go home early for regimental drill, but it was impossible to remain doing nothing, so when that was over I went up to town again, and, after waiting in expectation of news which never came, and missing the midnight train, I walked home. It was a hot sultry night, and I did not arrive till near sunrise. The whole town was quite still—the lull before the storm; and as I let myself in with my latch-key, and went softly upstairs to my room to avoid waking the sleeping household, I could not but contrast the peacefulness of the morning—no sound breaking the silence but the singing of birds in the garden—with the passionate remorse and indignation that would break out with the day. Perhaps the inmates of the house were as wakeful as myself; but the house in its stillness was just as it used to be when I came home alone from balls or parties in the happy days gone by. Tired though I was, I could not sleep, so I went down to the river and had a swim; and on returning found the household was assembling for early breakfast. A sorrowful household it was, although the burden pressing on each was partly an unseen one. My father, doubting whether his firm could last through the day; my mother, her distress about my brother, now with his regiment on the coast, already exceeding that which she felt for the public misfortune, had come down, although hardly fit to leave her room. My sister Clara was worst of all, for she could not but try to disguise her special interest in the fleet; and though we had all guessed that her heart was given to the young lieutenant in the flagship—the first vessel to go down—a love unclaimed could not be told, nor could we express the sympathy we felt for the poor girl. That breakfast, the last meal we ever had together, was soon ended, and my father and I went up to town by an early train, and got there just as the fatal announcement of the loss of the fleet was telegraphed from Portsmouth.

The panic and excitement of that day—how the funds went down to 35; the run upon the bank and its stoppage; the fall of half the houses in the city; how the Government issued a notification suspending specie payment and the tendering of bills—this last precaution too late for most firms, Carter & Co. among the number, which stopped payment as soon as my father got to the office; the call to arms, and the unanimous response of the country—all this is history which I need not repeat. You wish to hear about my own share in the business of the time. Well, volunteering had increased immensely from the day war was proclaimed, and our regiment went up in a day or two from its usual strength of 600 to nearly 1,000. But the stock of rifles was deficient. We were promised a further supply in a few days, which, however, we never received; and while waiting for them the regiment had to be divided into two parts, the recruits drilling with the rifles in the morning, and we old hands in the evening. The failures and stoppage of work on this black Friday threw an immense number of young men out of employment and we recruited up to 1,400 strong by the next day; but what was the use of all these men without arms? On the Saturday it was announced that a lot of smooth-bore muskets in store at the Tower would be served out to regiments applying for them, and a regular scramble took place among the volunteers for them, and our people got hold of a couple of hundred. But you might almost as well have tried to learn rifle-drill with a broom-stick as with old Brown Bess; besides, there was no smooth-bore ammunition in the country. A national subscription was opened up for the manufacture of rifles at Birmingham, which ran up to a couple of millions in two days, but, like everything else, this came too late.

To return to the volunteers: camps had been formed a fortnight before at Dover, Brighton, Harwich, and other places, of regulars and militia, and the headquarters of most of the volunteer regiments were attached to one or other of them, and the volunteers used to go down for drill from day to day, as they could spare time, and on Friday an order went out that they should be permanently embodied; but the metropolitan volunteers were still kept about London as a sort of reserve, till it could be seen at what point the invasion would take place. We were all told off to brigades and divisions. Our brigade consisted of the 4th Royal Surrey Militia, the 1st Surrey Administrative Battalion, as it was called, at Clapham, the 7th Surrey Volunteers at Southwark, and ourselves; but only our battalion and the militia were quartered in the same place, and the whole brigade had merely two or three afternoons together at brigade exercise in Bushey Park before the march took place. Our brigadier belonged to a line regiment in Ireland, and did not join till the very morning the order came. Meanwhile, during the preliminary fortnight, the militia colonel commanded. But though we volunteers were busy with our drill and preparations, those of us who, like myself, belonged to government offices had more than enough of office work to do, as you may suppose. The volunteer clerks were allowed to leave office at four o'clock, but the rest were kept hard at the desk far into the night. Orders to the lord-lieutenants, to the magistrates, notifications, all the arrangements for cleaning out the workhouses for hospitals—these and a hundred other things had to be managed in our office, and there was as much bustle indoors as out. Fortunate we were to be so busy— the people to be pitied were those who had nothing to do. And on Sunday (that was the 15th of August) work went on just as usual. We had an early parade and drill, and I went up to town by the nine o'clock train in my uniform, taking my rifle with me in case of accidents and, luckily too, as it turned out, a mackintosh overcoat.

When I got to Waterloo there were all sorts of rumour afloat. A fleet had been seen off the Downs, and some of the despatch-boats which were hovering about the coasts brought news that there was a large flotilla off Harwich, but nothing could be seen from the shore, as the weather was hazy. The enemy's light ships had taken and sunk all the fishing-boats they could catch, to prevent the news of their whereabouts reaching us; but a few escaped during the night and reported that the *Inconstant* frigate coming home from North America, without any knowledge of what had taken place, had sailed right into the enemy's fleet and been captured. In town the troops were all getting ready for a move; the Guards in the Wellington Barracks were under arms, and their baggage-waggons packed and drawn up in the Bird Cage Walk. The usual guard at the Horse Guards had been withdrawn, and orderlies and staff officers were going to and fro. All this I saw on the way to my office, where I worked away till twelve o'clock, and then, feeling hungry after my early breakfast, I went across Parliament Street to my club to get some luncheon. There were about half-a-dozen men in the coffee room, none of whom I knew; but in a minute or two Danvers of the Treasury entered in a tremendous hurry. From him I got the first bit of authentic news I had had that day. The enemy had landed in force near Harwich, and the metropolitan regiments were ordered down there to reinforce the troops already collected in that neighbourhood; his regiment was to parade at one o'clock, and he had come to get something to eat before starting. We bolted a hurried lunch, and were just leaving the club when a messenger from the Treasury came running into the hall.

'Oh, Mr Danvers,' said he, 'I've come to look for you, sir; the secretary says that all the gentlemen are wanted at the office, and that you must please not one of you go with the regiments.'

'The devil!' cried Danvers.

'Do you know if that order extends to all the public offices?' I asked.

'I don't know,' said the man, 'but I believe it do. I know there's messengers gone round to all the clubs and luncheon-bars to look for the gentlemen; the secretary says it's quite impossible any one can be spared just now, there's so much work to do; there's orders just come to send off our records to Birmingham tonight.'

I did not wait to condole with Danvers, but, just glancing up Whitehall to see if any of our messengers were in pursuit, I ran off as hard as I could for Westminster Bridge, and so to the Waterloo Station.

The place had quite changed its aspect since the morning. The regular service of trains had ceased, and the station and approaches were full of troops, among them the Guards and artillery. Everything was very orderly; the men had piled arms, and were standing about in groups. There was no sign of high spirits or enthusiasm. Matters had become too serious. Every man's face reflected the general feeling that we had neglected the warnings given us, and that now the danger so long derided as impossible and absurd had really come and found us unprepared. But the soldiers, if grave, looked determined, like men who meant to do their duty whatever might happen. A train full of guardsmen was just starting for Guildford. I was told it would stop at Surbiton, and, with several other volunteers, hurrying like myself to join our regiment, got a place in it. We did not arrive a moment too soon, for the regiment was marching from Kingston down to the station. The destination of our brigade was the east coast. Empty carriages were drawn up in the siding, and our regiment was to go first. A large crowd was assembled to see it off, including the recruits who had joined during the last fortnight, and who formed by far the largest part of our strength. They were to stay behind, and were certainly very much in the way already; for as all the officers and sergeants belonged to the active part, there was no one to keep discipline among them, and they came crowding around us, breaking the ranks and making it difficult to get into the train. Here I saw our new brigadier for the first time. He was a soldier-like man, and no doubt knew his duty, but he appeared new to volunteers, and did not seem to know how to deal with gentlemen privates. I wanted very much to run home and get my greatcoat and knapsack, which I had bought a few days ago, but feared to be left behind; a good-natured recruit volunteered to fetch them for me, but he had not returned before we started, and I began the campaign with a kit consisting of a mackintosh and a small pouch of tobacco.

It was a tremendous squeeze in the train; for, besides the ten men sitting down, there were three or four standing up in every compartment, and the afternoon was close and sultry, and there were so many stoppages on the way that we took nearly an hour and a half crawling up to Waterloo. It was between five and six in the afternoon when we arrived there, and it was nearly seven before we marched up to the Shoreditch station. The whole place was filled up with stores and ammunition, to be sent off to the east, so we piled arms in the street and scattered about to get food and drink, of which most of us stood in need, especially the latter, for some were already feeling the worse for the heat and crush. I was just stepping into a public-house with Travers, when who should drive up but his pretty wife? Most of our friends had paid their adieus at the Surbiton station, but she had driven up by the road in his brougham, bringing their little boy to have a last look at papa. She had also brought his knapsack and greatcoat, and, what was still more acceptable, a basket containing fowls, tongue, bread-and-butter, and biscuits, and a couple of bottles of claret—which priceless luxuries they insisted on my sharing.

Meanwhile the hours went on. The 4th Surrey Militia, which had marched all the way from Kingston, had come up, as well as the other volunteer corps; the station had been partly cleared of the stores that encumbered it; some artillery, two militia regiments, and a battalion of the line had been despatched, and our turn to start had come, and long lines of carriages were drawn up ready for us; but still we remained in the street. You may fancy the scene. There seemed to be as many people as ever in London, and we could hardly move for the crowds of spectators—fellows hawking fruits and volunteers' comforts, newsboys, and so forth, to say nothing of the cabs and omnibuses; while orderlies and staff-officers were constantly riding up with messages. A good many of the militiamen, and some of our people too, had taken more than enough to drink; perhaps a hot sun had told on empty stomachs; anyhow, they became very noisy. The din, dirt, and heat were indescribable.

So the evening wore on, and all the information our officers could get from the brigadier, who appeared to be acting under another general, was that orders had come to stand fast for the present. Gradually the street became quieter and cooler. The brigadier, who, by way of setting an example, had remained for some hours without leaving his saddle, had got a chair out of a shop, and sat nodding in it; most of the men were lying down or sitting on the pavement—some sleeping, some smoking. In vain had Travers begged his wife to go home. She declared that, having come so far, she would stay and see the last of us. The brougham had been sent away to a by-street, as it blocked up the road; so he sat on a doorstep, she by him on the knapsack. Little Arthur, who had been delighted at the bustle and the uniforms, and in high spirits, became at last very cross, and eventually cried himself to sleep in his father's arms, his golden hair and one little dimpled arm hanging over his shoulder. Thus went on the weary hours, till suddenly the assembly sounded, and we all started up. We were to return to Waterloo. The landing on the east was only a feint—so ran the rumour—the real attack was on the south. Anything seemed better than indecision and delay, and, tired though we were, the march back was gladly hailed. Mrs Travers, who made us take the remains of the luncheon with us, we left to look for her carriage; little Arthur, who was awake again, but very good and quiet, in her arms.

We did not reach Waterloo till nearly midnight, and there was some delay in starting again. Several volunteer and militia regiments had arrived from the north; the station and all its approaches were jammed up with men, and trains were being despatched away as fast as they could be made up. All this time no news had reached us since the first announcement; but the excitement then aroused had now passed away under the influence of fatigue and want of sleep, and most of us dozed off as soon as we got under way. I did, at any rate, and was awoke by the train stopping at Leatherhead. There was an up-train returning to town, and some persons in it were bringing up news from the coast. We could not, from our part of the train, hear what they said, but the rumour was passed up from one carriage to another. The enemy had landed in force at Worthing. Their position had been attacked by the troops from the camp near Brighton, and the action would be renewed in the morning. The volunteers had behaved very well. This was all the information we could get. So, then, the invasion had come at last. It was clear, at any rate, from what was said, that the enemy had not been driven back yet, and we should be in time most likely to take a share in the defence.

It was sunrise when the train crawled into Dorking, for there had been numerous stoppages on the way; and here it was pulled up for a long time, and we were told to get out and stretch ourselves—an order gladly responded to, for we had been very closely packed all night. Most of us, too, took the opportunity to make an early breakfast off the food we had brought from Shoreditch. I had the remains of Mrs Travers's fowl and some bread wrapped up in my waterproof, which I shared with one or two less provident comrades. We could see from our halting-place that the line was blocked with trains beyond and behind. It must have been about eight o'clock when we got orders to take our seats again, and the train began to move slowly on towards Horsham. Horsham Junction was the point to be occupied— so the rumour went; but about ten o'clock, when halting at a small station a few miles short of it, the order came to leave the train, and our brigade formed in column on the high road. Beyond us was some field-artillery; and further on, so we were told by a staff-officer, an-other brigade, which was to make up a division with ours.

After more delays the line began to move, but not forwards; our route was towards the north-west, and a sort of suspicion of the state of affairs flashed across my mind. Horsham was already occupied by the enemy's advanced-guard, and we were to fall back on Leith Common, and take up a position threatening his flank, should he advance either to Guildford or Dorking. This was soon confirmed by what the colonel was told by the brigadier and passed down the ranks; and just now, for the first time, the boom of artillery came up on the light south breeze. In about an hour the firing ceased. What did it mean? We could not tell. Meanwhile our march continued. The day was very close and sultry, and the clouds of dust stirred up by our feet almost suffocated us. I had saved a soda-water-bottleful of yesterday's claret; but this went only a short way, for there were many mouths to share it with, and the thirst soon became as bad as ever. Several of the regiment fell out from faintness, and we made frequent halts to rest and let the stragglers come up.

At last we reached the top of Leith Hill. It is a striking spot, being the highest point in the south of England. The view from it was splendid, and most lovely did the country look this summer day, although the grass was brown from the long drought. It was a great relief to get from the dusty road on to the common, and at the top of the hill there was a refreshing breeze. We could see now, for the first time, the whole of our division. Our own regiment did not muster more than 500, for it contained a large number of government office men who had been detained, like Danvers, for duty in town, and others were not much larger; but the militia regiment was very strong, and the whole division, I was told, mustered nearly 5,000 rank and file. We could see other troops also in extension of our division, and could count a couple of field-batteries of Royal Artillery, besides some heavy guns, belonging to the volunteers apparently, drawn by cart-horses. The cooler air, the sense of numbers, and the evident strength of the position we held raised our spirits, which, I am not ashamed to say, had all the morning been depressed. It was not that we were not eager to close with the enemy, but that the counter-marching and halting ominously betokened a vacillation of purpose in those who had the guidance of affairs. Here in two days the invaders had got more than twenty miles inland, and nothing effectual had been done to stop them. And the ignorance in which we volunteers, from the colonel downwards, were kept of their movements filled us with uneasiness. We could not but depict to ourselves the enemy as carrying out all the while firmly his well-considered scheme of attack, and contrasting it with our own uncertainty of purpose. The very silence with which his advance appeared to be conducted filled us with mysterious awe.

Meanwhile the day wore on, and we became faint with hunger, for we had eaten nothing since daybreak. No provisions came up, and there were no signs of any commissariat officers. It seems that when we were at the Waterloo station a whole trainful of provisions was drawn up there, and our colonel proposed that one of the trucks should be taken off and attached to our train, so that we might have some food at hand; but the officer in charge, an assistant-controller I think they called him—this control department was a newfangled affair which did us almost as much harm as the enemy in the long-run—said his orders were to keep all the stores together, and that he couldn't issue any without authority from the head of his department. So, we had to go without. Those who had tobacco smoked—indeed, there is no solace like a pipe under such circumstances. The militia regiment, I heard afterwards, had two days' provisions in their haversacks; it was we volunteers who had no haversacks, and nothing to put in them. All this time, I should tell you, while we were lying on the grass with our arms piled, the general, with the brigadiers and staff, was riding about slowly from point to point of the edge of the common, looking out with his glass towards the south valley. Orderlies and staff-officers were constantly coming, and about three o'clock there arrived up a road that led towards Horsham a small body of lancers and a regiment of yeomanry, who had, it appears, been out in advance, and now drew up a short way in front of us in column facing to the south. Whether they could see anything in their front I could not tell, for we were behind the crest of the hill ourselves, and so could not look into the valley below; but shortly afterwards the assembly sounded. Commanding officers were called out by the general, and received some brief instructions; and the column began to march again towards London, the militia this time coming last in our brigade.

A rumour regarding the object of this counter-march soon spread through the ranks. The enemy was not going to attack us here, but was trying to turn the position on both sides, one column pointing to Reigate, the other to Aldershot; and so we must fall back and take up a position at Dorking. The line of the great chalk-range was to be defended. A large force was concentrating at Guildford, another at Reigate, and we should find supports at Dorking. The enemy would be awaited in these positions. Such, so far as we privates could get at the facts, was to be the plan of operations. Down the hill, therefore, we marched. From one or two points we could catch a brief sight of the railway in the valley below running from Dorking to Horsham. Men in red were working upon it here and there. They were the Royal Engineers, someone said, breaking up the line. On we marched. The dust seemed worse than ever. In one village through which we passed—I forget the name now—there was a pump on the green. Here we stopped and had a good drink; and passing by a large farm, the farmer's wife and two or three of her maids stood at the gate and handed us hunches of bread and cheese out of some baskets. I got the share of a bit, but the bottom of the baskets must soon have been reached. Not a thing else was to be had till we got to Dorking about six o'clock; indeed, most of the farmhouses appeared deserted already.

On arriving there we were drawn up in the street, and just opposite was a baker's shop. Our fellows asked leave at first by twos and threes to go in and buy some loaves, but soon others began to break off and crowd into the shop, and at last a regular scramble took place. If there had been any order preserved, and a regular distribution arranged, they would no doubt have been steady enough, but hunger makes men selfish: each man felt that his stopping behind would do no good—he would simply lose his share; so it ended by almost the whole regiment joining in the scrimmage, and the shop was cleared out in a couple of minutes; while as for paying, you could not get your hand into your pocket for the crush. The colonel tried in vain to stop the row; some of the officers were as bad as the men. Just then a staff-officer rode by; he could scarcely make way for the crowd, and was pushed against rather rudely, and in a passion he called out to us to behave properly, like soldiers, and not like a parcel of roughs. 'Oh, blow it, governor,' says Dick Wake, 'you arn't agoing to come between a poor cove and his grub.' Wake was an articled attorney, and, as we used to say in those days, a cheeky young chap, although a good-natured fellow enough. At this speech, which was followed by some more remarks of the sort from those about him, the staff-officer became angrier still. 'Orderly,' cried he to the lancer riding behind him, 'take that man to the provost-marshal. As for you, sir,' he said, turning to our colonel, who sat on his horse silent with astonishment, 'if you don't want some of your men shot before their time, you and your precious officers had better keep this rabble in a little better order'; and poor Dick, who looked crest-fallen enough, would certainly have been led off at the tail of the sergeant's horse, if the brigadier had not come up and arranged matters, and marched us off to the hill beyond the town. This incident made us both angry and crest-fallen. We were annoyed at being so roughly spoken to: at the same time we felt we had deserved it, and were ashamed of the misconduct. Then, too, we had lost confidence in our colonel, after the poor figure he cut in the affair. He was a good fellow, the colonel, and showed himself a brave one next day; but he aimed too much at being popular, and didn't understand a bit how to command.

To resume: we had scarcely reached the hill above the town, which we were told was to be our bivouac for the night, when the welcome news came that a food-train had arrived at the station; but there were no carts to bring the things up, so a fatigue-party went down and carried back a supply to us in their arms—loaves, a barrel of rum, packets of tea, and joints of meat—abundance for all; but there was not a kettle or a cooking-pot in the regiment, and we could not eat the meat raw. The colonel and officers were no better off. They had arranged to have a regular mess, with crockery, steward, and all complete, but the establishment never turned up, and what had become of it no one knew. Some of us were sent back into the town to see what we could procure in the way of cooking utensils. We found the street full of artillery, baggage-waggons, and mounted officers, and volunteers shopping like ourselves; and all the houses appeared to be occupied by troops. We succeeded in getting a few kettles and saucepans, and I obtained for myself a leather bag, with a strap to go over the shoulder, which proved very handy afterwards; and thus laden, we trudged back to our camp on the hill, filling the kettles with dirty water from a little stream which runs between the hill and the town, for there was none to be had above. It was nearly a couple of miles each way; and, exhausted as we were with marching and want of rest, we were almost too tired to eat. The cooking was of the roughest, as you may suppose; all we could do was to cut off slices of the meat and boil them in saucepans, using our fingers for forks.

The tea, however, was very refreshing; and, thirsty as we were, we drank it by the gallon.

Just before it grew dark, the brigade-major came round, and, with the adjutant, showed our colonel how to set a picket in advance of our line a little way down the face of the hill. It was not necessary to place one, I suppose, because the town in our front was still occupied with troops; but no doubt the practice would be useful. We had also a quarter-guard, and a line of sentries in front and rear of our line, communicating with those of the regiments on our flanks. Firewood was plentiful, for the hill was covered with beautiful wood; but it took some time to collect it, for we had nothing but our pocket-knives to cut down the branches with.

So we lay down to sleep. My company had no duty, and we had the night undisturbed to ourselves; but, tired though I was, the excitement and the novelty of the situation made sleep difficult. And although the night was still and warm, and we were sheltered by the woods, I soon found it chilly with no better covering than my thin dust-coat, the more so as my clothes, saturated with perspiration during the day, had never dried; and before daylight I woke from a short nap, shivering with cold, and was glad to get warm with others by a fire. I then noticed that the opposite hills on the south were dotted with fires; and we thought at first they must belong to the enemy, but we were told that the ground up there was still held by a strong rear-guard of regulars, and that there need be no fear of surprise.

At the first sign of dawn the bugles of the regiments sounded the *reveillé*, and we were ordered to fall in, and the roll was called. About twenty men were absent, who had fallen out sick the day before; they had been sent up to London by train during the night, I believe. After standing in column for about half an hour, the brigade-major came down with orders to pile arms and stand easy; and perhaps half an hour afterwards we were told to get breakfast as quickly as possible, and to cook a day's food at the same time. This operation was managed pretty much in the same way as the evening before, except that we had our cooking pots and kettles ready. Meantime there was leisure to look around, and from where we stood there was a commanding view of one of the most beautiful scenes in England.

Our regiment was drawn up in the extremity of the ridge which

runs from Guildford to Dorking. This is indeed merely a part of the
great chalk-range which extends from beyond Aldershot east to the
Medway; but there is a gap in the ridge just here where the little
stream that runs past Dorking turns suddenly to the north, to find its
way to the Thames. We stood on the slope of the hill, as it trends
down eastward towards this gap, and had passed our bivouac in what
appeared to be a gentleman's park. A little way above us, and to our
right, was a very fine country-seat to which the park was attached,
now occupied by the headquarters of our division. From this house
the hill sloped steeply down southward to the valley below, which
runs nearly east and west parallel to the ridge, and carries the railway
and the road from Guildford to Reigate; and in which valley immediately in front of the chateau, and perhaps a mile and a half distant
from it, was the little town of Dorking, nestled in the trees, and rising
up the foot of the slopes on the other side of the valley which
stretched away to Leith Common, the scene of yesterday's march.
Thus, the main part of the town of Dorking was on our right front, but
the suburbs stretched away eastward nearly to our proper front, cul-
minating in a small railway station, from which the grassy slopes of
the park rose up dotted with shrubs and trees to where we were
standing. Round this railway station was a cluster of villas and one or
two mills, of whose gardens we thus had a bird's-eye view, their little
ornamental ponds glistening like looking glasses in the morning sun.
Immediately on our left the park sloped steeply down to the gap
before mentioned, through which ran the little stream, as well as the
railway from Epsom to Brighton, nearly due north and south, meeting
the Guildford and Reigate line at right angles. Close to the point of
intersection and the little station already mentioned was the station of
the former line where we had stopped the day before. Beyond the gap
on the east (our left), and in continuation of our ridge, rose the chalk-
hill again. The shoulder of this ridge overlooking the gap is called Box
Hill, from the shrubbery of box-wood with which it was covered. Its
sides were very steep, and the top of the ridge was covered with
troops.

The natural strength of our position was manifested at a glance; a
high grassy ridge steep to the south, with a stream in front, and but
little cover up the sides. It seemed made for a battle-field. The weak
point was the gap; the ground at the junction of the railways and the
roads immediately at the entrance of the gap formed a little valley,

dotted, as I have said, with buildings and gardens. This, in one sense, was the key of the position; for although it would not be tenable while we held the ridge commanding it, the enemy by carrying this point and advancing through the gap would cut our line in two. But you must not suppose I scanned the ground thus critically at the time. Anybody, indeed, might have been struck with the natural advantages of our position; but what, as I remember, most impressed me, was the peaceful beauty of the scene—the little town with the outline of the houses obscured by a blue mist, the massive crispness of the foliage, the outlines of the great trees, lighted up by the sun, and relieved by deep blue shade. So thick was the timber here, rising up the southern slopes of the valley, that it looked almost as if it might have been a primeval forest. The quiet of the scene was the more impressive because contrasted in the mind with the scenes we expected to follow; and I can remember, as if it were yesterday, the sensation of bitter regret that it should now be too late to avert this coming desecration of our country, which might so easily have been prevented. A little firmness, a little prevision on the part of our rulers, even a little common-sense, and this great calamity would have been rendered utterly impossible. Too late, alas! We were like the foolish virgins in the parable.

But you must not suppose the scene immediately around was gloomy; the camp was brisk and bustling enough. We had got over the stress of weariness; our stomachs were full; we felt a natural enthusiasm at the prospect of having so soon to take a part as the real defenders of the country, and we were inspirited at the sight of the large force that was now assembled. Along the slopes which trended off to the rear of our ridge, troops came marching up—volunteers, militia, cavalry, and guns; these, I heard, had come down from the north as far as Leatherhead the night before, and had marched over at daybreak. Long trains, too, began to arrive by the rail through the gap, one after another, containing militia and volunteers, who moved up to the ridge to the right and left, and took up their position, massed for the most part on the slopes which ran up from, and in rear of, where we stood. We now formed part of an army corps, we were told, consisting of three divisions, but what regiments composed the other two divisions I never heard.

All this movement we could distinctly see from our position, for we had hurried over our breakfast, expecting every minute that the battle would begin, and now stood or sat about on the ground near our piled arms. Early in the morning, too, we saw a very long train come along the valley from the direction of Guildford, full of redcoats. It halted at the little station at our feet, and the troops alighted. We could soon make out their bear-skins. They were the Guards, coming to reinforce this part of the line. Leaving a detachment of skirmishers to hold the line of the railway embankment, the main body marched up with a springy step and with the band playing, and drew up across the gap on our left, in prolongation of our line. There appeared to be three battalions of them, for they formed up in that number of columns at short intervals.

Shortly after this I was sent over to Box Hill with a message from our colonel to the colonel of a volunteer regiment stationed there, to know whether an ambulance-cart was obtainable, as it was reported this regiment was well supplied with carriage, whereas we were without any: my mission, however, was futile. Crossing the valley, I found a scene of great confusion at the railway station. Trains were still coming in with stores, ammunition, guns, and appliances of all sorts, which were being unloaded as fast as possible; but there were scarcely any means of getting the things off. There were plenty of waggons of all sorts, but hardly any horses to draw them, and the whole place was blocked up; while, to add to the confusion, a regular exodus had taken place of the people from the town, who had been warned that it was likely to be the scene of fighting. Ladies and women of all sorts and ages, and children, some with bundles, some empty-handed, were seeking places in the train, but there appeared no one on the spot authorized to grant them, and these poor creatures were pushing their way up and down, vainly asking for information and permission to get away. In the crowd I observed our surgeon, who likewise was in search of an ambulance of some sort: his whole professional apparatus, he said, consisted of a case of instruments.

Also in the crowd I stumbled upon Wood, Travers's old coachman. He had been sent down by his mistress to Guildford, because it was supposed our regiment had gone there, riding the horse, and laden with a supply of things—food, blankets, and, of course, a letter. He had also brought my knapsack; but at Guildford the horse was pressed for artillery work, and a receipt for it given him in exchange, so he had been obliged to leave all the heavy packages there, including my knapsack; but the faithful old man had brought on as many things as he could carry, and, hearing that we should be found in this part, had walked over thus laden from Guildford. He said that place was crowded with troops and that the heights were lined with them the whole way between the two towns; also, that some trains with wounded had passed up from the coast in the night, through Guildford. I led him off to where our regiment was, relieving the old man from part of the load he was staggering under. The food sent was not now so much needed, but the plates, knives, etc., and drinking-vessels promised to be handy—and Travers, you may be sure, was delighted to get his letter; while a couple of newspapers the old man had brought were eagerly competed for by all, even at this critical moment, for we had heard no authentic news since we left London on Sunday. And even at this distance of time, although I only glanced down the paper, I can remember almost the very words I read there. They were both copies of the same paper: the first, published on Sunday evening, when the news had arrived of the successful landing at three points, was written in a tone of despair. The country must confess that it had been taken by surprise. The conqueror would be satisfied with the humiliation inflicted by a peace dictated on our own shores; it was the clear duty of the Government to accept the best terms obtainable, and to avoid further bloodshed and disaster, and avert the fall of our tottering mercantile credit. The next morning's issue was in quite a different tone. Apparently the enemy had received a check, for we were here exhorted to resistance. An impregnable position was to be taken up along the Downs, a force was concentrating there far outnumbering the rash invaders, who, with an invincible line before them, and the sea behind, had no choice between destruction or surrender. Let there be no pusillanimous talk of negotiation: the fight must be fought out, and there could be but one issue. England, expectant but calm, awaited with confidence the result of the attack on its unconquerable volunteers. The writing appeared to me eloquent, but rather inconsistent. The same paper said the Government had sent off 500 workmen from Woolwich, to open a branch arsenal at Birmingham.

All this time we had nothing to do, except to change our position, which we did every few minutes, now moving up the hill farther to our right, now taking ground lower down to our left, as one order after another was brought down the line; but the staff-officers were galloping about perpetually with orders, while the rumble of the artillery as they moved about from one part of the field to another went on almost incessantly. At last the whole line stood to arms, the bands struck up, and the general commanding our army corps came riding down with his staff. We had seen him several times before, as we had been moving frequently about the position during the morning; but he now made a sort of formal inspection. He was a tall thin man, with long light hair, very well mounted, and as he sat his horse with an erect seat, and came prancing down the line, at a little distance he looked as if he might be five-and-twenty; but I believe he had served more than fifty years, and had been made a peer for services performed when quite an old man. I remember that he had more decorations than there was room for on the breast of his coat, and wore them suspended like a necklace round his neck. Like all the other generals, he was dressed in blue, with a cocked-hat and feathers—a bad plan, I thought, for it made them very conspicuous. The general halted before our battalion, and after looking at us a while made a short address: We had a post of honour next her Majesty's Guards, and would show ourselves worthy of it, and of the name of Englishmen. It did not need, he said, to be a general to see the strength of our position; it was impregnable, if properly held. Let us wait till the enemy was well pounded, and then the word would be given to go at him. Above everything, we must be steady. He then shook hands with our colonel, we gave him a cheer, and he rode on to where the Guards were drawn up.

Now then, we thought, the battle will begin. But still there were no signs of the enemy; and the air, though hot and sultry, began to be very hazy, so that you could scarcely see the town below, and the hills opposite were merely a confused blur, in which no features could be distinctly made out. After a while, the tension of feeling which followed the general's address relaxed, and we began to feel less as if everything depended on keeping our rifles firmly grasped: we were told to pile arms again, and got leave to go down by tens and twenties to the stream below to drink. This stream, and all the hedges and banks on our side of it, were held by our skirmishers, but the town had been abandoned. The position appeared an excellent one, except that the enemy, when they came, would have almost better cover than our men. While I was down at the brook, a column emerged from the town, making for our position. We thought for a moment it was the enemy, and you could not make out the colour of the uniforms for the dust; but it turned out to be our rear-guard, falling back from the opposite hills which they had occupied the previous night. One battalion of rifles halted for a few minutes at the stream to let the men drink, and I had a minute's talk with a couple of the officers. They had formed part of the force which had attacked the enemy on their first landing. They had it all their own way, they said, at first, and could have beaten the enemy back easily if they had been properly supported; but the whole thing was mismanaged. The volunteers came on very pluckily, they said, but they got into confusion, and so did the militia, and the attack failed with serious loss. It was the wounded of this force which had passed through Guildford in the night. The officers asked us eagerly about the arrangements for the battle, and when we said that the Guards were the only regular troops in this part of the field, shook their heads ominously.

While we were talking a third officer came up; he was a dark man with a smooth face and a curious excited manner. 'You are volunteers, I suppose,' he said, quickly, his eyes flashing the while. 'Well, now, look here; mind I don't want to hurt your feelings, or to say anything unpleasant, but I'll tell you what; if all you gentlemen were just to go back, and leave us to fight it out alone, it would be a devilish good thing. We could do it a precious deal better without you, I assure you. We don't want your help, I can tell you. We would much rather be left alone, I assure you. Mind I don't want to say anything rude, but that's a fact.' Having blurted out this passionately, he strode away before any one could reply, or the other officers could stop him. They apologized for his rudeness, saying that his brother, also in the regiment, had been killed on Sunday, and that this, and the sun, and marching, had affected his head. The officers told us that the enemy's advanced-guard was close behind, but that he had apparently been waiting for reinforcements, and would probably not attack in force until noon. It was, however, nearly three o'clock before the battle began. We had almost worn out the feeling of expectancy. For twelve hours had we been waiting for the coming struggle, till at last it seemed almost as if the invasion were but a bad dream, and the enemy, as yet unseen by us, had no real existence. So far things had not been very different, but for the numbers and for what we had been told, from a Volunteer review on Brighton Downs.

I remember that these thoughts were passing through my mind as we lay down in groups on the grass, some smoking, some nibbling at

their bread, some even asleep, when the listless state we had fallen
into was suddenly disturbed by a gunshot fired from the top of the hill
on our right, close by the big house. It was the first time I had ever
heard a shotted gun fired, and although it is fifty years ago, the angry
whistle of the shot as it left the gun is in my ears now. The sound was
soon to become common enough. We all jumped up at the report, and
fell in almost without the word being given, grasping our rifles tightly,
and the leading files peering forward to look for the approaching
enemy. This gun was apparently the signal to begin, for now our
batteries opened fire all along the line. What they were firing at I
could not see, and I am sure the gunners could not see much themselves. I have told you what a haze had come over the air since the
morning, and now the smoke from the guns settled like a pall over
the hill, and soon we could see little but the men in our ranks, and the
outline of some gunners in the battery drawn up next us on the slope
on our right. This firing went on, I should think, for nearly a couple of
hours, and still there was no reply. We could see the gunners—it was
a troop of horse-artillery—working away like fury, ramming, loading,
and running up with cartridges, the officer in command riding slowly
up and down just behind his guns, and peering out with his fieldglass
into the mist. Once or twice they ceased firing to let their smoke clear
away, but this did not do much good. For nearly two hours did this go
on, and not a shot came in reply. If a battle is like this, said Dick
Wake, who was my next-hand file, it's mild work, to say the least.

The words were hardly uttered when a rattle of musketry was
heard in front; our skirmishers were at it, and very soon the bullets
began to sing over our heads, and some struck the ground at our feet.
Up to this time we had been in column; we were now deployed into
line on the ground assigned to us. From the valley or gap on our left
there ran a lane right up the hill almost due west, or along our front.
This lane had a thick bank about four feet high, and the greater part
of the regiment was drawn up behind it; but a little way up the hill the
lane trended back out of the line, so the right of the regiment here left
it and occupied the open grass-land of the park. The bank had been
cut away at this point to admit of our going in and out. We had been
told in the morning to cut down the bushes on the top of the bank, so
as to make the space clear for firing over, but we had no tools to work
with; however, a party of sappers had come down and finished the
job. My company was on the right, and was thus beyond the shelter

of the friendly bank. On our right again was the battery of artillery already mentioned; then came a battalion of the line, then more guns, then a great mass of militia and volunteers and a few lined up to the big house. At least this was the order before the firing began; after that I do not know what changes took place.

And now the enemy's artillery began to open; where their guns were posted we could not see, but we began to hear the rush of the shells over our heads, and the bang as they burst just beyond. And now what took place I can really hardly tell you. Sometimes when I try and recall the scene, it seems as if it lasted for only a few minutes; yet I know, as we lay on the ground, I thought the hours would never pass away, as we watched the gunners still plying their task, firing at the invisible enemy, never stopping for a moment except when now and again a dull blow would be heard and a man fall down, then three or four of his comrades would carry him to the rear. The captain no longer rode up and down; what had become of him I do not know. Two of the guns ceased firing for a time; they had got injured in some way, and up rode an artillery general. I think I see him now, a very handsome man, with straight features and a dark moustache, his breast covered with medals. He appeared in a great rage at the guns stopping fire.

'Who commands this battery?' he cried.

'I do, Sir Henry,' said an officer, riding forward, whom I had not noticed before.

The group is before me at this moment, standing out clear against the background of smoke, Sir Henry erect on his splendid charger, his flashing eye, his left arm pointing towards the enemy to enforce something he was going to say, the young officer reining in his horse just beside him, and saluting with his right hand raised to his busby. This for a moment, then a dull thud, and both horses and riders are prostrate on the ground. A round shot had struck all four at the saddle line. Some of the gunners ran up to help, but neither officer could have lived many minutes. This was not the first I saw killed. Some time before this, almost immediately on the enemy's artillery opening, as we were lying, I heard something like the sound of steel striking steel, and at the same moment Dick Wake, who was next me in the ranks, leaning on his elbows, sank forward on his face. I looked round and saw what had happened; a shot fired at a high elevation, passing over his head, had struck the ground behind, nearly cutting his thigh off. It must have been the ball striking his sheathed bayonet which made the noise. Three of us carried the poor fellow to the rear, with difficulty for the shattered limb; but he was nearly dead from loss of blood when we got to the doctor, who was waiting in a sheltered hollow about two hundred yards in rear, with two other doctors in plain clothes, who had come up to help. We deposited our burden and returned to the front. Poor Wake was sensible when we left him, but apparently too shaken by the shock to be able to speak. Wood was there helping the doctors. I paid more visits to the rear of the same sort before the evening was over.

All this time we were lying there to be fired at without returning a shot, for our skirmishers were holding the line of walls and enclosures below. However, the bank protected most of us, and the brigadier now ordered our right company, which was in the open, to get behind it also; and there we lay about four deep, the shells crashing and bullets whistling over our heads, but hardly a man being touched. Our colonel was, indeed, the only one exposed, for he rode up and down the lane at a foot-pace as steady as a rock; but he made the major and adjutant dismount and take shelter behind the hedge, holding their horses. We were all pleased to see him so cool, and it restored our confidence in him, which had been shaken yesterday.

The time seemed interminable while we lay thus inactive. We could not, of course, help peering over the bank to try and see what was going on; but there was nothing to be made out, for now a tremendous thunderstorm, which had been gathering all day, burst on us, and a torrent of almost blinding rain came down, which obscured the view even more than the smoke, while the crashing of the thunder and the glare of the lightning could be heard and seen even above the roar and flashing of the artillery. Once the mist lifted, and I saw for a minute an attack on Box Hill, on the other side of the gap on our left. It was like the scene at a theatre—a curtain of smoke all round and a clear gap in the centre, with a sudden gleam of evening sunshine lighting it up. The steep smooth slope of the hill was crowded with the dark-blue figures of the enemy, whom I now saw for the first time—an irregular outline in front, but very solid in rear: the whole body was moving forward by fits and starts, the men firing and advancing, the officers waving their swords, the columns closing up and gradually making way. Our people were almost concealed by the bushes at the top, whence the smoke and their fire could be seen proceeding; presently from these bushes on the crest came out a red line, and dashed down the brow of the hill, a flame of fire belching out from the front as it advanced. The enemy hesitated, gave way, and finally ran back in a confused crowd down the hill. Then the mist covered the scene, but the glimpse of this splendid charge was inspiriting, and I hoped we should show the same coolness when it came to our turn.

It was about this time that our skirmishers fell back, a good many wounded, some limping along by themselves, others helped. The main body retired in very fair order, halting to turn round and fire; we could see a mounted officer of the Guards riding up and down encouraging them to be steady. Now came our turn. For a few minutes we saw nothing, but a rattle of bullets came through the rain and mist, mostly, however, passing over the bank. We began to fire in reply, stepping up against the bank to fire, and stooping down to load; but our brigade-major rode up with an order, and the word was passed through the men to reserve our fire. In a very few moments it must have been that, when ordered to stand, we could see the helmet-spikes and then the figures of the skirmishers as they came on: a lot of them there appeared to be, five or six deep I should say, but in loose order, each man stopping to aim and fire, and then coming forward a little. Just then the brigadier clattered on horseback up the lane. 'Now, then, gentlemen, give it them hot,' he cried; and fire away we did, as fast as ever we were able. A perfect storm of bullets seemed to be flying about us too, and I thought each moment must be the last; escape seemed impossible, but I saw no one fall, for I was too busy, and so were we all, to look to the right or left, but loaded and fired as fast as I could. How long this went on I know not—it could not have been long; neither side could have lasted many minutes under such a fire, but it ended by the enemy gradually falling back, and as soon as we saw this we raised a tremendous shout, and some of us jumped up on the bank to give them our parting shots. Suddenly the order was passed down the line to cease firing, and we soon discovered the cause; a battalion of the Guards was charging obliquely across from our left across our front. It was, I expect, their flank attack as much as our fire which had turned back the enemy; and it was a splendid sight to see their steady line as they advanced slowly across the smooth lawn below us, firing as they went, but as steady as if on parade. We felt a great elation at this moment; it seemed as if the battle was won.

Just then somebody called out to look to the wounded, and for the first time I turned to glance down the rank along the lane. Then I saw that we had not beaten back the attack without loss. Immediately before me lay Lawford of my office, dead on his back from a bullet through his forehead, his hand still grasping his rifle. At every step was some friend or acquaintance killed or wounded, and a few paces down the lane I found Travers, sitting with his back against the bank. A ball had gone through his lungs, and blood was coming from his mouth. I was lifting him up, but the cry of agony he gave stopped me. I then saw that this was not his only wound; his thigh was smashed by a bullet (which must have hit him when standing on the bank), and the blood streaming down mixed in a muddy puddle with the rain-water under him. Still he could not be left here, so, lifting him up as well as I could, I carried him through the gate which led out of the lane at the back to where our camp hospital was in the rear. The movement must have caused him awful agony, for I could not support the broken thigh, and he could not restrain his groans, brave fellow though he was; but how I carried him at all I cannot make out, for he was a much bigger man than myself. But I had not gone far, one of a stream of our fellows, all on the same errand, when a bandsman and Wood met me, bringing a hurdle as a stretcher, and on this we placed him. Wood had just time to tell me that he had got a cart down in the hollow, and would endeavour to take off his master at once to Kingston, when a staff-officer rode up to call us to the ranks. 'You really must not straggle in this way, gentlemen,' he said; 'pray keep your ranks.'

'But we can't leave our wounded to be trodden down and die,' cried one of our fellows.

'Beat off the enemy first, sir,' he replied. 'Gentlemen, do, pray, join your regiments, or we shall be a regular mob.' And no doubt he did not speak too soon; for besides our fellows straggling to the rear, lots of volunteers from the regiments in reserve were running forward to help, till the whole ground was dotted with groups of men. I hastened back to my post, but I had just time to notice that all the ground in our rear was occupied by a thick mass of troops, much more numerous than in the morning, and a column was moving down to the left of our line, to the ground before held by the Guards.

All this time, although the musketry had slackened, the artillery-fire seemed heavier than ever; the shells screamed overhead or burst

around; and I confess to feeling quite a relief at getting back to the
friendly shelter of the lane. Looking over the bank, I noticed for the
first time the frightful execution our fire had created. The space in
front was thickly strewed with dead and badly wounded, and beyond
the bodies of the fallen enemy could just be seen—for it was now
getting dusk—the bear-skins and red coats of our own gallant Guards
scattered over the slope, and marking the line of their victorious
advance. But hardly a minute could have passed in thus looking over
the field, when our brigade-major came moving up the lane on foot (I
suppose his horse had been shot) crying, 'Stand to your arms, Volunteers! they're coming on again!' and we found ourselves a second
time engaged in a hot musketry fire. How long it went on I cannot
now remember, but we could distinguish clearly the thick line of
skirmishers about sixty paces off, and mounted officers among them;
and we seemed to be keeping them well in check, for they were quite
exposed to our fire, while we were protected nearly up to our shoulders, when—I know not how—I became sensible that something had
gone wrong. 'We are taken in flank!' called out some one; and looking
along the left, sure enough there were dark figures jumping over the
bank into the lane and firing up along our line. The volunteers in
reserve, who had come down to take the place of the Guards, must
have given way at this point; the enemy's skirmishers had got through
our line, and turned our left flank.

How the next move came about I cannot recollect, or whether it
was without orders, but in a short time we found ourselves out of the
lane and drawn up in a straggling line about thirty yards in rear of it—
at our end, that is; the other flank had fallen back a good deal more—
and the enemy were lining the hedge, and numbers of them passing
over and forming up on our side. Beyond our left a confused mass
were retreating, firing as they went, followed by the advancing line of
the enemy. We stood in this way for a short space, firing at random as
fast as we could. Our colonel and major must have been shot, for there
was no one to give an order, when somebody on horseback called out
from behind—I think it must have been the brigadier—'Now, then,
Volunteers! give a British cheer, and go at them—charge!' and, with
a shout, we rushed at the enemy. Some of them ran, some stopped to
meet us, and for a moment it was a real hand-to-hand fight. I felt a
sharp sting in my leg, as I drove my bayonet right through the man in
front of me. I confess I shut my eyes, for I just got a glimpse of the

poor wretch as he fell back, his eyes starting out of his head, and, savage though we were, the sight was almost too horrible to look at. But the struggle was over in a second, and we had cleared the ground again right up to the rear hedge of the lane. Had we gone on, I believe we might have recovered the lane too, but we were now all out of order; there was no one to say what to do; the enemy began to line the hedge and open fire, and they were streaming past our left; and how it came about I know not, but we found ourselves falling back towards our right rear, scarce any semblance of a line remaining, and the volunteers who had given way on our left mixed up with us, and adding to the confusion.

It was now nearly dark. On the slopes which we were retreating to was a large mass of reserves drawn up in columns. Some of the leading files of these, mistaking us for the enemy, began firing at us; our fellows, crying out to them to stop, ran towards their ranks, and in a few moments the whole slope of the hill became a scene of confusion that I cannot attempt to describe, regiments and detachments mixed up in hopeless disorder. Most of us, I believe, turned towards the enemy and fired away our few remaining cartridges; but it was too late to take aim, fortunately for us, or the guns which the enemy had brought up through the gap, and were firing point-blank, would have done more damage. As it was, we could see little more than the bright flashes of their fire. In our confusion we had jammed up a line regiment immediately behind us, and its colonel and some staff-officers were in vain trying to make a passage for it, and their shouts to us to march to the rear and clear a road could be heard above the roar of the guns and the confused babel of sound. At last a mounted officer pushed his way through, followed by a company in sections, the men brushing past with firm-set faces, as if on a desperate task; and the battalion, when it got clear, appeared to deploy and advance down the slope. I have also a dim recollection of seeing the Life Guards trot past the front, and push on towards the town—a last desperate attempt to save the day—before we left the field.

Our adjutant, who had got separated from our flank of the regiment in the confusion, now came up, and managed to lead us, or at any rate some of us, up to the crest of the hill in the rear, to reform, as he said; but there we met a vast crowd of volunteers, militia, and waggons, all hurrying rearward from the direction of the big house, and we were borne in the stream for a mile at least before it was possible to stop.

At last the adjutant led us to an open space a little off the line of fugitives, and there we re-formed the remains of the companies. Telling us to halt, he rode off to try and obtain orders, and find out where the rest of our brigade was. From this point, a spur of high ground running off from the main plateau, we looked down through the dim twilight into the battlefield below. Artillery fire was still going on. We could see the flashes from the guns on both sides, and now and then a stray shell came screaming up and burst near us, but we were beyond the sound of musketry.

This halt first gave us time to think about what had happened. The long day of expectancy had been succeeded by the excitement of battle; and when each minute may be your last, you do not think much about other people, nor when you are facing another man with a rifle have you time to consider whether he or you are the invader, or that you are fighting for your home and hearths. All fighting is pretty much alike, I suspect, as to sentiment, when once it begins. But now we had time for reflection; and although we did not yet quite understand how far the day had gone against us, an uneasy feeling of self-condemnation must have come up in the minds of most of us; while, above all, we now began to realize what the loss of this battle meant to the country. Then, too, we knew not what had become of all our wounded comrades. Reaction, too, set in after the fatigue and excitement. For myself, I had found out for the first time that, besides the bayonet-wound in my leg, a bullet had gone through my left arm, just below the shoulder, and outside the bone. I remember feeling something like a blow just when we lost the lane, but the wound passed unnoticed till now, when the bleeding had stopped and the shirt was sticking to the wound.

This half-hour seemed an age, and while we stood on this knoll the endless tramp of men and rumbling of carts along the downs beside us told their own tale. The whole army was falling back. At last we could discern the adjutant riding up to us out of the dark. The army was to retreat, and take up a position on Epsom Downs, he said: we should join in the march, and try and find our brigade in the morning; and so we turned into the throng again, and make our way on as best we could. A few scraps of news he gave us as he rode alongside of our leading section; the army had held its position well for a time, but the enemy had at last broken through the line between us and Guildford, as well as in our front, and had poured his men through the point gained, throwing the line into confusion, and the first army corps near Guildford were also falling back to avoid being outflanked. The regular troops were holding the rear; we were to push on as fast as possible to get out of their way, and allow them to make an orderly retreat in the morning. The gallant old lord commanding our corps had been badly wounded early in the day, he heard, and carried off the field. The Guards had suffered dreadfully; the household cavalry had ridden down the Cuirassiers, but had got into broken ground and had been awfully cut up. Such were the scraps of news passed down our weary column. What had become of our wounded no one knew, and no one liked to ask. So we trudged on. It must have been midnight when we reached Leatherhead. Here we left the open ground and took to the road, and the block became greater. We pushed our way painfully along; several trains passed slowly ahead along the railway by the roadside, containing the wounded, we supposed—such of them, at least, as were lucky enough to be picked up.

It was daylight when we got to Epsom. The night had been bright and clear after the storm, with a cool air, which, blowing through my soaking clothes, chilled me to the bone. My wounded leg was stiff and sore, and I was ready to drop with exhaustion and hunger. Nor were my comrades in much better case; we had eaten nothing since breakfast the day before, and the bread we had put by had been washed away by the storm; only a little pulp remained at the bottom of my bag. The tobacco was all too wet to smoke. In this plight we were creeping along, when the adjutant guided us into a field by the roadside to rest awhile, and we lay down exhausted on the sloppy grass. The roll was here taken, and only 180 answered out of nearly 500 present on the morning of the battle. How many of these were killed and wounded no one could tell; but it was certain many must have got separated in the confusion of the evening. While resting here, we saw pass by, in the crowd of vehicles and men, a cart laden with commissariat stores, driven by a man in uniform. 'Food!' cried some one, and a dozen volunteers jumped up and surrounded the cart. The driver tried to whip them off; but he was pulled off his seat, and the contents of the cart thrown out in an instant. They were preserved meats in tins, which we tore open with our bayonets. The meat had been cooked before, I think; at any rate we devoured it. Shortly after this a general came by with three or four staff-officers. He stopped and spoke to our adjutant, and then rode into the field.

'My lads,' said he, 'you shall join my division for the present: fall in, and follow the regiment that is now passing.'

We rose up, fell in by companies, each about twenty strong, and turned once more into the stream moving along the road—regiments, detachments, single volunteers or militiamen, country people making off, some with bundles, some without, a few in carts, but most on foot; here and there waggons of stores, with men sitting wherever there was room, others crammed with wounded soldiers. Many blocks occurred from horses falling, or carts breaking down and filling up the road.

In the town the confusion was even worse, for all the houses seemed full of volunteers and militiamen, wounded or resting, or trying to find food, and the streets were almost choked up. Some officers were in vain trying to restore order, but the task seemed a hopeless one. One or two volunteer regiments which had arrived from the north the previous night, and had been halted here for orders, were drawn up along the roadside steadily enough, and some of the retreating regiments, including ours, may have preserved the semblance of discipline; but for the most part the mass pushing to the rear was a mere mob. The regulars, or what remained of them, were now, I believe, all in the rear, to hold the advancing enemy in check. A few officers among such a crowd could do nothing. To add to the confusion, several houses were being emptied of the wounded brought here the night before, to prevent their falling into the hands of the enemy, some in carts, some being carried to the railway by men. The groans of these poor fellows as they were jostled through the street went to our hearts, selfish though fatigue and suffering had made us.

At last, following the guidance of a staff-officer who was standing to show the way, we turned off from the main London road and took that towards Kingston. Here the crush was less, and we managed to move along pretty steadily. The air had been cooled by the storm, and there was no dust. We passed through a village where our new general had seized all the public-houses, and taken possession of the liquor; and each regiment as it came up was halted, and each man got a drink of beer, served out by companies. Whether the owner got paid, I know not, but it was like nectar.

It must have been about one o'clock in the afternoon that we came in sight of Kingston. We had been on our legs sixteen hours, and had got over about twelve miles of ground. There is a hill a little south of the Surbiton station, covered then mostly with villas, but open at the western extremity, where there was a clump of trees on the summit. We had diverged from the road towards this, and here the general halted us and disposed the line of the division along his front, facing to the south-west, the right of the line reaching down to the Thames, the left extending along the southern slope of the hill, in the direction of the Epsom road by which we had come. We were nearly in the centre, occupying the knoll just in front of the general, who dismounted on the top and tied his horse to a tree. It is not much of a hill, but commands an extensive view over the flat country around; and as we lay wearily on the ground we could see the Thames glistening like a silver field in the bright sunshine, the palace at Hampton Court, the bridge at Kingston, and the old church tower rising above the haze of the town, with the woods of Richmond Park behind it.

To most of us the scene could not but call up their associations of happy days of peace—days now ended and peace destroyed through national infatuation. We did not say this to each other, but a deep depression had come upon us, partly due to weakness and fatigue, no doubt, but we saw that another stand was going to be made, and we had no longer any confidence in ourselves. If we could not hold our own when stationary in line, on a good position, but had been broken up into a rabble at the first shock, what chance had we now of manoeuvring against a victorious enemy in this open ground? A feeling of desperation came over us, a determination to struggle on against hope; but anxiety for the future of the country, and our friends, and all dear to us, filled our thoughts now that we had time for reflection. We had had no news of any kind since Wood joined us the day before—we knew not what was doing in London, or what the Government was about, or anything else; and, exhausted though we were, we felt an intense craving to know what was happening in other parts of the country.

Our general had expected to find a supply of food and ammunition here, but nothing turned up. Most of us had hardly a cartridge left, so he ordered the regiment next to us, which came from the north and had not been engaged, to give us enough to make up twenty rounds a man, and he sent off a fatigue-party to Kingston to try and get provisions, while a detachment of our fellows was allowed to go foraging among the villas in our rear; and in about an hour they brought back some bread and meat, which gave us a slender meal all round. They said most of the houses were empty, and that many had been stripped of all eatables, and a good deal damaged already.

It must have been between three and four o'clock when the sound of cannonading began to be heard in the front, and we could see the smoke of guns rising above the woods of Esher and Claremont, and soon afterwards some troops emerged from the fields below us. It was the rear-guard of regular troops. There were some guns also, which were driven up the slope and took up their position round the knoll. There were three batteries, but they only counted eight guns amongst them. Behind them was posted the line; it was a brigade apparently of four regiments, but the whole did not look to be more than eight or nine hundred men. Our regiment and another had been moved a little to the rear to make way for them, and presently we were ordered down to occupy the railway station on our right rear. My leg was now so stiff I could no longer march with the rest, and my left arm was very swollen and sore, and almost useless; but anything seemed better than being left behind, so I limped after the battalion as best I could down to the station. There was a goods shed a little in advance of it down the line, a strong brick building, and here my company was posted. The rest of our men lined the wall of the enclosure. A staff-officer came with us to arrange the distribution; we should be supported by line troops, he said; and in a few minutes a train full of them came slowly up from Guildford way. It was the last; the men got out, the train passed on, and a party began to tear up the rails, while the rest were distributed among the houses on each side. A sergeant's party joined us in our shed, and an engineer officer with sappers came to knock holes in the wall for us to fire from; but there were only half-a-dozen of them, so progress was not rapid, and as we had no tools we could not help.

It was while we were watching this job that the adjutant, who was as active as ever, looked in, and told us to muster in the yard. The fatigue-party had come back from Kingston, and a small baker's hand-cart of food was made over to us as our share. It contained loaves, flour, and some joints of meat. The meat and the flour we had not time or means to cook. The loaves we devoured; and there was a tap of water in the yard, so we felt refreshed by the meal. I should have liked to wash my wounds, which were becoming very offensive, but I dare not take off my coat, feeling sure I should not be able to get it on again. It was while we were eating our bread that the rumour first reached us of another disaster, even greater than that we had witnessed ourselves. Whence it came I know not; but a whisper went down the ranks that Woolwich had been captured. We all knew that it was our only arsenal, and understood the significance of the blow. No hope, if this were true, of saving the country. Thinking over this, we went back to the shed.

Although this was only our second day of war, I think we were already old soldiers so far that we had come to be careless about fire, and the shot and shell that now began to open on us made no sensation. We felt, indeed, our need of discipline, and we saw plainly enough the slender chance of success coming out of such a rabble as we were; but I think we were all determined to fight on as long as we could. Our gallant adjutant gave his spirit to everybody; and the staff-officer commanding was a very cheery fellow, and went about as if we were certain of victory. Just as the firing began he looked in to say that we were as safe as in a church, that we must be sure and pepper the enemy well, and that more cartridges would soon arrive. There were some steps and benches in the shed, and on these a part of our men were standing, to fire through the upper loop-holes, while the line soldiers and others stood on the ground, guarding the second row. I sat on the floor, for I could not now use my rifle, and besides, there were more men than loop-holes.

The artillery fire which had opened now on our position was from a longish range; and occupation for the riflemen had hardly begun, when there was a crash in the shed, and I was knocked down by a blow on the head. I was almost stunned for a time, and could not make out what had happened. A shot or shell had hit the shed without quite penetrating the wall, but the blow had upset the steps resting against it, and the men standing on them, bringing down a cloud of plaster and brickbats, one of which had struck me. I felt now past being of use. I could not use my rifle, and could barely stand; and after a time I thought I would make for my own house, on the chance of finding some one still there. I got up therefore, and staggered homewards. Musketry fire had now commenced, and our side were blazing away from the windows of the houses, and from behind walls, and from the shelter of some trucks still standing in the station. A couple of field-pieces in the yard were firing, and in the open space in rear a reserve was drawn up. There, too, was the staff-officer on horseback, watching the fight through his field-glass. I remember having still enough sense to feel that the position was a hopeless one. That straggling line of houses and gardens would surely be broken through at some point, and then the line must give way like a rope of sand. It was about a mile to our house, and I was thinking how I could possibly drag myself so far when I suddenly recollected that I was passing Travers's house—one of the first of a row of villas then leading from the station to Kingston. Had he been brought home, I wondered, as his faithful old servant promised, and was his wife still here? I remember to this day the sensation of shame I felt, when I recollected that I had not once given him—my greatest friend—a thought since I carried him off the field the day before. But war and suffering make men selfish. I would go in now at any rate and rest awhile, and see if I could be of use.

The little garden before the house was as trim as ever—I used to pass it every day on my way to the train, and knew every shrub in it—and a blaze of flowers, but the hall-door stood ajar. I stepped in and saw little Arthur standing in the hall. He had been dressed as neatly as ever that day, and as he stood there in his pretty blue frock and white trousers and socks showing his chubby little legs, with his golden locks, fair face, and large dark eyes, the picture of childish beauty, in the quiet hall, just as it used to look—the vases of flowers, the hat and coats hanging up, the familiar pictures on the walls—this vision of peace in the midst of war made me wonder for a moment, faint and giddy as I was, if the pandemonium outside had any real existence, and was not merely a hideous dream. But the roar of the guns making the house shake, and the rushing of the shot, gave a ready answer. The little fellow appeared almost unconscious of the scene around him, and was walking up the stairs holding by the railing, one step at a time, as I had seen him do a hundred times before, but turned round as I came in. My appearance frightened him, and staggering as I did into the hall, my face and clothes covered with blood and dirt, I must have looked an awful object to the child, for he gave a cry and turned to run toward the basement stairs. But he stopped on hearing my voice calling him back to his god-papa, and after a while came timidly up to me. Papa had been to the battle, he said, and was very ill; mamma was with papa; Wood was out; Lucy was in the cellar, and had taken him there, but he wanted to go to mamma.

Telling him to stay in the hall for a minute till I called him, I climbed up-stairs and opened the bedroom-door. My poor friend lay there, his body resting on the bed, his head supported on his wife's shoulder as she sat by the bedside. He breathed heavily, but the pallor of his face, the closed eyes, the prostrate arms, the clammy foam she was wiping from his mouth, all spoke of approaching death. The good old servant had done his duty, at least—he had brought his master home to die in his wife's arms. The poor woman was too intent on her charge to notice the opening of the door, and as the child would be better away, I closed it gently and went down to the hall to take little Arthur to the shelter below, where the maid was hiding. Too late! He lay at the foot of the stairs on his face, his little arms stretched out, his hair dabbled in blood. I had not noticed the crash among the other noises, but a splinter of a shell must have come through the open doorway; it had carried away the back of his head. The poor child's death must have been instantaneous. I tried to lift up the little corpse with my one arm, but even this load was too much for me, and while stooping down I fainted away.

When I came to my senses again it was quite dark, and for some time I could not make out where I was; I lay indeed for some time like one half asleep, feeling no inclination to move. By degrees I became aware that I was on the carpeted floor of a room. All noise of battle had ceased, but there was a sound as of many people close by. At last I sat up and gradually got to my feet. The movement gave me intense pain, for my wounds were now highly inflamed, and my clothes sticking to them made them dreadfully sore. At last I got up and groped my way to the door, and opening it at once saw where I was, for the pain had brought back my senses. I had been lying in Travers's little writing-room at the end of the passage, into which I make my way. There was no gas, and the drawing-room door was closed; but from the open dining-room the glimmer of a candle feebly lighted up the hall, in which half-a-dozen sleeping figures could be discerned, while the room itself was crowded with men. The table was covered with plates, glasses, and bottles; but most of the men were asleep in the chairs or on the floor, a few were smoking cigars, and one or two with their helmets on were still engaged at supper, occasionally grunting out an observation between the mouthfuls.

'*Sind wackere Soldaten, diese Englischen Freiwilligen,*' said a broad-shouldered brute, stuffing a great hunch of beef into his mouth with a silver fork, an implement I should think he must have been using for the first time in his life.

'*Ja, ja,*' replied a comrade, who was lolling back in his chair with a pair of very dirty legs on the table, and one of poor Travers's best cigars in his mouth, '*Sie so gut laufen können.*'

'*Ja wohl,*' responded the first speaker, '*aber sind nicht eben so schnell wie die Französischen Mobloten.*'

'*Gewiss,*' grunted a hulking lout from the floor, leaning on his elbow, and sending out a cloud of smoke from his ugly jaws, '*und da sind hier etwa gute Schützen.*'

'*Hast recht, lange Peter,*' answered number one, '*wenn die Schurken so gut exerciren wie schützen könnten, so wären wir heute nicht hier!*'

'*Recht! Recht!*' said the second, '*das exerciren macht den guten Soldaten.*'

What more criticisms on the shortcomings of our unfortunate volunteers might have passed I did not stop to hear, being interrupted by a sound on the stairs. Mrs Travers was standing on the landing-place; I limped up the stairs to meet her. Among the many pictures of those fatal days engraven on my memory, I remember none more clearly than the mournful aspect of my poor friend, widowed and childless within a few moments, as she stood there in her white dress, coming forth like a ghost from the chamber of the dead, the candle she held lighting up her face, and contrasting its pallor with the dark hair that fell disordered round it, its beauty radiant even through features worn with fatigue and sorrow. She was calm and even tearless, though the trembling lip told of the effort to restrain the emotion she felt.

'Dear friend,' she said, taking my hand, 'I was coming to seek you; forgive my selfishness in neglecting you so long; but you will understand'—glancing at the door above—'how occupied I have been.'

'Where', I began, 'is'—

'my boy?' she answered, anticipating my question. 'I have laid him by his father. But now your wounds must be cared for; how pale and faint you look!—rest here for a moment'—and, descending to the dining-room, she returned with some wine, which I gratefully drank, and then, making me sit down on the top step of the stairs, she brought water and linen, and, cutting off the sleeve of my coat, bathed and bandaged my wounds. 'Twas I who felt selfish for thus adding to her troubles; but in truth I was too weak to have much will left, and stood in need of the help which she forced me to accept; and the dressing of my wounds afforded indescribable relief. While thus tending me, she explained in broken sentences how matters stood. Every room but her own, and the little parlour into which she with Wood's help had carried me, was full of soldiers. Wood had been taken away to work at repairing the railroad, and Lucy had run off from fright; but the cook had stopped at her post, and had served up supper and had opened the cellar for the soldiers' use; she did not understand what they said, and they were rough and boorish, but not uncivil. I should now go, she said, when my wounds were dressed, to look after my own home, where I might be wanted; for herself, she wished only to be allowed to remain watching there—pointing to the room where lay the bodies of her husband and child—where she would not be molested. I felt that her advice was good. I could be of no use as protection, and I had an anxious longing to know what had become of my sick mother and sister; besides, some arrangement must be made for the burial. I therefore limped away. There was no need to express thanks on either side, and the grief was too deep to be reached by any outward show of sympathy.

Outside the house there was a good deal of movement and bustle; many carts going along, the waggoners, from Sussex and Surrey, evidently impressed and guarded by soldiers; and although no gas was burning, the road towards Kingston was well lighted by torches held by persons standing at short intervals in line, who had been seized for the duty, some of them the tenants of neighbouring villas. Almost the first of these torch-bearers I came to was an old gentleman whose face I was well acquainted with, from having frequently travelled up and down in the same train with him. He was a senior clerk in a government office, I believe, and was a mild-looking old man with a prim face and a long neck, which he used to wrap in a wide double neckcloth, a thing even in those days seldom seen. Even in that moment of bitterness I could not help being amused by the absurd figure this poor old fellow presented, with his solemn face and long cravat doing penance with a torch in front of his own door, to light up the path of our conquerors.

But a more serious object now presented itself, a corporal's guard passing by, with two English volunteers in charge, their hands tied behind their backs. They cast an imploring glance at me, and I stepped into the road to ask the corporal what was the matter, and even ventured, as he was passing on, to lay my hand on his sleeve. '*Auf dem Wege, Spitzbube!*' cried the brute, lifting his rifle as if to knock me down. 'Must one prisoners who fire at us let shoot,' he went on to add; and shot the poor fellows would have been, I suppose, if I had not interceded with an officer who happened to be riding by. '*Herr Hauptmann*,' I cried, as loud as I could, 'is this your discipline, to let unarmed prisoners be shot without orders?' The officer, thus appealed to, reined in his horse, and halted the guard till he heard what I had to say. My knowledge of other languages here stood me in good stead, for the prisoners, north-country factory hands apparently, were of course utterly unable to make themselves understood, and did not even know in what they had offended. I therefore interpreted their explanation; they had been left behind while skirmishing near Ditton, in a barn, and coming out of their hiding-place in the midst of a party of the enemy, with their rifles in their hands, the latter thought they were going to fire at them from behind. It was a wonder they were not shot down on the spot.

The captain heard the tale, and then told the guard to let them go, and they slunk off at once into a by-road. He was a fine soldier-like man, but nothing could exceed the insolence of his manner, which was perhaps all the greater because it seemed not intentional, but to arise from a sense of immeasurable superiority. Between lame *Freiwilliger* pleading for his comrades and the captain of the conquering army, there was, in his view, an infinite gulf. Had the two men been dogs, their fate could not have been decided more contemptuously. They were let go simply because they were not worth keeping as prisoners, and perhaps to kill any living thing without cause went against the *Hauptmann's* sense of justice. But why speak of this insult in particular? Had not every man who lived then his tale to tell of humiliation and degradation? For it was the same story everywhere. After the first stand in line, and when once they had got us on the march, the enemy laughed at us. Our handful of regular troops was sacrificed almost to a man in a vain conflict with numbers; our volunteers and militia, with officers who did not know their work, without ammunition or equipment, or staff to superintend, starving in the midst of plenty, we had soon become a helpless mob, fighting desperately here and there, but with whom, as a manoeuvring army, the disciplined invaders did just what they pleased. Happy those whose bones whitened the fields of Surrey; they at least were spared the disgrace we lived to endure. Even you, who have never known what it is to live otherwise than on sufferance, even your cheeks burn when we talk of these days; think, then, what those endured who, like your grandfather, had been citizens of the proudest nation on earth, which had never known disgrace or defeat, and whose boast it used to be that they bore a flag on which the sun never set! We had heard of generosity in war; we found none: the war was made by us, it was said, and we must take the consequences. London and our only arsenal captured, we were at the mercy of our captors, and right heavily did they tread on our necks.

Need I tell you the rest?—of the ransom we had to pay, and the taxes raised to cover it, which keep us paupers to this day?—the brutal frankness that announced we must give place to a new naval Power, and be made harmless for revenge?—the victorious troops living at free quarters, the yoke they put on us made the more galling that their requisitions had a semblance of method and legality? Better have been robbed at first hand by the soldiery themselves, than through our own magistrates made the instruments for extortion. How we lived through the degradation we daily and hourly underwent, I hardly even now understand. And what was there left to us to live for? Stripped of our colonies; Canada and the West Indies gone to America; Australia forced to separate; India lost for ever, after the English there had all been destroyed, vainly trying to hold the country when cut off from aid by their countrymen; Gibraltar and Malta ceded to the new naval Power; Ireland independent and in perpetual anarchy and revolution. When I look at my country as it is now—its trade gone, its factories silent, its harbours empty, a prey to pauperism and decay—when I see all this, and think what Great Britain was in my youth, I ask myself whether I have really a heart or any sense of patriotism that I should have witnessed such degradation and still care to live!

France was different. There, too, they had to eat the bread of tribulation under the yoke of the conqueror; their fall was hardly more sudden or violent than ours; but war could not take away their rich soil; they had no colonies to lose; their broad lands, which made their wealth, remained to them; and they rose again from the blow. But our people could not be got to see how artificial our prosperity was—that it all rested on foreign trade and financial credit; that the course of trade once turned away from us, even for a time, it might never return; and that our credit once shaken might never be restored. To hear men talk in those days, you would have thought that Providence had ordained that our Government should always borrow at three per cent, and that trade came to us because we lived in a foggy little island set in a boisterous sea. They could not be got to see that the wealth heaped up on every side was not created in the country, but in India and China, and other parts of the world; and that it would be quite possible for the people who made money by buying and selling the natural treasures of the earth, to go and live in other places, and take their profits with them. Nor would men believe that there could ever be an end to our coal and iron, or that they would get to be so much dearer than the coal and iron of America that it would no longer be worth while to work them, and that therefore we ought to insure against the loss of our artificial position as the great centre of trade, by making ourselves secure and strong and respected.

We thought we were living in a commercial millennium, which must last for a thousand years at least. After all, the bitterest part of our reflection is that all this misery and decay might have been so easily prevented, and that we brought it about ourselves by our own shortsighted recklessness. There, across the narrow Straits, was the writing on the wall; but we would not choose to read it. The warnings of the few were drowned in the voice of the multitude. Power was then passing away from the class which had been used to rule, and to face political dangers, and which had brought the nation with honour unsullied through former struggles, into the hands of the lower classes, uneducated, untrained to the use of political rights, and swayed by demagogues; and the few who were wise in their generation were denounced as alarmists, or as aristocrats who sought their own aggrandizement by wasting public money on bloated armaments. The rich were idle and luxurious; the poor grudged the cost of defence. Politics had become a mere bidding for Radical votes, and those who should have led the nation stooped rather to pander to the selfishness of the day, and humoured the popular cry which denounced those who would secure the defence of the nation by enforced arming of its manhood, as interfering with the liberties of the people.

Truly the nation was ripe for a fall; but when I reflect how a little firmness and self-denial, or political courage and foresight, might have averted the disaster, I feel that the judgement must have really been deserved. A nation too selfish to defend its liberty could not have been fit to retain it. To you, my grandchildren, who are now going to seek a new home in a more prosperous land, let not this bitter lesson be lost upon you in the country of your adoption. For me, I am too old to begin life again in a strange country; and, hard and evil as have been my days, it is not much to await in solitude the time which cannot now be far off, when my old bones will be laid to rest in the soil I have loved so well, and whose happiness and honour I have so long survived.

When William Came

A Story of London under the Hohenzollerns

CONTENTS

CHAPTER I

The Singing-Bird and the Barometer

Cicely Yeovil sat in a low swing chair, alternately looking at herself in a mirror and at the other occupant of the room in the flesh. Both prospects gave her undisguised satisfaction. Without being vain she was duly appreciative of good looks, whether in herself or in another, and the reflection that she saw in the mirror, and the young man whom she saw seated at the piano, would have come with credit out of a more severely critical inspection. Probably she looked longer and with greater appreciation at the piano-player than at her own image; her good looks were an inherited possession, that had been with her more or less all her life, while Ronnie Storre was a comparatively new acquisition, discovered and achieved, so to speak, by her own enterprise, selected by her own good taste. Fate had given her adorable eyelashes and an excellent profile. Ronnie was an indulgence she had bestowed on herself.

Cicely had long ago planned out for herself a complete philosophy of life, and had resolutely set to work to carry her philosophy into practice. 'When love is over how little of love even the lover understands,' she quoted to herself from one of her favourite poets, and transposed the saying into 'While life is with us how little of life even the materialist understands.' Most people that she knew took endless pains and precautions to preserve and prolong their lives and keep their powers of enjoyment unimpaired; few, very few, seemed to make any intelligent effort at understanding what they really wanted in the way of enjoying their lives, or to ascertain what were the best means for satisfying those wants. Fewer still bent their whole energies to the one paramount aim of getting what they wanted in the fullest possible measure. Her scheme of life was not a wholly selfish one; no one could understand what she wanted as well as she did herself, therefore she felt that she was the best person to pursue her own ends and cater for her own wants. To have others thinking and acting for one merely meant that one had to be perpetually grateful for a lot of well-meant and usually unsatisfactory services. It was like the case of a rich man giving a community a free library, when probably the community only wanted free fishing or reduced tram-fares. Cicely studied her own whims and wishes, experimented in the best method of carrying them into effect, compared the accumulated results of her experiments, and gradually arrives at a very clear idea of what she wanted in life, and how best to achieve it. She was not by disposition a self-centred soul, therefore she did not make the mistake of supposing that one can live successfully and gracefully in a crowded world without taking due notice of the other human elements around one. She was instinctively far more thoughtful for others than many a person who is genuinely but unseeingly addicted to unselfishness. Also she kept in her armoury the weapon which can be so mightily effective if used sparingly by a really sincere individual—the knowledge of when to be a humbug.

Ambition entered to a certain extent into her life, and governed it perhaps rather more than she knew. She desired to escape from the doom of being a nonentity, but the escape would have to be effected in her own way and in her own time; to be governed by ambition was only a shade or two better than being governed by convention.

The drawing-room in which she and Ronnie were sitting was of such proportions that one hardly knew whether it was intended to be one room or several, and it had the merit of being moderately cool at two o'clock on a particularly hot July afternoon. In the coolest of its many alcoves servants had noiselessly set out an improvised luncheon table: a tempting array of caviare, crab and mushroom salads, cold asparagus, slender hock bottles, and high-stemmed wine goblets peeped out from amid a setting of Charlotte Klemm roses.

Cicely rose from her seat and went over to the piano.

'Come,' she said, touching the young man lightly with a finger-tip on the top of his very sleek, copper-hued head, 'we're going to have picnic-lunch to-day up here; it's so much cooler than any of the downstairs rooms, and we shan't be bothered with the servants trotting in and out all the time. Rather a good idea of mine, wasn't it?'

Ronnie, after looking anxiously to see that the word 'picnic' did not portend tongue sandwiches and biscuits, gave the idea his blessing.

'What is young Storre's profession?' some one had once asked concerning him.

'He has a great many friends who have independent incomes,' had been the answer.

The meal was begun in an appreciative silence; a picnic in which three kinds of red pepper were available, for the caviare demanded a certain amount of respectful attention.

'My heart ought to be like a singing-bird to-day, I suppose,' said Cicely presently.

'Because your good man is coming home?' asked Ronnie.

Cicely nodded.

'He's expected some time this afternoon, though I'm rather vague as to which train he arrives by. Rather a stifling day for railway travelling.'

'And *is* your heart doing the singing-bird business?' asked Ronnie.

'That depends,' said Cicely, 'if I may choose the bird. A missel-thrush would do, perhaps; it sings loudest in stormy weather, I believe.'

Ronnie disposed of two or three stems of asparagus before making any comment on this remark.

'Is there going to be stormy weather?' he asked.

'The domestic barometer is set rather that way,' said Cicely. 'You see, Murrey has been away for ever so long, and, of course, there will be lots of things he won't be used to, and I'm afraid matters may be rather strained and uncomfortable for a time.'

'Do you mean that he will object to me?' asked Ronnie.

'Not in the least,' said Cicely, 'he's quite broad-minded on most subjects, and he realizes that this is an age in which sensible people know thoroughly well what they want, and are determined to get what they want. It pleases me to see a lot of you, and to spoil you and pay you extravagant compliments about your good looks and your music, and to imagine at times that I'm in danger of getting fond of you; I don't see any harm in it, and I don't suppose Murrey will either—in fact, I shouldn't be surprised if he takes rather a liking to you. No, it's the general situation that will trouble and exasperate him; he's not had time to get accustomed to the *fait accompli* like we have. It will break on him with horrible suddenness.'

'He was somewhere in Russia when the war broke out, wasn't he?' said Ronnie.

'Somewhere in the wilds of Eastern Siberia, shooting and bird collecting, miles away from a railway or telegraph line, and it was all over before he knew anything about it; it didn't last very long, when you come to think of it. He was due home somewhere about that time, and when the weeks slipped by without my hearing from him, I quite thought he'd been captured in the Baltic or somewhere on the way back. It turned out that he was down with marsh fever in some out-of-the-way spot, and everything was over and finished with before he got back to civilization and newspapers.'

'It must have been a bit of a shock,' said Ronnie, busy with a well-devised salad; 'still, I don't see why there should be domestic storms when he comes back. You are hardly responsible for the catastrophe that has happened.'

'No,' said Cicely, 'but he'll come back naturally feeling sore and savage with everything he sees around him, and he won't realize just at once that we've been through all that ourselves, and have reached the stage of sullen acquiescence in what can't be helped. He won't understand, for instance, how we can be enthusiastic and excited over Gorla Mustelford's début, and things of that sort; he'll think we are a set of callous revellers, fiddling while Rome is burning.'

'In this case,' said Ronnie, 'Rome isn't burning, it's burnt. All that remains to be done is to rebuild it—when possible.'

'Exactly, and he'll say we're not doing much towards helping at that.'

'But,' protested Ronnie, 'the whole thing has only just happened. "Rome wasn't built in a day," and we can't rebuild our Rome in a day.'

'I know,' said Cicely, 'but so many of our friends, and especially Murrey's friends, have taken the thing in a tragical fashion, and cleared off to the Colonies, or shut themselves up in their country houses, as though there was a sort of moral leprosy infecting London.'

'I don't see what good that does,' said Ronnie.

'It doesn't do any good, but it's what a lot of them have done because they felt like doing it, and Murrey will feel like doing it too. That is where I foresee trouble and disagreement.'

Ronnie shrugged his shoulders.

'I would take things tragically if I saw the good of it,' he said; 'as matters stand it's too late in the day and too early to be anything but philosophical about what one can't help. For the present we've just got to make the best of things. Besides, you can't very well turn down Gorla at the last moment.'

'I'm not going to turn down Gorla, or anybody,' said Cicely with decision. 'I think it would be silly, and silliness doesn't appeal to me. That is why I foresee storms on the domestic horizon. After all, Gorla has her career to think of. Do you know,' she added, with a change of tone, 'I rather wish you would fall in love with Gorla; it would make me horribly jealous, and a little jealousy is such a good tonic for any woman who knows how to dress well. Also, Ronnie, it would prove that you are capable of falling in love with some one, of which I've grave doubts up to the present.'

'Love is one of the few things in which the make-believe is superior to the genuine,' said Ronnie, 'it lasts longer, and you get more fun out of it, and it's easier to replace when you've done with it.'

'Still, it's rather like playing with coloured paper instead of playing with fire,' objected Cicely.

A footman came round the corner with the trained silence that tactfully contrives to make itself felt.

'Mr Luton to see you, madam,' he announced, 'shall I say you are in?'

'Mr Luton? Oh, yes,' said Cicely, 'he'll probably have something to tell us about Gorla's concert,' she added, turning to Ronnie.

Tony Luton was a young man who had sprung from the people, and had taken care that there should be no recoil. He was scarcely twenty years of age, but a tightly packed chronicle of vicissitudes lay behind his sprightly insouciant appearance. Since his fifteenth year he had lived, Heaven knew how, getting sometimes a minor engagement at some minor music-hall, sometimes a temporary job as secretary-valet-companion to a roving invalid, dining now and then on plovers' eggs and asparagus at one of the smarter West End restaurants, at other times devouring a kipper or a sausage in some stuffy Edgware Road eating-house; always seemingly amused by life, and always amusing. It is possible that somewhere in such heart as he possessed there lurked a rankling bitterness against the hard things of life, or a scrap of gratitude towards the one or two friends who had helped him disinterestedly, but his most intimate associates could not have guessed at the existence of such feelings. Tony Luton was just a merry-eyed dancing faun, whom Fate had surrounded with streets instead of woods, and it would have been in the highest degree inartistic to have sounded him for a heart or a heartache.

The dancing of the faun took one day a livelier and more assured turn, the joyousness became more real, and the worst of the vicissitudes seemed suddenly over. A musical friend, gifted with mediocre but marketable abilities, supplied Tony with a song, for which he obtained a trial performance at an East End hall. Dressed as a jockey, for no particular reason except that the costume suited him, he sang, 'They quaff the gay bubbly in Eccleston Square' to an appreciative audience, which included the manager of a famous West End theatre of varieties. Tony and his song won the managerial favour, and were immediately transplanted to the West End house, where they scored a success of which the drooping music-hall industry was at the moment badly in need.

It was just after the great catastrophe, and men of the London world were in no humour to think; they had witnessed the inconceivable befall them, they had nothing but political ruin to stare at, and they were anxious to look the other way. The words of Tony's song were more or less meaningless, though he sang them remarkably well, but the tune, with its air of slyness and furtive joyousness, appealed in some unaccountable manner to people who were furtively unhappy, and who were trying to appear stoically cheerful.

'What must be, must be,' and 'It's a poor heart that never rejoices,' were the popular expressions of the London public at that moment, and the men who had to cater for that public were thankful when they were able to stumble across anything that fitted in with the prevailing mood. For the first time in his life Tony Luton discovered that agents and managers were a leisured class, and that office boys had manners.

He entered Cicely's drawing-room with the air of one to whom assurance of manner has become a sheathed weapon, a court accessory rather than a trade implement. He was more quietly dressed than the usual run of music-hall successes; he had looked critically at life from too many angles not to know that though clothes cannot make a man they can certainly damn him.

'Thank you, I have lunched already,' he said in answer to a question from Cicely. 'Thank you,' he said again in a cheerful affirmative, as the question of hock in a tall ice-cold goblet was propounded to him.

'I've come to tell you the latest about the Gorla Mustelford evening,' he continued. 'Old Laurent is putting his back into it, and it's really going to be rather a big affair. She's going to out-Russian the Russians. Of course, she hasn't their technique nor a tenth of their training, but she's having tons of advertisement. The name Gorla is almost an advertisement in itself, and then there's the fact that she's the daughter of a peer.'

'She has temperament,' said Cicely, with the decision of one who makes a vague statement in a good cause.

'So Laurent says,' observed Tony. 'He discovers temperament in every one that he intends to boom. He told me that I had temperament to the finger-tips, and I was too polite to contradict him. But I haven't told you the really important thing about the Mustelford début. It is a profound secret, more or less, so you must promise not to breathe a word about it till half-past four, when it will appear in all the six o'clock newspapers.'

Tony paused for dramatic effect, while he drained his goblet, and then made his announcement.

'Majesty is going to be present. Informally and unofficially, but still present in the flesh. A sort of casual dropping in, carefully heralded by unconfirmed rumour a week ahead.'

'Heavens!' exclaimed Cicely, in genuine excitement, 'what a bold stroke. Lady Shalem has worked that, I bet. I suppose it will go down all right.'

'Trust Laurent to see to that,' said Tony, 'he knows how to fill his house with the right sort of people, and he's not the one to risk a fiasco. He knows what he's about. I tell you, it's going to be a big evening.'

'I say!' exclaimed Ronnie suddenly, 'give a supper party here for Gorla on the night, and ask the Shalem woman and all her crowd. It will be awful fun.'

Cicely caught at the suggestion with some enthusiasm. She did not particularly care for Lady Shalem, but she thought it would be just as well to care for her as far as outward appearances went.

Grace, Lady Shalem, was a woman who had blossomed into sudden importance by constituting herself a sort of foster-mother to the *fait accompli*. At a moment when London was denuded of most of its aforetime social leaders she had seen her opportunity, and made the most of it. She had not contented herself with bowing to the inevitable, she had stretched out her hand to it, and forced herself to smile graciously at it, and her polite attentions had been reciprocated. Lady Shalem, without being a beauty or a wit, or a grand lady in the traditional sense of the word, was in a fair way to becoming a power in the land; others, more capable and with stronger claims to social recognition, would doubtless overshadow her and displace her in due course, but for the moment she was a person whose good graces counted for something, and Cicely was quite alive to the advantage of being in those good graces.

'It would be rather fun,' she said, running over in her mind the possibilities of the suggested super-party.

'It would be jolly useful,' put in Ronnie eagerly; 'you could get all sorts of interesting people together, and it would be an excellent advertisement for Gorla.'

Ronnie approved of supper-parties on principle, but he was also thinking of the advantage which might accrue to the drawing-room concert which Cicely had projected (with himself as the chief performer), if he could be brought into contact with a wider circle of music patrons.

'I know it would be useful,' said Cicely, 'it would be almost historical; there's no knowing who might not come to it—and things are dreadfully slack in the entertaining line just now.'

The ambitious note in her character was making itself felt at that moment.

'Let's go down to the library, and work out a list of people to invite,' said Ronnie.

A servant entered the room and made a brief announcement.

'Mr Yeovil has arrived, madam.'

'Bother,' said Ronnie sulkily. 'Now you'll cool off about that supper party, and turn down Gorla and the rest of us.'

It was certainly true that the supper already seemed a more difficult proposition in Cicely's eye than it had a moment or two ago.

> ' "You'll not forget my only daughter,
>   E'en though Saphia has crossed the sea," '

quoted Tony, with mocking laughter in his voice and eyes.

Cicely went down to greet her husband. She felt that she was probably very glad that he was home once more; she was angry with herself for not feeling greater certainty on the point. Even the well-beloved, however, can select the wrong moment for return. If Cicely Yeovil's heart was like a singing-bird, it was of a kind that has frequent lapses into silence.

CHAPTER II

The Homecoming

Murrey Yeovil got out of the boat-train at Victoria Station, and stood waiting, in an attitude something between listlessness and impatience, while a porter dragged his light travelling kit out of the railway carriage and went in search of his heavier baggage with a hand-truck. Yeovil was a grey-faced young man, with restless eyes, and a rather wistful mouth, and an air of lassitude that was evidently only a temporary characteristic. The hot dusty station, with its blended crowds of dawdling and scurrying people, its little streams of suburban passengers pouring out every now and then from this or that platform, like ants swarming across a garden path, made a wearisome climax to what had been a rather wearisome journey. Yeovil glanced quickly, almost furtively, around him in all directions, with the air of a man who is constrained by morbid curiosity to look for things that he would rather not see. The announcements placed in German alternatively with English over the booking office, left-luggage office, refreshment buffets, and so forth, the crowned eagle and monogram displayed on the post boxes, caught his eye in quick succession.

He turned to help the porter to shepherd his belongings on to the truck, and followed him to the outer yard of the station, where a string of taxi-cabs was being slowly absorbed by an outpouring crowd of travellers.

Portmanteaux, wraps, and a trunk or two, much be-labelled and travel-worn, were stowed into a taxi, and Yeovil turned to give the direction to the driver.

'Twenty-eight, Berkshire Street.'

'Berkschirestrasse, acht-und-zwanzig,' echoed the man, a bulky spectacled individual of unmistakable Teuton type.

'Twenty-eight, Berkshire Street,' repeated Yeovil, and got into the cab, leaving the driver to re-translate the direction into his own language.

A succession of cabs leaving the station blocked the roadway for a moment or two, and Yeovil had leisure to observe the fact that

Viktoria Strasse was lettered side by side with the familiar English name of the street. A notice directing the public to the neighboring swimming baths was also written up in both languages. London had become a bilingual city, even as Warsaw.

The cab threaded its way swiftly along Buckingham Palace Road towards the Mall. As they passed the long front of the Palace the traveller turned his head resolutely away, that he might not see the alien uniforms at the gates and the eagle standard flapping in the sunlight. The taxi driver, who seemed to have combative instincts, slowed down as he was turning into the Mall, and pointed to the white pile of memorial statuary in front of the palace gates.

'Grossmutter Denkmal, yes,' he announced, and resumed his journey.

Arrived at his destination, Yeovil stood on the steps of his house and pressed the bell with an odd sense of forlornness, as though he were a stranger drifting from nowhere into a land that had no cognizance of him; a moment later he was standing in his own hall, the object of respectful solicitude and attention. Sprucely garbed and groomed lackeys busied themselves with his battered travel-soiled baggage; the door closed on the guttural-voiced taxi driver, and the glaring July sunshine. The wearisome journey was over.

'Poor dear, how dreadfully pulled-down you look,' said Cicely, when the first greetings had been exchanged.

'It's been a slow business, getting well,' said Yeovil. 'I'm only three-quarter way there yet.'

He looked at his reflection in a mirror and laughed ruefully.

'You should have seen what I looked like five or six weeks ago,' he added.

'You ought to have let me come out and nurse you,' said Cicely; 'you know I wanted to.'

'Oh, they nursed me well enough,' said Yeovil, 'and it would have been a shame dragging you out there; a small Finnish health resort, out of the season, is not a very amusing place, and it would have been worse for anyone who didn't talk Russian.'

'You must have been buried alive there,' said Cicely, with commiseration in her voice.

'I wanted to be buried alive,' said Yeovil. 'The news from the outer world was not of a kind that helped a despondent invalid towards convalescence. They spoke to me as little as possible about what was happening, and I was grateful for your letters because they also told me very little. When one is abroad, among foreigners, one's country's misfortunes cause one an acuter, more personal distress, than they would at home even.'

'Well, you are at home now, anyway,' said Cicely, 'and you can jog along the road to complete recovery at your own pace. A little quiet shooting this autumn and a little hunting, just enough to keep you fit and not to overtire you; you mustn't overtax your strength.'

'I'm getting my strength back all right,' said Yeovil. 'This journey hasn't tired me half as much as one might have expected. It's the awful drag of listlessness, mental and physical, that is the worst after-effect of these marsh fevers; they drain the energy out of you in bucketfuls, and it trickles back again in teaspoonfuls. And just now untiring energy is what I shall need, even more than strength; I don't want to degenerate into a slacker.'

'Look here, Murrey,' said Cicely, 'after we've had dinner together to-night, I'm going to do a seemingly unwifely thing. I'm going to go out and leave you alone with an old friend. Doctor Holham is coming in to drink coffee and smoke with you. I arranged this because I knew it was what you would like. Men can talk these things over best by themselves, and Holham can tell you everything that happened—since you went away. It will be a dreary story, I'm afraid, but you will want to hear it all. It was a nightmare time, but now one sees it in a calmer perspective.'

'I feel in a nightmare still,' said Yeovil.

'We all felt like that,' said Cicely, rather with the air of an elder person who tells a child that it will understand things better when it grows up; 'time is always something of a narcotic, you know. Things seem absolutely unbearable, and then bit by bit we find out that we are bearing them. And now, dear, I'll fill up your notification paper and leave you to superintend your unpacking. Robert will give you any help you want.'

'What is the notification paper?' asked Yeovil.

'Oh, a stupid form to be filled up when anyone arrives, to say where they come from, and their business and nationality and religion, and all that sort of thing. We're rather more bureaucratic than we used to be, you know.'

Yeovil said nothing, but into the sallow greyness of his face there crept a dark flush, that faded presently and left his colour more grey and bloodless than before.

The journey seemed suddenly to have recommenced; he was under his own roof, his servants were waiting on him, his familiar possessions were in evidence around him, but the sense of being at home had vanished. It was as though he had arrived at some wayside hotel, and been asked to register his name and status and destination. Other things of disgust and irritation he had foreseen in the London he was coming to—the alterations on stamps and coinage, the intrusive Teuton element, the alien uniforms cropping up everywhere, the new orientation of social life; such things he was prepared for, but this personal evidence of his subject state came on him unawares, at a moment when he had, so to speak, laid his armour aside. Cicely spoke lightly of the hateful formality that had been forced on them; would he, too, come to regard things in the same acquiescent spirit?

CHAPTER III

'The Metskie Tsar'

'I was in the early stages of my fever when I got the first inkling of what was going on,' said Yeovil to the doctor, as they sat over their coffee in a recess of the big smoking-room; 'just able to potter about a bit in the daytime, fighting against depression and inertia, feverish as evening came on, and delirious in the night. My game tracker and my attendant were both Buriats, and spoke very little Russian, and that was the only language we had in common to converse in. In matters concerning food and sport we soon got to understand each other, but on other subjects we were not easily able to exchange ideas. One day my tracker had been to a distant trading-store to get some things of which we were in need; the store was eighty miles from the nearest point of railroad, eighty miles of terribly bad roads, but it was in its way a centre and transmitter of news from the outside world. The tracker brought back with him vague tidings of a conflict of some sort between the "Metskie Tsar" and the "Angliskie Tsar," and kept repeating the Russian word for defeat. The "Angliskie Tsar" I recognized, of course, as the King of England, but my brain was too sick and dull to read any further meaning into the man's reiterated gabble. I grew so ill just then that I had to give up the struggle against fever, and make my way as best I could towards the nearest point where nursing and doctoring could be had. It was one evening, in a lonely rest-hut on the edge of a huge forest, as I was waiting for my boy to bring the meal for which I was feverishly impatient, and which I knew I should loathe as soon as it was brought, that the explanation of the word "Metskie" flashed on me. I had thought of it as referring to some Oriental potentate, some rebellious rajah perhaps, who was giving trouble, and whose followers had possibly discomfited an isolated British force in some out-of-the-way corner of our Empire. And all of a sudden I knew that "Nemetskie Tsar," German Emperor, had been the name that the man had been trying to convey to me. I shouted for the tracker, and put him through a breathless cross-examination; he confirmed what my fears had told me. The "Metskie Tsar" was a big European ruler, he had been in conflict with the "Angliskie Tsar," and the latter had been defeated, swept away; the man spoke the word that he used for ships, and made energetic pantomime to express the sinking of a fleet. Holham, there was nothing for it but to hope that this was a false, groundless rumour, that had somehow crept to the confines of civilization. In my saner balanced moments it was possible to disbelieve it, but if you have ever suffered from delirium you will know what raging torments of agony I went through in the nights, how my brain fought and refought that rumoured disaster.'

The doctor gave a murmur of sympathetic understanding.

'Then,' continued Yeovil, 'I reached the small Siberian town towards which I had been struggling. There was a little colony of Russians there, traders, officials, a doctor or two, and some army officers. I put up at the primitive hotel-restaurant, which was the general gathering-place of the community. I knew quickly that the news was true. Russians are the most tactful of any European race that I have ever met; they did not stare with insolent or pitying curiosity, but there was something changed in their attitude which told me that the travelling Briton was no longer in their eyes the interesting respect-commanding personality that he had been in past days. I went to my own room, where the samovar was bubbling its familiar tune and a smiling red-shirted Russian boy was helping my Buriat servant to unpack my wardrobe, and I asked for any back numbers of newspapers that could be supplied at a moment's notice. I was given a bundle of well-thumbed sheets, odd pieces of the *Novoe Vremya*, the *Moskovskie Viedomosti*, one or two complete numbers of local papers published at Perm and Tobolsk. I do not read Russian well, though I speak it fairly readily, but from the fragments of disconnected telegrams that I pieced together I gathered enough information to acquaint me with the extent of the tragedy that had been worked out in a few crowded hours in a corner of North-Western Europe. I searched frantically for telegrams of later dates that would put a better complexion on the matter, that would retrieve something from the ruin; presently I came across a page of the illustrated supplement that the *Novoe Vremya* publishes once a week. There was a photograph of a long-fronted building with a flag flying over it, labelled "The new standard floating over Buckingham Palace." The picture was not much more than a smudge, but the flag, possibly touched up, was unmistakable. It was the eagle of the Nemetskie Tsar. I have a vivid recollection of that plainly furnished little room, with the inevitable gilt ikon in one corner, and the samovar hissing and gurgling on the table, and the thrumming music of a balalaika orchestra coming up from the restaurant below; the next coherent thing I can remember was weeks and weeks later, discussing in an impersonal detached manner whether I was strong enough to stand the fatigue of the long railway journey to Finland.

'Since then, Holham, I have been encouraged to keep my mind as much off the war and public affairs as possible, and I have been glad to do so. I knew the worst and there was no particular use in deepening my despondency by dragging out the details. But now I am more or less a live man again, and I want to fill in the gaps in my knowledge of what happened. You know how much I know, and how little; those fragments of Russian newspapers were about all the information that I had. I don't even know clearly how the whole thing started.'

Yeovil settled himself back in his chair with the air of a man who has done some necessary talking, and now assumes the rôle of listener.

'It started,' said the doctor, 'with a wholly unimportant disagreement about some frontier business in East Africa; there was a slight attack of nerves in the stock markets, and then the whole thing seemed in a fair way towards being settled. Then the negotiations over the affair began to drag unduly, and there was a further flutter of nervousness in the money world. And then one morning the papers reported a highly menacing speech by one of the German Ministers, and the situation began to look black indeed. "He will be disavowed," every one said over here, but in less than twenty-four hours those who knew anything knew that the crisis was on us—only their knowledge came too late. "War between two such civilized and enlightened nations is an impossibility," one of our leaders of public opinion had declared on the Saturday; by the following Friday the war had indeed become an impossibility, because we could no longer carry it on. It burst on us with calculated suddenness, and we were just not enough, everywhere where the pressure came. Our ships were good against their ships, our seamen were better than their seamen, but our ships were not able to cope with their ships plus their superiority in aircraft. Our trained men were good against their trained men, but they could not be in several places at once, and the enemy could. Our half-trained men and our untrained men could not master the science of war at a moment's notice, and a moment's notice was all they got. The enemy were a nation apprenticed in arms, we were not even the idle apprentice: we had not deemed apprenticeship worth our while. There was courage enough running loose in the land, but it was like unharnessed electricity, it controlled no forces, it struck no blows. There was no time for the heroism and the devotion which a drawn-out struggle, however hopeless, can produce; the war was over almost as soon as it had begun. After the reverses which happened with lightning rapidity in the first three days of warfare, the newspapers made no effort to pretend that the situation could be retrieved; editors and public alike recognized that these were blows over the heart, and that it was a matter of moments before we were counted out. One might liken the whole affair to a snap checkmate early in a game of chess; one side had thought out the moves, and brought the requisite pieces into play, the other side was hampered and helpless, with its resources unavailable, its strategy discounted in advance. That, in a nutshell, is the history of the war.'

Yeovil was silent for a moment or two, then he asked:

'And the sequel, the peace?'

'The collapse was so complete that I fancy even the enemy were hardly prepared for the consequences of their victory. No one had quite realized what one disastrous campaign would mean for an island nation with a closely packed population. The conquerors were in a position to dictate what terms they pleased, and it was not wonderful that their ideas of aggrandizement expanded in the hour of intoxication. There was no European combination ready to say them nay, and certainly no one Power was going to be rash enough to step in to contest the terms of the treaty that they imposed on the conquered. Annexation had probably never been a dream before the war; after the war it suddenly became temptingly practical. *Warum nicht?* became the theme of leader-writers in the German Press; they pointed out that Britain, defeated and humiliated, but with enormous powers of recuperation, would be a dangerous and inevitable enemy for the Germany of to-morrow, while Britain incorporated within the Hohenzollern Empire would merely be a disaffected province, without a navy to make its disaffection a serious menace, and with great tax-paying capabilities, which would be available for relieving the burdens of the other Imperial States. Wherefore, why not annex? The *warum nicht?* party prevailed. Our King, as you know, retired with his Court to Delhi, as Emperor in the East, with most of his overseas dominions still subject to his sway. The British Isles came under the German Crown as a *Reichsland*, a sort of Alsace-Lorraine washed by the North Sea instead of the Rhine. We still retain our Parliament, but it is a clipped and pruned-down shadow of its former self, with most of its functions in abeyance; when the elections were held it was difficult to get decent candidates to come forward or to get people to vote. It makes one smile bitterly to think that a year or two ago we were seriously squabbling as to who should have votes. And, of course, the old party divisions have more or less crumbled away. The Liberals naturally are under the blackest of clouds, for having steered the country to disaster, though to do them justice it was no more their fault than the fault of any other party. In a democracy such as ours the Government of the day must more or less reflect the ideas and temperament of the nation in all vital matters, and the British nation in those days could not have been persuaded of the urgent need for military apprenticeship or of the deadly nature of its danger. It was willing now and then to be half-frightened and to have half-measures, or, one might better say, quarter-measures taken to reassure it, and the governments of the day were willing to take them, but any political party or group of statesmen that had said "the danger is enormous and immediate, the sacrifices and burdens must be enormous and immediate," would have met with certain defeat at the polls. Still, of course, the Liberals, as the party that had held office for nearly a decade, incurred the odium of a people maddened by defeat and humiliation; one Minister, who had had less responsibility for military organization than perhaps any of them, was attacked and nearly killed at Newcastle, another was hiding for three days on Exmoor, and escaped in disguise.'

'And the Conservatives?'

'They are also under eclipse, but it is more or less voluntary in their case. For generations they had taken their stand as supporters of Throne and Constitution, and when they suddenly found the Constitution gone and the Throne filled by an alien dynasty, their political orientation had vanished. They are in much the same position as the Jacobites occupied after the Hanoverian accession. Many of the leading Tory families have emigrated to the British lands beyond the seas, others are shut up in their country houses, retrenching their expenses, selling their acres, and investing their money abroad. The Labour faction, again, are almost in as bad odour as the Liberals, because of having hob-nobbed too effusively and ostentatiously with the German democratic parties on the eve of the war, exploiting an evangel of universal brotherhood which did not blunt a single Teuton bayonet when the hour came. I suppose in time party divisions will reassert themselves in some form or other; there will be a Socialist Party, and the mercantile and manufacturing interests will evolve a sort of bourgeoisie party, and the different religious bodies will try to get themselves represented——'

Yeovil made a movement of impatience.

'All these things that you forecast,' he said, 'must take time, considerable time; is this nightmare, then, to go on for ever?'

'It is not a nightmare, unfortunately,' said the doctor, 'it is a reality.'

'But, surely—a nation such as ours, a virile, highly civilized nation with an age-long tradition of mastery behind it, cannot be held under for ever by a few thousand bayonets and machine guns. We must surely rise up one day and drive them out.'

'Dear man,' said the doctor, 'we might, of course, at some given moment overpower the garrison that is maintained here, and seize the forts, and perhaps we might be able to mine the harbours; what then? In a fortnight or so we could be starved into unconditional submission. Remember, all the advantages of isolated position that told in our favour while we had the sea dominion, tell against us now that the sea dominion is in other hands. The enemy would not need to mobilize a single army corps or to bring a single battleship into action; a fleet of nimble cruisers and destroyers circling round our coasts would be sufficient to shut out our food supplies.'

'Are you trying to tell me that this is a final overthrow?' said Yeovil in a shaking voice; 'are we to remain a subject race like the Poles?'

'Let us hope for a better fate,' said the doctor. 'Our opportunity may come if the Master Power is ever involved in an unsuccessful naval war with some other nation, or perhaps in some time of European crisis, when everything hung in the balance, our latent hostility might have to be squared by a concession of independence. That is what we have to hope for and watch for. On the other hand, the conquerors have to count on time and tact to weaken and finally obliterate the old feelings of nationality; the middle-aged of to-day will grow old and acquiescent in the changed state of things; the young generations will grow up never having known anything different. It's a far cry to Delhi, as the old Indian proverb says, and the strange half-European, half-Asiatic Court out there will seem more and more a thing exotic and unreal. "The King across the water" was a rallying-cry once upon a time in our history, but a king on the farther side of the Indian Ocean is a shadowy competitor for one who alternates between Potsdam and Windsor.'

'I want you to tell me everything,' said Yeovil, after another pause; 'tell me, Holham, how far has this obliterating process of "time and tact" gone? It seems to be pretty fairly started already. I bought a newspaper as soon as I landed, and I read it in the train coming up. I read things that puzzled and disgusted me. There were announcements of concerts and plays and first-nights and private views; there were even small dances. There were advertisements of house-boats and weekend cottages and string bands for garden parties. It struck me that it was rather like merry-making with a dead body lying in the house.'

'Yeovil,' said the doctor, 'you must bear in mind two things. First, the necessity for the life of the country going on as if nothing had happened. It is true that many thousands of our working men and women have emigrated and thousands of our upper and middle class too; they were the people who were not tied down by business, or who could afford to cut those ties. But those represent comparatively a few out of the many. The great businesses and the small businesses must go on, people must be fed and clothed and housed and medically treated, and their thousand-and-one wants and necessities supplied. Look at me, for instance; however much I loathe coming under a foreign domination and paying taxes to an alien government, I can't abandon my practice and my patients, and set up anew in Toronto or Allahabad, and if I could, some other doctor would have to take my place here. I or that other doctor must have our servants and motors and food and furniture and newspapers, even our sport. The golf links and the hunting field have been wellnigh deserted since the war, but they are beginning to get back their votaries because outdoor sport has become a necessity, and a very rational necessity, with numbers of men who have to work otherwise under unnatural and exacting conditions. That is one factor of the situation. The other affects London more especially, but through London it influences the rest of the country to a certain extent. You will see around you here much that will strike you as indications of heartless indifference to the calamity that has befallen our nation. Well, you must remember that many things in modern life, especially in the big cities, are not national but international. In the world of music and art and the drama, for instance, the foreign names are legion, they confront you at every turn, and some of our British devotees of such arts are more acclimatized to the ways of Munich or Moscow than they are familiar with the life, say, of Stirling or York. For years they have lived and thought and spoken in an atmosphere and jargon of denationalized culture—even those of them who have never left our shores. They would take pains to be intimately familiar with the domestic affairs and views of life of some Galician gipsy dramatist, and gravely quote and discuss his opinions on debts and mistresses and cookery, while they would shudder at "D'ye ken John Peel?" as a piece of uncouth barbarity. You cannot expect a world of that sort to be permanently concerned or downcast because the Crown of Charlemagne takes its place now on the top of the Royal box in the theatres, or at the head of programmes at State concerts. And then there are the Jews.'

'There are many in the land, or at least in London,' said Yeovil.

'There are even more of them now than there used to be,' said Holham. 'I am to a great extent a disliker of Jews myself, but I will be fair to them, and admit that those of them who were in any genuine sense British have remained British and have stuck by us loyally in our misfortune; all honour to them. But of the others, the men who by temperament and everything else were far more Teuton or Polish or Latin than they were British, it was not to be expected that they would be heart-broken because London had suddenly lost its place among the political capitals of the world, and became a cosmopolitan city. They had appreciated the free and easy liberty of the old days, under British rule, but there was a stiff insularity in the ruling race that they chafed against. Now, putting aside some petty Government restrictions that Teutonic bureaucracy has brought in, there is really, in their eyes, more licence and social adaptability in London than before. It has taken on some of the aspects of a No-Man's-Land, and the Jew, if he likes, may almost consider himself as of the dominant race; at any rate he is ubiquitous. Pleasure, of the café and cabaret and boulevard kind, the sort of thing that gave Berlin the aspect of the gayest capital in Europe within the last decade, that is the insidious leaven that will help to denationalize London. Berlin will probably climb back to some of its old austerity and simplicity, a world-ruling city with a great sense of its position and its responsibilities, while London will become more and more the centre of what these people understand by life.'

Yeovil made a movement of impatience and disgust.

'I know, I know,' said the doctor, sympathetically; 'life and enjoyment mean to you the howl of a wolf in a forest, the call of a wild swan on the frozen tundras, the smell of a wood fire in some little inn among the mountains. There is more music to you in the quick thud, thud of hoofs on desert mud as a free-stepping horse is led up to your tent door than in all the dronings and flourishes that a highly paid orchestra can reel out to an expensively fed audience. But the tastes of modern London, as we see them crystallized around us, lie in a very different direction. People of the world that I am speaking of, our dominant world at the present moment, herd together as closely packed to the square yard as possible, doing nothing worth doing, and saying nothing worth saying, but doing it and saying it over and over again, listening to the same melodies, watching the same artistes, echoing the same catchwords, ordering the same dishes in the same restaurants, suffering each other's cigarette smoke and perfumes and conversation, feverishly, anxiously making arrangements to meet each other again to-morrow, next week, and the week after next, and repeat the same gregarious experience. If they were not herded together in a corner of western London, watching each other with restless intelligent eyes, they would be herded together at Brighton or Dieppe, doing the same thing. Well, you will find that life of that sort goes forward just as usual, only it is even more prominent and noticeable now because there is less public life of other kinds.'

Yeovil said something which was possibly the Buriat word for the nether world.

Outside in the neighbouring square a band had been playing at intervals during the evening. Now it struck up an air that Yeovil had already heard whistled several times since his landing, an air with a captivating suggestion of slyness and furtive joyousness running through it.

He rose and walked across to the window, opening it a little wider. He listened till the last notes had died away.

'What is that tune they have just played?' he asked.

'You'll hear it often enough,' said the doctor. 'A Frenchman writing in the *Matin* the other day called it the "National Anthem of the *fait accompli*".'

CHAPTER IV

'Es ist Verboten'

Yeovil wakened next morning to the pleasant sensation of being in a household where elaborate machinery for the smooth achievement of one's daily life was noiselessly and unceasingly at work. Fever and the long weariness of convalescence in indifferently comfortable surroundings had given luxury a new value in his eyes. Money had not always been plentiful with him in his younger days; in his twenty-eighth year he had inherited a fairly substantial fortune, and he had married a wealthy woman a few months later. It was characteristic of the man and his breed that the chief use to which he had put his newly acquired wealth had been in seizing the opportunity which it gave him for indulging in unlimited travel in wild, out-of-the-way regions, where the comforts of life were meagrely represented. Cicely occasionally accompanied him to the threshold of his expeditions, such as Cairo or St Petersburg or Constantinople, but her own tastes in the matter of roving were more or less condensed within an area that comprised Cannes, Homburg, the Scottish Highlands, and the Norwegian Fiords. Things outlandish and barbaric appealed to her chiefly when presented under artistic but highly civilized stage management on the boards of Covent Garden, and if she wanted to look at wolves or sand grouse, she preferred doing so in the company of an intelligent Fellow of the Zoological Society on some fine Sunday afternoon in Regent's Park. It was one of the bonds of union and good-fellowship between her husband and herself that each understood and sympathized with the other's tastes without in the least wanting to share them; they went their own ways and were pleased and comrade-like when the ways happened to run together for a span, without self-reproach or heart-searching when the ways diverged. Moreover, they had separate and adequate banking accounts, which constitute, if not the keys of the matrimonial Heaven, at least the oil that lubricates them.

Yeovil found Cicely and breakfast waiting for him in the cool breakfast-room, and enjoyed, with the appreciation of a recent invalid, the comfort and resources of a meal that had not to be ordered or thought about in advance, but seemed as though it were there, foreordained from the beginning of time in its smallest detail. Each desire of the breakfasting mind seemed to have its realization in some dish, lurking unobtrusively in hidden corners until asked for. Did one want grilled mushrooms, English fashion, they were there, black and moist and sizzling, and extremely edible; did one desire mushrooms *à la Russe*, they appeared, blanched and cool and toothsome under their white blanketing of sauce. At one's bidding was a service of coffee, prepared with rather more forethought and circumspection than would go to the preparation of a revolution in a South American Republic.

The exotic blooms that reigned in profusion over the other parts of the house were scrupulously banished from the breakfast-room; bowls of wild thyme and other flowering weeds of the meadow and hedgerow gave it an atmosphere of country freshness that was in keeping with the morning meal.

'You look dreadfully tired still,' said Cicely critically, 'otherwise I would recommend a ride in the Park, before it gets too hot. There is a new cob in the stable that you will just love, but he is rather lively, and you had better content yourself for the present with some more sedate exercise than he is likely to give you. He is apt to try and jump out of his skin when the flies tease him. The Park is rather jolly for a walk just now.'

'I think that will be about my form after my long journey,' said Yeovil, 'an hour's stroll before lunch under the trees. That ought not to fatigue me unduly. In the afternoon I'll look up one or two people.'

'Don't count on finding too many of your old set,' said Cicely rather hurriedly. 'I dare say some of them will find their way back some time, but at present there's been rather an exodus.'

'The Bredes,' said Yeovil, 'are they here?'

'No, the Bredes are in Scotland, at their place in Sutherlandshire; they don't come south now, and the Ricardes are farming somewhere in East Africa, the whole lot of them. Valham has got an appointment of some sort in the Straits Settlement, and has taken his family with him. The Collards are down at their mother's place in Norfolk; a German banker has bought their house in Manchester Square.'

'And the Hebways?' asked Yeovil.

'Dick Hebway is in India,' said Cicely, 'but his mother lives in

Paris; poor Hugo, you know, was killed in the war. My friends the Allinsons are in Paris too. It's rather a clearance, isn't it? However, there are some left, and I expect others will come back in time. Pitherby is here; he's one of those who are trying to make the best of things under the new *régime*.'

'He would be,' said Yeovil, shortly.

'It's a difficult question,' said Cicely, 'whether one should stay at home and face the music or go away and live a transplanted life under the British flag. Either attitude might be dictated by patriotism.'

'It is one thing to face the music, it is another thing to dance to it,' said Yeovil.

Cicely poured out some more coffee for herself and changed the conversation.

'You'll be in to lunch, I suppose? The Clubs are not very attractive just now, I believe, and the restaurants are mostly hot in the middle of the day. Ronnie Storre is coming in; he's here pretty often these days. A rather good-looking young animal with something midway between talent and genius in the piano-playing line.'

'Not long-haired and Semitic or Tcheque or anything of that sort, I suppose?' asked Yeovil.

Cicely laughed at the vision of Ronnie conjured up by her husband's words.

'No, beautifully groomed and clipped and Anglo-Saxon. I expect you'll like him. He plays bridge almost as well as he plays the piano. I suppose you wonder at anyone who can play bridge well wanting to play the piano.'

'I'm not quite so intolerant as all that,' said Yeovil; 'anyhow I promise to like Ronnie. Is anyone else coming to lunch?'

'Joan Mardle will probably drop in, in fact I'm afraid she's a certainty. She invited herself in that way of hers that brooks of no refusal. On the other hand, as a mitigating circumstance, there will be a *point d'asperge* omelette such as few kitchens could turn out, so don't be late.'

Yeovil set out for his morning walk with the curious sensation of one who starts on a voyage of discovery in a land that is well known to him. He turned into the Park at Hyde Park Corner and made his way along the familiar paths and alleys that bordered the Row. The familiarity vanished when he left the region of fenced-in lawns and rhododendron bushes and came to the open space that stretched away beyond the bandstand. The bandstand was still there, and a military band, in sky-blue Saxon uniform, was executing the first item in the forenoon programme of music. Around it, instead of the serried rows of green chairs that Yeovil remembered, was spread out an acre or so of small round tables, most of which had their quota of customers, engaged in a steady consumption of lager beer, coffee, lemonade, and syrups. Farther in the background, but well within earshot of the band, a gaily painted pagoda-restaurant sheltered a number of more commodious tables under its awnings, and gave a hint of convenient indoor accommodation for wet or windy weather. Movable screens of trellis-trained foliage and climbing roses formed little hedges by means of which any particular table could be shut off from its neighbours if semi-privacy were desired. One or two decorative advertisements of popularized brands of champagne and Rhine wines adorned the outside walls of the building, and under the central gable of its upper storey was a flamboyant portrait of a stern-faced man, whose image and superscription might also be found on the newer coinage of the land. A mass of bunting hung in folds round the flag-pole on the gable, and blew out now and then on a favouring breeze, a long three-coloured strip, black, white, and scarlet, and over the whole scene the elm trees towered with an absurd sardonic air of nothing having changed around their roots.

Yeovil stood for a minute or two, taking in every detail of the unfamiliar spectacle.

'They have certainly accomplished something that we never attempted,' he muttered to himself. Then he turned on his heel and made his way back to the shady walk that ran alongside the Row. At first sight little was changed in the aspect of the well-known exercising ground. One or two riding masters cantered up and down as of yore, with their attendant broods of anxious-faced young girls and awkwardly bumping women pupils, while horsey-looking men put marketable animals through their paces or drew up to the rails for long conversations with horsey-looking friends on foot. Sportingly attired young women, sitting astride of their horses, careered by at intervals as though an extremely game fox were leading hounds a merry chase a short way ahead of them; it all seemed much as usual.

Presently, from the middle distance a bright patch of colour set in a whirl of dust drew rapidly nearer and resolved itself into a group of cavalry officers extending their chargers in a smart gallop. They were well mounted and sat their horses to perfection, and they made a brave show as they raced past Yeovil with a clink and clatter and rhythmic thud, thud of hoofs, and became once more a patch of colour in a whirl of dust. An answering glow of colour seemed to have burned itself into the grey face of the young man, who had seen them pass without appearing to look at them, a stinging rush of blood, accompanied by a choking catch in the throat and a hot white blindness across the eyes. The weakness of fever broke down at times the rampart of outward indifference that a man of Yeovil's temperament builds coldly round his heartstrings.

The Row and its riders had become suddenly detestable to the wanderer; he would not run the risk of seeing that insolently joyous cavalcade come galloping past again. Beyond a narrow stretch of tree-shaded grass lay the placid sunlit water of the Serpentine, and Yeovil made a short cut across the turf to reach its gravelled bank.

'Can't you read either English or German?' asked a policeman who confronted him as he stepped off the turf.

Yeovil stared at the man and then turned to look at the small neatly printed notice to which the official was imperiously pointing; in two languages it was made known that it was forbidden and *verboten*, punishable and *straffbar*, to walk on the grass.

'Three shilling fine,' said the policeman, extending his hand for the money.

'Do I pay you?' asked Yeovil, feeling almost inclined to laugh; 'I'm rather a stranger to the new order of things.'

'You pay me,' said the policeman, 'and you receive a quittance for the sum paid,' and he proceeded to tear a counterfoil receipt for a three shilling fine from a small pocket book.

'May I ask,' said Yeovil, as he handed over the sum demanded and received his quittance, 'what the red and white band on your sleeve stands for?'

'Bi-lingual,' said the constable, with an air of importance. 'Preference is given to members of the Force who qualify in both languages. Nearly all the police engaged on Park duty are bi-lingual. About as many foreigners as English use the parks nowadays; in fact, on a fine Sunday afternoon, you'll find three foreigners to every two English. The park habit is more Continental than British, I take it.'

'And are there many Germans in the Police Force?' asked Yeovil.

'Well, yes, a good few; there had to be,' said the constable; 'there were such a lot of resignations when the change came, and they had to be filled up somehow. Lots of men what used to be in the Force emigrated or found work of some other kind, but everybody couldn't take that line; wives and children had to be thought of. 'Tisn't every head of a family that can chuck up a job on the chance of finding another. Starvation's been the lot of a good many what went out. Those of us that stayed on got better pay than we did before, but then of course the duties are much more multitudinous.'

'They must be,' said Yeovil, fingering his three shilling State document; 'by the way,' he asked, 'are all the grass plots in the Park out of bounds for human feet?'

'Everywhere where you see the notices,' said the policeman, 'and that's about three-fourths of the whole grass space; there's been a lot of new gravel walks opened up in all directions. People don't want to walk on the grass when they've got clean paths to walk on.'

And with this parting reproof the bi-lingual constable strode heavily away, his loss of consideration and self-esteem as a unit of a sometime ruling race evidently compensated for to some extent by his enhanced importance as an official.

'The women and children,' thought Yeovil, as he looked after the retreating figure; 'yes, that is one side of the problem. The children that have to be fed and schooled, the women folk that have to be cared for, an old mother, perhaps, in the home that cannot be broken up. The old case of giving hostages.'

He followed the path alongside the Serpentine, passing under the archway of the bridge and continuing his walk into Kensington Gardens. In another moment he was within view of the Peter Pan statue and at once observed that it had companions. On one side was a group representing a scene from one of the Grimm fairy stories, on the other was Alice in conversation with Gryphon and Mockturtle, the episode looking distressingly stiff and meaningless in its sculptured form. Two other spaces had been cleared in the neighbouring turf, evidently for the reception of further statue groups, which Yeovil mentally assigned to Struwelpeter and Little Lord Fauntleroy.

'German middle-class taste,' he commented, 'but in this matter we certainly gave them a lead. I suppose the idea is that childish fancy is dead and that it is only decent to erect some sort of memorial to it.'

The day was growing hotter, and the Park had ceased to seem a desirable place to loiter in. Yeovil turned his steps homeward, passing on his way the bandstand with its surrounding acreage of tables. It was now nearly one o'clock, and luncheon parties were beginning to assemble under the awnings of the restaurant. Lighter refreshments, in the shape of sausages and potato salads, were being carried out by scurrying waiters to the drinkers of lager beer at the small tables. A park orchestra, in brilliant trappings, had taken the place of the military band. As Yeovil passed the musicians launched out into the tune which the doctor had truly predicted he would hear to repletion before he had been many days in London; the 'National Anthem of the *fait accompli*.'

CHAPTER V

L'Art d'etre Cousine

Joan Mardle had reached forty in the leisurely untroubled fashion of a woman who intends to be comely and attractive at fifty. She cultivated a jovial, almost joyous manner, with a top-dressing of hearty good will and good nature which disarmed strangers and recent acquaintances; on getting to know her better they hastily re-armed themselves. Some one had once aptly described her as a hedgehog with the protective mimicry of a puffball. If there was an awkward remark to be made at an inconvenient moment before undesired listeners, Joan invariably made it, and when the occasion did not present itself she was usually capable of creating it. She was not without a certain popularity, the sort of popularity that a dashing highwayman sometimes achieved among those who were not in the habit of travelling on his particular highway. A great-aunt on her mother's side of the family had married so often that Joan imagined herself justified in claiming cousinship with a large circle of disconnected houses, and treating them all on a relationship footing, which theoretical kinship enabled her to exact luncheons and other accommodations under the plea of keeping the lamp of family life aglow.

'I felt I simply had to come to-day,' she chuckled at Yeovil; 'I was just dying to see the returned traveller. Of course, I know perfectly well that neither of you want me, when you haven't seen each other for so long and must have heaps and heaps to say to one another, but I thought I would risk the odium of being the third person on an occasion when two are company and three are a nuisance. Wasn't it brave of me?'

She spoke in full knowledge of the fact that the luncheon party would not in any case have been restricted to Yeovil and his wife, having seen Ronnie arrive in the hall as she was being shown upstairs.

'Ronnie Storre is coming, I believe,' said Cicely, 'so you're not breaking into a tête-à-tête.'

'Ronnie, oh I don't count him,' said Joan gaily; 'he's just a boy who looks nice and eats asparagus. I hear he's getting to play the piano really well. Such a pity. He will grow fat; musicians always do, and it will ruin him. I speak feelingly because I'm gravitating towards plumpness myself. The Divine Architect turns us out fearfully and wonderfully built, and the result is charming to the eye, and then He adds another chin and two or three extra inches round the waist, and the effect is ruined. Fortunately you can always find another Ronnie when this one grows fat and uninteresting; the supply of boys who look nice and eat asparagus is unlimited. Hullo, Mr Storre, we were all talking about you.'

'Nothing very damaging, I hope?' said Ronnie, who had just entered the room.

'No, we were merely deciding that, whatever you may do with your life, your chin must remain single. When one's chin begins to lead a double life one's own opportunities for depravity are insensibly narrowed. You needn't tell me that you haven't any hankerings after depravity; people with your coloured eyes and hair are always depraved.'

'Let me introduce you to my husband, Ronnie,' said Cicely, 'and then let's go and begin lunch.'

'You two must almost feel as if you were honeymooning again,' said Joan as they sat down; 'you must have quite forgotten each other's tastes and peculiarities since you last met. Old Emily Fronding was talking about you yesterday, when I mentioned that Murrey was expected home; "curious sort of marriage tie," she said, in that stupid staring way of hers, "when husband and wife spend most of their time in different continents. I don't call it marriage at all." "Nonsense," I said, "it's the best way of doing things. The Yeovils will be a united and devoted couple long after heaps of their married contemporaries have trundled through the Divorce Court." I forgot at the moment that her youngest girl had divorced her husband last year, and that her second girl is rumoured to be contemplating a similar step. One can't remember everything.'

Joan Mardle was remarkable for being able to remember the smallest details in the family lives of two or three hundred acquaintances.

From personal matters she went with a bound to the political small talk of the moment.

'The Official Declaration as to the House of Lords is out at last,' she said; 'I bought a paper just before coming here, but I left it in the

Tube. All existing titles are to lapse if three successive holders, including the present ones, fail to take the oath of allegiance.'

'Have any taken it up to the present?' asked Yeovil.

'Only about nineteen, so far, and none of them representing very leading families; of course others will come in gradually, as the change of Dynasty becomes more and more an accepted fact, and of course there will be lots of new creations to fill up the gaps. I hear for certain that Pitherby is to get a title of some sort, in recognition of his literary labours. He has written a short history of the House of Hohenzollern, for use in schools you know, and he's bringing out a popular Life of Frederick the Great—at least he hopes it will be popular.'

'I didn't know that writing was much in his line,' said Yeovil, 'beyond the occasional editing of a company prospectus.'

'I understand his historical researches have given every satisfaction in exalted quarters,' said Joan; 'something may be lacking in the style, perhaps, but the august approval can make good that defect with the style of Baron. Pitherby has such a kind heart; "kind hearts are more than coronets," we all know, but the two go quite well together. And the dear man is not content with his services to literature, he's blossoming forth as a liberal patron of the arts. He's taken quite a lot of tickets for dear Gorla's début; half the second row of the dress-circle.'

'Do you mean Gorla Mustelford?' asked Yeovil, catching at the name; 'what on earth is she having a début about?'

'What?' cried Joan, in loud-voiced amazement; 'haven't you heard? Hasn't Cicely told you? How funny that you shouldn't have heard. Why, it's going to be one of the events of the season. Everybody's talking about it. She's going to do suggestion dancing at the Caravansery Theatre.'

'Good Heavens, what is suggestion dancing?' asked Yeovil.

'Oh, something quite new,' explained Joan; 'at any rate the name is quite new and Gorla is new as far as the public are concerned, and that is enough to establish the novelty of the thing. Among other things she does a dance suggesting the life of a fern; I saw one of the rehearsals, and to me it would have equally well suggested the life of John Wesley. However, that is probably the fault of my imagination— I've either got too much or too little. Anyhow it is an understood thing that she is to take London by storm.'

'When I last saw Gorla Mustelford,' observed Yeovil, 'she was a rather serious flapper who thought the world was in urgent need of regeneration and was not certain whether she would regenerate it or take up miniature painting. I forget which she attempted ultimately.'

'She is quite serious about her art,' put in Cicely; 'she's studied a good deal abroad and worked hard at mastering the technique of her profession. She's not a mere amateur with a hankering after the footlights. I fancy she will do well.'

'But what do her people say about it?' asked Yeovil.

'Oh, they're simply furious about it,' answered Joan; 'the idea of a daughter of the house of Mustelford prancing and twisting about the stage for Prussian officers and Hamburg Jews to gaze at is a dreadful cup of humiliation for them. It's unfortunate, of course, that they should feel so acutely about it, but still one can understand their point of view.'

'I don't see what other point of view they could possibly take,' said Yeovil sharply; 'if Gorla thinks that the necessities of art, or her own inclinations, demand that she should dance in public, why can't she do it in Paris or even Vienna? Anywhere would be better, one would think, than in London under present conditions.'

He had given Joan the indication that she was looking for as to his attitude towards the *fait accompli*. Without asking a question she had discovered that husband and wife were divided on the fundamental issue that underlay all others at the present moment. Cicely was weaving social schemes for the future, Yeovil had come home in a frame of mind that threatened the destruction of those schemes, or at any rate a serious hindrance to their execution. The situation presented itself to Joan's mind with an alluring piquancy.

'You are giving a grand supper-party for Gorla on the night of her début, aren't you?' she asked Cicely; 'several people spoke to me about it, so I suppose it must be true.'

Tony Luton and young Storre had taken care to spread the news of the projected supper function, in order to ensure against a change of plans on Cicely's part.

'Gorla is a great friend of mine,' said Cicely, trying to talk as if the conversation had taken a perfectly indifferent turn; 'also I think she deserves a little encouragement after the hard work she has been through. I thought it would be doing her a kindness to arrange a supper party for her on her first night.'

There was a moment's silence. Yeovil said nothing, and Joan understood the value of being occasionally tongue-tied.

'The whole question is,' continued Cicely as the silence became oppressive, 'whether one is to mope and hold aloof from the national life, or take our share in it; the life has got to go on whether we participate in it or not. It seems to me to be more patriotic to come down into the dust of the market-place than to withdraw oneself behind walls or beyond the seas.'

'Of course the industrial life of the country has to go on,' said Yeovil; 'no one could criticize Gorla if she interested herself in organizing cottage industries or anything of that sort, in which she would be helping her own people. That one could understand, but I don't think a cosmopolitan concern like the music-hall business calls for personal sacrifices from young women of good family at a moment like the present.'

'It is just at a moment like the present that the people want something to interest them and take them out of themselves,' said Cicely argumentatively; 'what has happened, has happened, and we can't undo it or escape the consequences. What we can do, or attempt to do, is to make things less dreary, and make people less unhappy.'

'In a word, more contented,' said Yeovil; 'if I were a German statesman, that is the end I would labour for and encourage others to labour for, to make the people forget that they were discontented. All this work of regalvanizing the social side of London life may be summed up in the phrase "*travailler pour le roi de Prusse*".'

'I don't think there is any use in discussing the matter further,' said Cicely.

'I can see that grand supper-party not coming off,' said Joan provocatively.

Ronnie looked anxiously at Cicely.

'You can see it coming on, if you're gifted with prophetic vision of a reliable kind,' said Cicely; 'of course as Murrey doesn't take kindly to the idea of Gorla's enterprise I won't have the party here. I'll give it at a restaurant, that's all. I can see Murrey's point of view, and sympathize with it, but I'm not going to throw Gorla over.'

There was another pause of uncomfortably protracted duration.

'I say, this is a top-hole omelette,' said Ronnie.

It was his only contribution to the conversation, but it was a valuable one.

CHAPTER VI

Herr von Kwarl

Herr von Kwarl sat at his favourite table in the Brandenburg Café, the new building that made such an imposing show (and did such thriving business) at the lower end of what most of its patrons called the Regentstrasse. Though the establishment was new it had already achieved its unwritten code of customs, and the sanctity of Herr von Kwarl's specially reserved table had acquired the authority of a tradition. A set of chess-men, a copy of the *Kreuz Zeitung* and the *Times*, and a slim-necked bottle of Rhenish wine, ice-cool from the cellar, were always to be found there early in the forenoon, and the honoured guest for whom these preparations were made usually arrived on the scene shortly after eleven o'clock. For an hour or so he would read and silently digest the contents of his two newspapers, and then at the first sign of flagging interest on his part, another of the café's regular customers would march across the floor, exchange a word or two on the affairs of the day, and be bidden with a wave of the hand into the opposite seat. A waiter would instantly place the chess-board with its marshalled ranks of combatants in the required position, and the contest would begin.

Herr von Kwarl was a heavily built man of mature middle-age, of the blond North-German type, with a facial aspect that suggested stupidity and brutality. The stupidity of his mien masked an ability and shrewdness that was distinctly above the average and the suggestion of brutality was belied by the fact that von Kwarl was as kind-hearted a man as one could meet with in a day's journey. Early in life, almost before he was in his teens, Fritz von Kwarl had made up his mind to accept the world as it was, and to that philosophical resolution, steadfastly adhered to, he attributed his excellent digestion and his unruffled happiness. Perhaps he confused cause and effect; the excellent digestion may have been responsible for at least some of the philosophical serenity.

He was a bachelor of the type that is called confirmed, and which might better be labelled consecrated; from his early youth onward to his present age he had never had the faintest flickering intention of marriage. Children and animals he adored, women and plants he accounted somewhat of a nuisance. A world without women and roses and asparagus would, he admitted, be robbed of much of its charm, but with all their charm these things were tiresome and thorny and capricious, always wanting to climb or creep in places where they were not wanted, and resolutely drooping and fading away when they were desired to flourish. Animals, on the other hand, accepted the world as it was and made the best of it, and children, at least nice children, uncontaminated by grown-up influences, lived in worlds of their own making.

Von Kwarl held no acknowledged official position in the country of his residence, but it was an open secret that those responsible for the real direction of affairs sought his counsel on nearly every step that they meditated, and that his counsel was very rarely disregarded. Some of the shrewdest and most successful enactments of the ruling power were believed to have originated in the brain-cells of the bovine-fronted *Stammgast* of the Brandenburg Café.

Around the wood-panelled walls of the Café were set at intervals well-mounted heads of boar, elk, stag, roebuck, and other game-beasts of a northern forest, while in between were carved armorial escutcheons of the principal cities of the lately expanded realm, Magdeburg, Manchester, Hamburg, Bremen, Bristol and so forth. Below these came shelves on which stood a wonderful array of stone beer-mugs, each decorated with some fantastic device or motto, and most of them pertaining individually and sacredly to some regular and unfailing customer. In one particular corner of the highest shelf, greatly at his ease and in nowise to be disturbed, slept Wotan, the huge grey house-cat, dreaming doubtless of certain nimble and audacious mice down in the cellar three floors below, whose nimbleness and audacity were as precious to him as the forwardness of the birds is to a skilled gun on a grouse moor. Once every day Wotan came marching in stately fashion across the polished floor, halted midway to resume an unfinished toilet operation, and then proceeded to pay his leisurely respects to his friend von Kwarl. The latter was said to be prouder of this daily demonstration of esteem than of his many coveted orders of merit. Several of his friends and acquaintances shared with him the distinction of having achieved the Black Eagle, but not one of them had ever succeeded in obtaining the slightest recognition of their existence from Wotan.

The daily greeting had been exchanged and the proud grey beast had marched away to the music of a slumberous purr. The *Kreuz Zeitung* and the *Times* underwent a final scrutiny and were pushed aside, and von Kwarl glanced aimlessly out at the July sunshine bathing the walls and windows of the Piccadilly Hotel. Herr Rebinok, the plump little Pomeranian banker, stepped across the floor, almost as noiselessly as Wotan had done, though with considerably less grace, and some half-minute later was engaged in sliding pawns and knights and bishops to and fro on the chess-board in a series of lightning moves bewildering to look on. Neither he nor his opponent played with the skill that they severally brought to bear on banking and statecraft, nor did they conduct their game with the politeness that they punctiliously observed in other affairs of life. A running fire of contemptuous remarks and aggressive satire accompanied each move, and the mere record of the conversation would have given an uninitiated onlooker the puzzling impression that an easy and crushing victory was assured to both the players.

'Aha, he is puzzled. Poor man, he doesn't know what to do. . . . Oho, he thinks he will move there, does he? Much good that will do him. . . . Never have I seen such a mess as he is in . . . he cannot do anything, he is absolutely helpless, helpless.'

'Ah, you take my bishop, do you? Much I care for that. Nothing. See, I give you check. Ah, now he is in a fright! He doesn't know where to go. What a mess he is in. . . .'

So the game proceeded, with a brisk exchange of pieces and incivilities and a fluctuation of fortunes, till the little banker lost his queen as the result of an incautious move, and, after several woebegone contortions of his shoulders and hands, declined further contest. A sleek-headed piccolo rushed forward to remove the board, and the erstwhile combatants resumed the courteous dignity that they discarded in their chess-playing moments.

'Have you seen the *Germania* to-day?' asked Herr Rebinok, as soon as the boy had receded to a respectful distance.

'No,' said von Kwarl, 'I never see the *Germania*. I count on you to tell me if there is anything noteworthy in it.'

'It has an article to-day headed, "Occupation or Assimilation",' said the banker. 'It is of some importance, and well written. It is very pessimistic.'

'Catholic papers are always pessimistic about the things of this world,' said von Kwarl, 'just as they are unduly optimistic about the things of the next world. What line does it take?'

'It says that our conquest of Britain can only result in a temporary occupation, with a "notice to quit" always hanging over our heads; that we can never hope to assimilate the people of these islands in our Empire as a sort of maritime Saxony or Bavaria, all the teaching of history is against it; Saxony and Bavaria are part of the Empire because of their past history. England is being bound into the Empire in spite of her past history; and so forth.'

'The writer of the article has not studied history very deeply,' said von Kwarl. 'The impossible thing that he speaks of has been done before, and done in these very islands, too. The Norman Conquest became an assimilation in comparatively few generations.'

'Ah, in those days, yes,' said the banker, 'but the conditions were altogether different. There was not the rapid transmission of news and the means of keeping the public mind instructed in what was happening; in fact, one can scarcely say that the public mind was there to instruct. There was not the same strong bond of brotherhood between men of the same nation that exists now. Northumberland was almost as foreign to Devon or Kent as Normandy was. And the Church in those days was a great international factor, and the Crusades bound men together fighting under one leader for a common cause. Also there was not a great national past to be forgotten as there is in this case.'

'There are many factors, certainly, that are against us,' conceded the statesman, 'but you must also take into account those that will help us. In most cases in recent history where the conquered have stood out against all attempts at assimilation, there has been a religious difference to add to the racial one—take Poland, for instance, and the Catholic parts of Ireland. If the Bretons ever seriously begin to assert their nationality as against the French, it will be because they have remained more Catholic in practice and sentiment than their neighbours. Here there is no such complication; we are in the bulk a Protestant nation with a Catholic minority, and the same may be said of the British. Then in modern days there is the alchemy of Sport and the Drama to bring men of different races amicably together. One or two sportsmanlike Germans in a London football team will do more to break down racial antagonism than anything that Governments or Councils can effect. As for the Stage, it has long been international in its tendencies. You can see that every day.'

The banker nodded his head.

'London is not our greatest difficulty,' continued von Kwarl. 'You must remember the steady influx of Germans since the war; whole districts are changing the complexion of their inhabitants, and in some streets you might almost fancy yourself in a German town. We can scarcely hope to make much impression on the country districts and the provincial towns at present, but you must remember that thousands and thousands of the more virile and restless-souled men have emigrated, and thousands more will follow their example. We shall fill up their places with our own surplus population, as the Teuton races colonized England in the old pre-Christian days. That is better, is it not, to people the fat meadows of the Thames valley and the healthy downs and uplands of Sussex and Berkshire than to go hunting for elbow-room among the flies and fevers of the tropics? We have somewhere to go to, now, better than the scrub and the veldt and the thorn-jungles.'

'Of course, of course,' assented Herr Rebinok, 'but while this desirable process of infiltration and assimilation goes on, how are you going to provide against the hostility of the conquered nation? A people with a great tradition behind them and the ruling instinct strongly developed, won't sit with their eyes closed and their hands folded while you carry on the process of Germanization. What will keep them quiet?'

'The hopelessness of the situation. For centuries Britain has ruled the seas, and been able to dictate to half the world in consequence; then she let slip the mastery of the seas, as something too costly and onerous to keep up, something which aroused too much jealousy and uneasiness in others, and now the seas rule her. Every wave that breaks on her shore rattles the keys of her prison. I am no fire-eater, Herr Rebinok, but I confess that when I am at Dover, say, or South-ampton, and see those dark blots on the sea and those grey specks in the sky, our battleships and cruisers and aircraft, and realize what they mean to us, my heart beats just a little quicker. If every German was flung out of England to-morrow, in three weeks' time we should be coming in again on our own terms. With our sea scouts and air scouts spread in organized network around, not a shipload of food-stuff could reach the country. They know that; they can calculate how many days of independence and starvation they could endure, and they will make no attempt to bring about such a certain fiasco. Brave men fight for a forlorn hope, but the bravest do not fight for an issue they know to be hopeless.'

'That is so,' said Herr Rebinok, 'as things are at present they can do nothing from within, absolutely nothing. We have weighed all that beforehand. But, as the *Germania* points out, there is another Britain beyond the seas. Supposing the Court at Delhi were to engineer a league——'

'A league? A league with whom?' interrupted the statesman. 'Russia we can watch and hold. We are rather nearer to its western frontier than Delhi is, and we could throttle its Baltic trade at five hours' notice. France and Holland are not inclined to provoke our hostility; they would have everything to lose by such a course.'

'There are other forces in the world that might be arrayed against us,' argued the banker; 'the United States, Japan, Italy, they all have navies.'

'Does the teaching of history show you that it is the strong Power, armed and ready, that has to suffer from the hostility of the world?' asked von Kwarl. 'As far as sentiment goes, perhaps, but not in practice. The danger has always been for the weak, dismembered nation. Think you a moment, has the enfeebled scattered British Empire overseas no undefended territories that are a temptation to her neighbours? Has Japan nothing to glean where we have har-vested? Are there no North American possessions which might slip into other keeping? Has Russia herself no traditional temptations beyond the Oxus? Mind you, we are not making the mistake Napo-leon made, when he forced all Europe to be for him or against him. We threaten no world aggressions, we are satiated where he was insatiable. We have cast down one overshadowing Power from the face of the world, because it stood in our way, but we have made no attempt to spread our branches over all the space that it covered. We have not tried to set up a tributary Canadian republic or to partition South Africa; we have dreamed no dream of making ourselves Lords of Hindostan. On the contrary, we have given proof of our friendly intentions towards our neighbours. We backed France up the other day in her squabble with Spain over the Moroccan boundaries, and proclaimed our opinion that the Republic had as indisputable a mission on the North Africa coast as we have in the North Sea. That is not the action or the language of aggression. No,' continued von Kwarl, after a moment's silence, 'the world may fear us and dislike us, but, for the present at any rate, there will be no leagues against us. No, there is one rock on which our attempt at assimilation will founder or find firm anchorage.'

'And that is——?'

'The youth of the country, the generation that is at the threshold now. It is them that we must capture. We must teach them to learn, and coax them to forget. In course of time Anglo-Saxon may blend with German, as the Elbe Saxons and the Bavarians and Swabians have blended with the Prussians into a loyal united people under the sceptre of the Hohenzollerns. Then we should be doubly strong, Rome and Carthage rolled into one, an Empire of the West greater than Charlemagne ever knew. Then we could look Slav and Latin and Asiatic in the face and keep our place as the central dominant force of the civilized world.'

The speaker paused for a moment and drank a deep draught of wine, as though he were invoking the prosperity of that future world-power. Then he resumed in a more level tone:

'On the other hand, the younger generation of Britons may grow up in hereditary hatred, repulsing all our overtures, forgetting nothing and forgiving nothing, waiting and watching for the time when some weakness assails us, when some crisis entangles us, when we cannot be everywhere at once. Then our work will be imperilled, perhaps undone. There lies the danger, there lies the hope, the younger generation.'

'There is another danger,' said the banker, after he had pondered over von Kwarl's remarks for a moment or two amid the incense-clouds of a fat cigar; 'a danger that I foresee in the immediate future; perhaps not so much a danger as an element of exasperation which may ultimately defeat your plans. The law as to military service will have to be promulgated shortly, and that cannot fail to be bitterly unpopular. The people of these islands will have to be brought into line with the rest of the Empire in the matter of military training and military service, and how will they like that? Will not the enforcing of such a measure infuriate them against us? Remember, they have made great sacrifices to avoid the burden of military service.'

'Dear God,' exclaimed Herr von Kwarl, 'as you say, they have made sacrifices on that altar!'

CHAPTER VII

The Lure

Cicely had successfully insisted on having her own way concerning the projected supper-party; Yeovil had said nothing further in opposition to it, whatever his feelings on the subject might be. Having gained her point, however, she was anxious to give her husband the impression of having been consulted, and to put her victory as far as possible on the footing of a compromise. It was also rather a relief to be able to discuss the matter out of range of Joan's disconcerting tongue and observant eyes.

'I hope you are not really annoyed about this silly supper-party,' she said on the morning before the much-talked-of first night. 'I had pledged myself to give it, so I couldn't back out without seeming mean to Gorla, and in any case it would have been impolitic to cry off.'

'Why impolitic?' asked Yeovil coldly.

'It would give offence in quarters where I don't want to give offence,' said Cicely.

'In quarters where the *fait accompli* is an object of solicitude,' said Yeovil.

'Look here,' said Cicely in her most disarming manner, 'it's just as well to be perfectly frank about the whole matter. If one wants to live in the London of the present day one must make up one's mind to accept the *fait accompli* with as good a grace as possible. I do want to live in London, and I don't want to change my way of living and start under different conditions in some other place. I can't face the prospect of tearing up my life by the roots; I feel certain that I shouldn't bear transplanting. I can't imagine myself recreating my circle of interests in some foreign town or colonial centre or even in a country town in England. India I couldn't stand. London is not merely a home to me, it is a world, and it happens to be just the world that suits me and that I am suited to. The German occupation, or whatever one likes to call it, is a calamity, but it's not like a molten deluge from Vesuvius that need send us all scuttling away from another Pompeii.

Of course,' she added, 'there are things that jar horribly on one, even when one has got more or less accustomed to them, but one must just learn to be philosophical and bear them.'

'Supposing they are not bearable?' said Yeovil; 'during the few days that I've been in the land I've seen things that I cannot imagine will ever be bearable.'

'That is because they're new to you,' said Cicely.

'I don't wish that they should ever come to seem bearable,' retorted Yeovil. 'I've been bred and reared as a unit of a ruling race; I don't want to find myself settling down resignedly as a member of an enslaved one.'

'There's no need to make things out worse than they are,' protested Cicely. 'We've had a military disaster on a big scale, and there's been a great political dislocation in consequence. But there's no reason why everything shouldn't right itself in time, as it has done after other similar disasters in the history of nations. We are not scattered to the winds or wiped off the face of the earth, we are still an important racial unit.'

'A racial unit in a foreign Empire,' commented Yeovil.

'We may arrive at the position of being the dominant factor in that Empire,' said Cicely, 'impressing our national characteristics on it, and perhaps dictating its dynastic future and the whole trend of its policy. Such things have happened in history. Or we may become strong enough to throw off the foreign connection at a moment when it can be done effectually and advantageously. But meanwhile it is necessary to preserve our industrial life and our social life, and for that reason we must accommodate ourselves to present circumstances, however distasteful they may be. Emigration to some colonial wilderness, or holding ourselves rigidly aloof from the life of the capital, won't help matters. Really, Murrey, if you will think things over a bit, you will see that the course I am following is the one dictated by sane patriotism.'

'Whom the gods wish to render harmless they first afflict with sanity,' said Yeovil bitterly. 'You may be content to wait for a hundred years or so, for this national revival to creep and crawl us back into a semblance of independence and world-importance. I'm afraid I haven't the patience or the philosophy to sit down comfortably and wait for a change of fortune that won't come in my time—if it comes at all.'

Cicely changed the drift of the conversation; she had only intro-duced the argument for the purpose of defining her point of view and accustoming Yeovil to it, as one leads a nervous horse up to an unfamiliar barrier that he is required eventually to jump.

'In any case,' she said, 'from the immediately practical standpoint England is the best place for you till you have shaken off all traces of that fever. Pass the time away somehow till the hunting begins, and then go down to the East Wessex country; they are looking out for a new master after this season, and if you were strong enough you might take it on for a while. You could go to Norway for fishing in the summer and hunt the East Wessex in the winter. I'll come down and do a bit of hunting too, and we'll have house-parties, and get a little golf in between whiles. It will be like old times.'

Yeovil looked at his wife and laughed.

'Who was that old fellow who used to hunt his hounds regularly through the fiercest times of the great Civil War? There is a picture of him, by Caton Woodville, I think, leading his pack between King Charles's army and the Parliament forces just as some battle was going to begin. I have often thought that the King must have disliked him rather more than he disliked the men who were in arms against him; they at least cared, one way or the other. I fancy that old chap would have a great many imitators nowadays, though, when it came to be a question of sport against soldiering. I don't know whether any-one has said it, but one might almost assert that the German victory was won on the golf-links of Britain.'

'I don't see why you should saddle one particular form of sport with a special responsibility,' protested Cicely.

'Of course not,' said Yeovil, 'except that it absorbed perhaps more of the energy and attention of the leisured class than other sports did, and in this country the leisured class was the only bulwark we had against official indifference. The working classes had a big share of the apathy, and, indirectly, a greater share of the responsibility, be-cause the voting power was in their hands. They had not the leisure, however, to sit down and think clearly what the danger was; their own industrial warfare was more real to them than anything that was threatening from the nation that they only knew from samples of German clerks and German waiters.'

'In any case,' said Cicely, 'as regards the hunting, there is no Civil War or national war raging just now, and there is no immediate

likelihood of one. A good many hunting seasons will have to come
and go before we can think of a war of independence as even a distant
possibility, and in the meantime hunting and horse-breeding and
country sports generally are the things most likely to keep Englishmen together on the land. That is why so many men who hate the
German occupation are trying to keep field sports alive, and in the
right hands. However, I won't go on arguing. You and I always think
things out for ourselves and decide for ourselves, which is much the
best way in the long run.'

   Cicely slipped away to her writing-room to make final arrangements over the telephone for the all-important supper-party, leaving
Yeovil to turn over in his mind the suggestion that she had thrown
out. It was an obvious lure, a lure to draw him away from the fret and
fury that possessed him so inconveniently, but its obvious nature did
not detract from its effectiveness. Yeovil had pleasant recollections of
the East Wessex, a cheery little hunt that afforded good sport in an
unpretentious manner, a joyous thread of life running through a
rather sleepy countryside, like a merry brook careering through a
placid valley. For a man coming slowly and yet eagerly back to the
activities of life from the weariness of a long fever, the prospect of a
leisurely season with the East Wessex was singularly attractive, and
side by side with its attractiveness there was a tempting argument in
favour of yielding to its attractions. Among the small squires and
yeoman farmers, doctors, country tradesmen, auctioneers and so forth
who would gather at the covert-side and at the hunt breakfasts, there
might be a local nucleus of revolt against the enslavement of the land,
a discouraged and leaderless band waiting for some one to mould
their resistance into effective shape and keep their loyalty to the old
dynasty and the old national cause steadily burning. Yeovil could see
himself taking up that position, stimulating the spirit of hostility to
the *fait accompli*, organizing stubborn opposition to every Germanizing influence that was brought into play, schooling the youth of the
countryside to look steadily Delhiward. That was the bait that Yeovil
threw out to his conscience, while slowly considering the other bait
that was appealing so strongly to his senses. The dry warm scent of
the stable, the nip of the morning air, the pleasant squelch-squelch of
the saddle leather, the moist earthy fragrance of the autumn woods
and wet fallows, the cold white mists of winter days, the whimper of
hounds and the hot restless pushing of the pack through ditch and

hedgerow and undergrowth, the birds that flew up and clucked and chattered as you passed, the hearty greeting and pleasant gossip in farmhouse kitchens and market-day bar-parlours—all these remembered delights of the chase marshalled themselves in the brain, and made a cumulative appeal that came with special intensity to a man who was a little tired of his wanderings, more than a little drawn away from the jarring centres of life. The hot London sunshine baking the soot-grimed walls and the ugly incessant hoot and grunt of the motor traffic gave an added charm to the vision of hill and hollow and copse that flickered in Yeovil's mind. Slowly, with a sensuous lingering over detail, his imagination carried him down to a small, sleepy, yet withal pleasantly bustling market town, and placed him unerringly in a wide straw-littered yard, half-full of men and quarter-full of horses, with a bob-tailed sheep-dog or two trying not to get in everybody's way, but insisting on being in the thick of things. The horses gradually detached themselves from the crowd of unimportant men and came one by one into momentary prominence, to be discussed and appraised for their good points and bad points, and finally to be bid for. And always there was one horse that detached itself conspicuously from the rest, the ideal hunter, or at any rate, Yeovil's ideal of the ideal hunter. Mentally it was put through its paces before him, its pedigree and brief history recounted to him; mentally he saw a stable lad put it over a jump or two, with credit to all concerned, and inevitably he saw himself outbidding less discerning rivals and securing the desired piece of horseflesh, to be the chief glory and mainstay of his hunting stable, to carry him well and truly and cleverly through many a joyous long-to-be-remembered run. That scene had been one of the recurring half-waking dreams of his long days of weakness in the far-away Finnish nursing-home, a dream sometimes of tantalizing mockery, sometimes of pleasure in the foretaste of a joy to come. And now it need scarcely be a dream any longer, he had only to go down at the right moment and take an actual part in his oft-rehearsed vision. Everything would be there, exactly as his imagination had placed it, even down to the bob-tailed sheep-dogs; the horse of his imagining would be there waiting for him, or if not absolutely the ideal animal, something very like it. He might even go beyond the limits of his dream and pick up a couple of desirable animals—there would probably be fewer purchasers for good class hunters in these days than of yore. And with the coming of this reflection his dream faded suddenly and his mind came back with a throb of pain to the things he had for the moment forgotten, the weary, hateful things that were symbolized for him by the standard that floated yellow and black over the frontage of Buckingham Palace.

Yeovil wandered down to his snuggery, a mood of listless dejection possessing him. He fidgeted aimlessly with one or two books and papers, filled a pipe, and half filled a waste-paper basket with torn circulars and accumulated writing-table litter. Then he lit the pipe and settled down in his most comfortable arm-chair with an old notebook in his hand. It was a sort of disjointed diary, running fitfully through the winter months of some past years, and recording noteworthy days with the East Wessex.

And over the telephone Cicely talked and arranged and consulted with men and women to whom the joys of a good gallop or the love of a stricken fatherland were as letters in an unknown alphabet.

CHAPTER VIII

The First Night

Huge posters outside the Caravansery Theatre of Varieties announced the first performance of the uniquely interesting Suggestion Dances, interpreted by the Hon. Gorla Mustelford. An impressionist portrait of a rather severe-looking young woman gave the public some idea of what the *danseuse* might be like in appearance, and the further information was added that her performance was the greatest dramatic event of the season. Yet another piece of information was conveyed to the public a few minutes after the doors had opened, in the shape of large notices bearing the brief announcement, 'house full'. For the first-night function most of the seats had been reserved for specially invited guests or else bespoken by those who considered it due to their own importance to be visible on such an occasion.

Even at the commencement of the ordinary programme of the evening (Gorla was not due to appear till late in the list) the theatre was crowded with a throng of chattering, expectant human beings; it seemed as though every one had come early to see every one else arrive. As a matter of fact it was the rumour-heralded arrival of one personage in particular that had drawn people early to their seats and given a double edge to the expectancy of the moment.

At first sight and first hearing the bulk of the audience seemed to comprise representatives of the chief European races in well-distributed proportions, but if one gave it closer consideration it could be seen that the distribution was geographically rather than ethnographically diversified. Men and women there were from Paris, Munich, Rome, Moscow, and Vienna, from Sweden and Holland and divers other cities and countries, but in the majority of cases the Jordan Valley had supplied their forefathers with a common cradle-ground. The lack of a fire burning on a national altar seemed to have drawn them by universal impulse to the congenial flare of the footlights, whether as artists, producers, impresarios, critics, agents, go-betweens, or merely as highly intelligent and fearsomely well-informed spectators. They were prominent in the chief seats, they were represented, more sparsely but still in fair numbers, in the cheaper places, and everywhere they were voluble, emphatic, sanguine or sceptical, prodigal of word and gesture, with eyes that seemed to miss nothing and acknowledge nothing, and a general restless dread of not being seen and noticed. Of the theatre-going London public there was also a fair muster, more particularly centred in the less expensive parts of the house, while in boxes, stalls, and circles a sprinkling of military uniforms gave an unfamiliar tone to the scene in the eyes of those who had not previously witnessed a first-night performance under the new conditions.

Yeovil, while standing aloof from his wife's participation in this social event, had made private arrangements for being a personal spectator of the scene; as one of the ticket-buying public he had secured a seat in the back row of a low-priced gallery, whence he might watch, observant and unobserved, the much-talked-of début of Gorla Mustelford, and the writing of a new chapter in the history of the *fait accompli*. Around him he noticed an incessant undercurrent of jangling laughter, an unending give-and-take of meaningless mirthless jest and catchword. He had noticed the same thing in streets and public places since his arrival in London, a noisy, empty interchange of chaff and laughter that he had been at a loss to account for. The Londoner is not well adapted for the irresponsible noisiness of jesting tongue that bubbles up naturally in a Southern race, and the effort to be volatile was the more noticeable because it so obviously was an effort. Turning over the pages of a book that told the story of Bulgarian social life in the days of Turkish rule, Yeovil had that morning come across a passage that seemed to throw some light on the thing that had puzzled him:

'Bondage has this one advantage: it makes a nation merry. Where far-reaching ambition has no scope for its development the community squanders its energy on the trivial and personal cares of its daily life, and seeks relief and recreation in simple and easily obtained material enjoyment.' The writer was a man who had known bondage, so he spoke at any rate with authority. Of the London of the moment it could not, however, be said with any truth that it was merry, but merely that its inhabitants made desperate endeavour not to appear crushed under their catastrophe. Surrounded as he was now with a babble of tongues and shrill mechanical repartee, Yeovil's mind went back to the book and its account of a theatre audience in the Turkish days of Bulgaria, with its light and laughing crowd of critics and spectators. Bulgaria! The thought of that determined little nation came to him with a sharp sense of irony. There was a people who had not thought it beneath the dignity of their manhood to learn the trade and discipline of arms. They had their reward; torn and exhausted and debt-encumbered from their campaigns, they were masters in their own house, the Bulgarian flag flew over the Bulgarian mountains. And Yeovil stole a glance at the crown of Charlemagne set over the Royal box.

In a capacious box immediately opposite the one set aside for royalty the Lady Shalem sat in well-considered prominence, confident that every Press critic and reporter would note her presence, and that one or two of them would describe, or misdescribe, her toilet. Already quite a considerable section of the audience knew her by name, and the frequency with which she graciously nodded towards various quarters of the house suggested the presence of a great many personal acquaintances. She had attained to that desirable feminine altitude of purse and position when people who go about everywhere know you well by sight and have never met your dress before.

Lady Shalem was a woman of commanding presence, of that type which suggests a consciousness that the command may not necessarily be obeyed; she had observant eyes and a well-managed voice. Her successes in life had been worked for, but they were also to some considerable extent the result of accident. Her public history went back to the time when, in the person of her husband, Mr Conrad Dort, she had contested two hopeless and very expensive Parliamentary elections on behalf of her party; on each occasion the declaration of the poll had shown a heavy though reduced majority on the wrong side, but she might have perpetrated an apt misquotation of the French monarch's traditional message after the defeat of Pavia, and assured the world 'all is lost save honours'. The forthcoming Honours List had duly proclaimed the fact that Conrad Dort, Esquire, had entered Parliament by another door as Baron Shalem of Wireskiln, in the county of Suffolk. Success had crowned the lady's efforts as far as the achievement of the title went, but her social ambitions seemed unlikely to make further headway. The new Baron and his wife, their title and money notwithstanding, did not 'go down' in their particular segment of county society, and in London there were other titles and incomes to compete with. People were willing to worship the Golden

Calf, but allowed themselves a choice of altars. No one could justly say that the Shalems were either oppressively vulgar or insufferably bumptious; probably the chief reason for their lack of popularity was their intense and obvious desire to be popular. They kept open house in such an insistently open manner that they created a social draught. The people who accepted their invitations for the second or third time were not the sort of people whose names gave importance to a dinner party or a house gathering. Failure, in a thinly disguised form, attended the assiduous efforts of the Shalems to play a leading rôle in the world that they had climbed into. The Baron began to observe to his acquaintances that 'gadding about' and entertaining on a big scale was not much in his line; a quiet after-dinner pipe and talk with some brother legislator was his ideal way of spending an evening.

Then came the great catastrophe, involving the old order of society in the national overthrow. Lady Shalem, after a decent interval of patriotic mourning, began to look around her and take stock of her chances and opportunities under the new régime. It was easier to achieve distinction as a titled oasis in the social desert that London had become than it had been to obtain recognition as a new growth in a rather overcrowded field. The observant eyes and agile brain quickly noted this circumstance, and her ladyship set to work to adapt herself to the altered conditions that governed her world. Lord Shalem was one of the few Peers who kissed the hand of the new Sovereign, his wife was one of the few hostesses who attempted to throw a semblance of gaiety and lavish elegance over the travesty of a London season following the year of disaster. The world of trades-men and purveyors and caterers, and the thousands who were de-pendent on them for employment, privately blessed the example set by Shalem House, whatever their feelings might be towards the *fait accompli*, and the august new-comer who had added an old Saxon kingdom and some of its accretions to the Teutonic realm of Charle-magne was duly beholden to an acquired subject who was willing to forget the bitterness of defeat and to help others to forget it also. Among other acts of Imperial recognition an earldom was being held in readiness for the Baron who had known how to accept accom-plished facts with a good grace. One of the wits of the Cockatrice Club had asserted that the new earl would take as supporters for his coat of arms a lion and a unicorn oublié.

In the box with Lady Shalem was the Gräfin von Tolb, a well-dressed woman of some fifty-six years, comfortable and placid in appearance, yet alert withal, rather suggesting a thoroughly wide-awake dormouse. Rich, amiable, and intelligent were the adjectives which would best have described her character and her life-story. In her own rather difficult social circle at Paderborn she had earned for herself the reputation of being one of the most tactful and discerning hostesses in Germany, and it was generally suspected that she had come over and taken up her residence in London in response to a wish expressed in high quarters; the lavish hospitality which she dispensed at her house in Berkeley Square was a considerable rein-forcement to the stricken social life of the metropolis.

In a neighbouring box Cicely Yeovil presided over a large and lively party, which of course included Ronnie Storre, who was for once in a way in a chattering mood, and also included an American dowager, who had never been known to be in anything else. A tone of literary distinction was imparted to the group by the presence of Augusta Smith, better known under her pen-name of Rhapsodie Pantril, author of a play that had had a limited but well-advertised success in Sheffield and the United States of America, author also of a book of reminiscences, entitled 'Things I Cannot Forget'. She had beautiful eyes, a knowledge of how to dress, and a pleasant disposi-tion, cankered just a little by a perpetual dread of the non-recognition of her genius. As the woman, Augusta Smith, she probably would have been unreservedly happy; as the super-woman, Rhapsodie Pantril, she lived within the border-line of discontent. Her most ordinary remarks were framed with the view of arresting attention; some one once said of her that she ordered a sack of potatoes with the air of one who is making inquiry for a love-philtre.

'Do you see what colour the curtain is?' she asked Cicely, throwing a note of intense meaning into her question.

Cicely turned quickly and looked at the drop-curtain.

'Rather a nice blue,' she said.

'Alexandrine blue—*my* colour—the colour of hope,' said Rhapsodie impressively.

'It goes well with the general colour-scheme,' said Cicely, feeling that she was hardly rising to the occasion.

'Say, is it really true that His Majesty is coming?' asked the lively

American dowager. 'I've put on my nooest frock and my best diamonds on purpose, and I shall be mortified to death if he doesn't see them.'

'There!' pouted Ronnie, 'I felt certain you'd put them on for me.'

'Why no, I should have put on rubies and orange opals for you. People with our colour of hair always like barbaric display——'

'They don't,' said Ronnie, 'they have chaste cold tastes. You are absolutely mistaken.'

'Well, I think I ought to know!' protested the dowager; 'I've lived longer in the world than you have, anyway.'

'Yes,' said Ronnie with devastating truthfulness, 'but my hair has been this colour longer than yours has.'

Peace was restored by the opportune arrival of a middle-aged man of blond North-German type, with an expression of brutality on his rather stupid face, who sat in the front of the box for a few minutes on a visit of ceremony to Cicely. His appearance caused a slight buzz of recognition among the audience, and if Yeovil had cared to make enquiry of his neighbours he might have learned that this decorated and obviously important personage was the redoubtable von Kwarl, artificer and shaper of much of the statecraft for which other men got the public credit.

The orchestra played a selection from the 'Gondola Girl,' which was the leading musical-comedy of the moment. Most of the audience, those in the more expensive seats at any rate, heard the same airs two or three times daily, at restaurant lunches, teas, dinners, and suppers, and occasionally in the Park; they were justified therefore in treating the music as a background to slightly louder conversation than they had hitherto indulged in. The music came to an end, episode number two in the evening's entertainment was signalled, the curtain of Alexandrine blue rolled heavily upward, and a troupe of performing wolves was presented to the public. Yeovil had encountered wolves in North Africa deserts and in Siberian forest and wold, he had seen them at twilight stealing like dark shadows across the snow, and heard their long whimpering howl in the darkness amid the pines; he could well understand how a magic lore had grown up round them through the ages among the peoples of four continents, how their name had passed into a hundred strange sayings and inspired a hundred traditions. And now he saw them ride round the stage on tricycles, with grotesque ruffles round their necks and clown caps on their heads, their eyes blinking miserably in the blaze of the foot-lights. In response to the applause of the house a stout, atrociously smiling man in evening dress came forward and bowed; he had had nothing to do either with the capture or the training of the animals, having bought them ready for use from a continental emporium where wild beasts were prepared for the music-hall market, but he continued bowing and smiling till the curtain fell.

Two American musicians with comic tendencies (denoted by the elaborate rags and tatters of their costumes) succeeded the wolves. Their musical performance was not without merit, but their comic 'business' seemed to have been invented long ago by some man who had patented a monopoly of all music-hall humour and forthwith retired from the trade. Some day, Yeovil reflected, the rights of the monopoly might expire and new 'business' become available for the knockabout profession.

The audience brightened considerably when item number five of the programme was signalled. The orchestra struck up a rollicking measure and Tony Luton made his entrance amid a rousing storm of applause. He was dressed as an errand-boy of some West End shop, with a livery and box-tricycle, as spruce and decorative as the most ambitious errand-boy could see himself in his most ambitious dreams. His song was a lively and very audacious chronicle of life behind the scenes of a big retail establishment, and sparkled with allusions which might fitly have been described as suggestive—at any rate they appeared to suggest meanings to the audience quite as clearly as Gorla Mustelford's dances were likely to do, even with the aid, in her case, of long explanations on the programmes. When the final verse seemed about to reach an unpardonable climax a stage policeman opportunely appeared and moved the lively songster on for obstructing the imaginary traffic of an imaginary Bond Street. The house received the new number with genial enthusiasm, and mingled its applause with demands for an earlier favourite. The orchestra struck up the familiar air, and in a few moments the smart errand-boy, transformed now into a smart jockey, was singing 'They quaff the gay bubbly in Eccleston Square' to an audience that hummed and nodded its unstinted approval.

The next number but one was the Gorla Mustelford début, and the house settled itself down to yawn and fidget and chatter for ten or twelve minutes while a troupe of talented Japanese jugglers performed some artistic and quite uninteresting marvels with fans and butterflies and lacquer boxes. The interval of waiting was not destined, however, to be without its interest; in its way it provided the one really important and dramatic moment of the evening. One or two uniforms and evening toilettes had already made their appearance in the Imperial box; now there was observable in that quarter a slight commotion, an unobtrusive reshuffling and reseating, and then every eye in the suddenly quiet semi-darkened house focused itself on one figure. There was no public demonstration from the newly loyal, it had been particularly wished that there should be none, but a ripple of whisper went through the vast audience from end to end. Majesty had arrived. The Japanese marvel-workers went through their display with even less attention than before. Lady Shalem, sitting well in the front of her box, lowered her observant eyes to her programme and her massive bangles. The evidence of her triumph did not need staring at.

CHAPTER IX

An Evening 'to be Remembered'

To the uninitiated or unappreciative the dancing of Gorla Mustelford did not seem widely different from much that had been exhibited aforetime by exponents of the posturing school. She was not naturally graceful of movement, she had not undergone years of arduous tutelage, she had not the instinct for sheer joyous energy of action that is stored in some natures; out of these unpromising negative qualities she had produced a style of dancing that might best be labelled a conscientious departure from accepted methods. The highly imaginative titles that she had bestowed on her dances, the 'Life of a fern', the 'Soul-dream of a topaz', and so forth, at least gave her audience and her critics something to talk about. In themselves they meant absolutely nothing, but they induced discussion, and that to Gorla meant a great deal. It was a season of dearth and emptiness in the footlights and box-office world, and her performance received a welcome that would scarcely have befallen it in a more crowded and prosperous day. Her success, indeed, had been waiting for her, ready-made, as far as the managerial profession was concerned, and nothing had been left undone in the way of advertisement to secure for it the appearance, at any rate, of popular favour. And loud above the interested applause of those who had personal or business motives for acclaiming a success swelled the exaggerated enthusiasm of the fairly numerous art-satellites who are unstinted in their praise of anything that they are certain they cannot understand. Whatever might be the subsequent verdict of the theatre-filling public the majority of the favoured first-night audience was determined to set the seal of its approval on the suggestion dances, and a steady roll of applause greeted the conclusion of each item. The dancer gravely bowed her thanks; in marked contradistinction to the gentleman who had 'presented' the performing wolves she did not permit herself the luxury of a smile.

'It teaches us a great deal,' said Rhapsodie Pantril vaguely, but impressively, after the Fern dance had been given and applauded.

'At any rate we know now that a fern takes life very seriously,' broke in Joan Mardle, who had somehow wriggled herself into Cicely's box.

As Yeovil, from the back of his gallery, watched Gorla running and ricochetting about the stage, looking rather like a wagtail in energetic pursuit of invisible gnats and midges, he wondered how many of the middle-aged women who were eagerly applauding her would have taken the least notice of similar gymnastics on the part of their offspring in nursery or garden, beyond perhaps asking them not to make so much noise. And a bitterer tinge came to his thoughts as he saw the bouquets being handed up, thoughts of the brave old dowager down at Torywood, the woman who had worked and wrought so hard and so unsparingly in her day for the well-being of the State— the State that had fallen helpless into alien hands before her tired eyes. Her eldest son lived invalid-wise in the South of France, her second son lay fathoms deep in the North Sea, with the hulk of a broken battleship for a burial-vault; and now the granddaughter was standing here in the limelight, bowing her thanks for the patronage and favour meted out to her by this cosmopolitan company, with its lavish sprinkling of the uniforms of an alien army.

Prominent among the flowers at her feet was one large golden-petalled bouquet of gorgeous blooms, tied with a broad streamer of golden riband, the tribute rendered by Cæsar to the things that were Cæsar's. The new chapter of the *fait accompli* had been written that night and written well. The audience poured slowly out with the triumphant music of Jancovius's *Kaiser Wilhelm* march, played by the orchestra as a happy inspiration, pealing in its ears.

'It has been a great evening, a most successful evening,' said Lady Shalem to Herr von Kwarl, whom she was conveying in her electric brougham to Cicely Yeovil's supper party; 'an important evening,' she added, choosing her adjectives with deliberation. 'It should give pleasure in high quarters, should it not?'

And she turned her observant eyes on the impassive face of her companion.

'Gracious lady,' he replied with deliberation and meaning, 'it has given pleasure. It is an evening to be remembered.'

The gracious lady suppressed a sigh of satisfaction. Memory in high places was a thing fruitful and precious beyond computation.

Cicely's party at the Porphyry Restaurant had grown to imposing dimensions. Every one whom she had asked had come, and so had Joan Mardle. Lady Shalem had suggested several names at the last moment, and there was quite a strong infusion of the Teutonic military and official world. It was just as well, Cicely reflected, that the supper was being given at a restaurant and not in Berkshire Street.

'Quite like ole times,' purred the beaming proprietor in Cicely's ear, as the staircase and cloakrooms filled up with a jostling, laughing throng.

The guests settled themselves at four tables, taking their places where chance or fancy led them, late comers having to fit in wherever they could find room. A babel of tongues in various languages reigned round the tables, amid which the rattle of knives and forks and plates and the popping of corks made a subdued hubbub. Gorla Mustelford, the motive for all this sound and movement, this chatter of guests and scurrying of waiters, sat motionless in the fatigued self-conscious silence of a great artist who has delivered a great message.

'Do sit at Lady Peach's table, like a dear boy,' Cicely begged of Tony Luton, who had come in late; 'she and Gerald Drowly have got together, in spite of all my efforts, and they are both so dull. Try and liven things up a bit.'

A loud barking sound, as of fur-seals calling across Arctic ice, came from another table, where Mrs Mentieth-Mendlesohnn (one of the Mendlesohnns of Invergordon, as she was wont to describe herself) was proclaiming the glories and subtleties of Gorla's achievement.

'It was a revelation,' she shouted; 'I sat there and saw a whole new scheme of thought unfold itself before my eyes. One could not define it, it was thought translated into action—the best art cannot be defined. One just sat there and knew that one was seeing something one had never seen before, and yet one felt that one had seen it in one's brain, all one's life. That was what was so wonderful—yes, please,' she broke off sharply as a fat quail in aspic was presented to her by a questioning waiter.

The voice of Mr Mauleverer Morle came across the table, like another seal barking at a greater distance.

'Rostand', he observed with studied emphasis, 'has been called *le Prince de l'adjectif Inopinè*; Miss Mustelford deserves to be described as the Queen of Unexpected Movement.'

'Oh, I say, do you hear that?' exclaimed Mrs Mentieth-

Mendlesohnn to as wide an audience as she could achieve; 'Rostand
has been called—tell them what you said, Mr Morle,' she broke off,
suddenly mistrusting her ability to handle a French sentence at the
top of her voice.

Mr Morle repeated his remark.

'Pass it on to the next table,' commanded Mrs Mentieth-
Mendlesohnn. 'It's too good to be lost.'

At the next table, however, a grave impressive voice was dwelling
at length on a topic remote from the event of the evening. Lady
Peach considered that all social gatherings, of whatever nature, were
intended for the recital of minor domestic tragedies. She lost no time
in regaling the company around her with the detailed history of an
interrupted week-end in a Norfolk cottage.

'The most charming and delightful old-world spot that you could
imagine, clean and quite comfortable, just a nice distance from the
sea and within an easy walk of the Broads. The very place for the
children. We'd brought everything for a four days' stay and meant to
have a really delightful time. And then on Sunday morning we found
that some one had left the springhead, where our only supply of
drinking water came from, uncovered, and a dead bird was floating in
it; it had fallen in somehow and got drowned. Of course we couldn't
use the water that a dead body had been floating in, and there was no
other supply for miles round, so we had to come away then and there.
Now what do you say to that?'

' "Ah, that a linnet should die in the Spring," ' quoted Tony Luton
with intense feeling.

There was an immediate outburst of hilarity where Lady Peach
had confidently looked for expressions of concern and sympathy.

'Isn't Tony just perfectly cute? Isn't he?' exclaimed a young
American woman, with an enthusiasm to which Lady Peach entirely
failed to respond. She had intended following up her story with the
account of another tragedy of a similar nature that had befallen her
three years ago in Argyllshire, and now the opportunity had gone. She
turned morosely to the consolations of a tongue salad.

At the centre table the excellent von Tolb led a chorus of congratulation and compliment, to which Gorla listened with an air of polite
detachment, much as the Sheikh Ul Islam might receive the homage
of a Wesleyan Conference. To a close observer it would have seemed
probable that her attitude of fatigued indifference to the flattering

remarks that were showered on her had been as carefully studied and rehearsed as any of her postures on the stage.

'It is something that one will appreciate more and more fully every time one sees it. . . . One cannot see it too often. . . . I could have sat and watched it for hours. . . . Do you know, I am just looking forward to to-morrow evening, when I can see it again. . . . I knew it was going to be good, but I had no idea——' so chimed the chorus, between mouthfuls of quail and bites of asparagus.

'Weren't the performing wolves wonderful?' exclaimed Joan in her fresh joyous voice, that rang round the room like laughter of the woodpecker.

If there is one thing that disturbs the complacency of a great artist of the Halls it is the consciousness of sharing his or her triumphs with performing birds and animals, but of course Joan was not to be expected to know that. She pursued her subject with the assurance of one who has hit on a particularly acceptable topic.

'It must have taken them years of training and concentration to master those tricycles,' she continued in high-pitched soliloquy. 'The nice thing about them is that they don't realize a bit how clever and educational they are. It would be dreadful to have them putting on airs, wouldn't it? And yet I suppose the knowledge of being able to jump through a hoop better than any other wolf would justify a certain amount of "side".'

Fortunately at this moment a young Italian journalist at another table rose from his seat and delivered a two-minute oration in praise of the heroine of the evening. He spoke in rapid nervous French, with a North Italian accent, but much of what he said could be understood by the majority of those present, and the applause was unanimous. At any rate he had been brief and it was permissible to suppose that he had been witty.

It was the opening for which Mr Gerald Drowly had been watching and waiting. The moment that the Italian enthusiast had dropped back into his seat amid a rattle of hand-clapping and rapping of forks and knives on the tables, Drowly sprang to his feet, pushed his chair well away, as for a long separation, and begged to endorse what had been so very aptly and gracefully, and, might he add, truly said by the previous speaker. This was only the prelude to the real burden of his message; with the dexterity that comes of practice he managed, in a couple of hurried sentences, to divert the course of his remarks to his own personality and career, and to inform his listeners that he was an actor of some note and experience, and had had the honour of acting under—and here followed a string of names of eminent actor managers of the day. He thought he might be pardoned for mentioning the fact that his performance of 'Peterkin' in the 'Broken Nutshell', had won the unstinted approval of the dramatic critics of the Provincial Press. Towards the end of what was a long speech, and which seemed even longer to its hearers, he reverted to the subject of Gorla's dancing and bestowed on it such laudatory remarks as he had left over. Drawing his chair once again into his immediate neighbourhood he sat down, aglow with the satisfied consciousness of a good work worthily performed.

'I once acted a small part in some theatricals got up for a charity,' announced Joan in a ringing, confidential voice; 'the *Clapham Courier* said that all the minor parts were very creditably sustained. Those were its very words. I felt I must tell you that, and also say how much I enjoyed Miss Mustelford's dancing.'

Tony Luton cheered wildly.

'That's the cleverest speech so far,' he proclaimed. He had been asked to liven things up at his table and was doing his best to achieve that result, but Mr Gerald Drowly joined Lady Peach in the unfavourable opinion she had formed of that irrepressible youth.

Ronnie, on whom Cicely kept a solicitous eye, showed no sign of any intention of falling in love with Gorla. He was more profitably engaged in paying court to the Gräfin von Tolb, whose hospitable mansion in Belgrave Square invested her with a special interest in his eyes. As a professional Prince Charming he had every inducement to encourage the cult of Fairy Godmother.

'Yes, yes, agreed, I will come and hear you play, that is a promise,' said the Gräfin, 'and you must come and dine with me one night and play to me afterwards, that is a promise, also, yes? That is very nice of you, to come and see a tiresome old woman. I am passionately fond of music; if I were honest I would tell you also that I am very fond of good-looking boys, but this is not the age of honesty, so I must leave you to guess that. Come on Thursday in next week, you can? That is nice. I have a reigning Prince dining with me that night. Poor man, he wants cheering up; the art of being a reigning Prince is not a very pleasing one nowadays. He has made it a boast all his life that he is Liberal and his subjects Conservative; now that is all changed—no, not all; he is still Liberal, but his subjects unfortunately are become Socialists. You must play your best for him.'

'Are there many Socialists over there, in Germany I mean?' asked Ronnie, who was rather out of his depth where politics were concerned.

'*Ueberall*,' said the Gräfin with emphasis; 'everywhere, I don't know what it comes from; better education and worse digestions I suppose. I am sure digestion has a good deal to do with it. In my husband's family for example, his generation had excellent digestions, and there wasn't a case of Socialism or suicide among them; the younger generation have no digestions worth speaking of, and there have been two suicides and three Socialists within the last six years. And now I must really be going. I am not a Berliner and late hours don't suit my way of life.'

Ronnie bent low over the Gräfin's hand and kissed it, partly because she was the kind of woman who naturally invoked such homage, but chiefly because he knew that the gesture showed off his smooth burnished head to advantage.

The observant eyes of Lady Shalem had noted the animated conversation between the Gräfin and Ronnie, and she had overheard fragments of the invitation that had been accorded to the latter.

'Take us the little foxes, the little foxes that spoil the vines,' she quoted to herself; 'not that that music-boy would do much in the destructive line, but the principle is good.'

CHAPTER X

Some Reflections and a 'Te Deum'

Cicely awoke, on the morning after the 'memorable evening', with the satisfactory feeling of victory achieved, tempered by a troubled sense of having achieved it in the face of a reasonably grounded opposition. She had burned her boats, and was glad of it, but the reek of their burning drifted rather unpleasantly across the jubilant incense-swinging of her *Te Deum* service.

Last night had marked an immense step forward in her social career; without running after the patronage of influential personages she had seen it quietly and tactfully put at her service. People such as the Gräfin von Tolb were going to be a power in the London world for a very long time to come. Herr von Kwarl, with all his useful qualities of brain and temperament, might conceivably fall out of favour in some unexpected turn of the political wheel, and the Shalems would probably have their little day and then a long afternoon of diminishing social importance; the placid dormouse-like Gräfin would outlast them all. She had the qualities which make either for contented mediocrity or else for very durable success, according as circumstances may dictate. She was one of those characters that can neither thrust themselves to the front, nor have any wish to do so, but being there, no ordinary power can thrust them away.

With the Gräfin as her friend Cicely found herself in altogether a different position from that involved by the mere interested patronage of Lady Shalem. A vista of social success was opened up to her, and she did not mean it to be just the ordinary success of a popular and influential hostess moving in an important circle. That people with naturally bad manners should have to be polite and considerate in their dealings with her, that people who usually held themselves aloof should have to be gracious and amiable, that the self-assured should have to be just a little humble and anxious where she was concerned, these things of course she intended to happen; she was a woman. But, she told herself, she intended a great deal more than that when she traced the pattern for her scheme of social influence. In her heart she detested the German occupation as a hateful necessity, but while her heart registered the hatefulness the brain recognized the necessity. The great fighting-machines that the Germans had built up and maintained, on land, on sea, and in air, were three solid crushing facts that demonstrated the hopelessness of any immediate thought of revolt. Twenty years hence, when the present generation was older and greyer, the chances of armed revolt would probably be equally hopeless, equally remote-seeming. But in the meantime something could have been effected in another way. The conquerors might partially Germanize London, but, on the other hand, if the thing were skilfully managed, the British element within the Empire might impress the mark of its influence on everything German. The fighting men might remain Prussian or Bavarian, but the thinking men, and eventually the ruling men, could gradually come under British influence, or even be of British blood. An English Liberal-Conservative 'Centre' might stand as a bulwark against the Junker-dom and Socialism of Continental Germany. So Cicely reasoned with herself, in a fashion induced perhaps by an earlier apprenticeship to the reading of *Nineteenth Century* articles, in which the possible politi-cal and racial developments of various countries were examined and discussed and put away in the pigeon-holes of probable happenings. She had sufficient knowledge of political history to know that such a development might possibly come to pass, she had not sufficient insight into actual conditions to know that the possibility was as remote as that of armed resistance. And the rôle which she saw herself playing was that of a deft and courtly political intriguer, rallying the British element and making herself agreeable to the German ele-ment, a political inspiration to the one and a social distraction to the other. At the back of her mind there lurked an honest confession that she was probably overrating her powers of statecraft and personality, that she was more likely to be carried along by the current of events than to control or divert its direction; the political day-dream re-mained, however, as day-dreams will, in spite of the clear light of probability shining through them. At any rate she knew, as usual, what she wanted to do, and as usual she had taken steps to carry out her intentions. Last night remained in her mind a night of important victory. There also remained the anxious proceeding of finding out if the victory had entailed any serious losses.

Cicely was not one of those ill-regulated people who treat the first meal of the day as a convenient occasion for serving up any differences or contentions that have been left over from the day before or overlooked in the press of other matters. She enjoyed her breakfast and gave Yeovil unhindered opportunity for enjoying his; a discussion as to the right cooking of a dish that he had first tasted among the Orenburg Tartars was the prevailing topic on this particular morning, and blended well with trout and toast and coffee. In the cosy nook of the smoking-room, in participation of the after-breakfast cigarettes, Cicely made her dash into debatable ground.

'You haven't asked me how my supper-party went off,' she said.

'There is a notice of it in two of the morning papers, with a list of those present,' said Yeovil; 'the conquering race seems to have been very well represented.'

'Several races were represented,' said Cicely; 'a function of that sort, celebrating a dramatic first-night, was bound to be cosmopolitan. In fact, blending of races and nationalities is the tendency of the age we live in.'

'The blending of races seems to have been consummated already in one of the individuals at your party,' said Yeovil drily; 'the name Mentieth-Mendlesohnn struck me as a particularly happy obliteration of racial landmarks.'

Cicely laughed.

'A noisy and very wearisome sort of woman,' she commented; 'she reminds one of garlic that's been planted by mistake in a conservatory. Still, she's useful as an advertising agent to anyone who rubs her the right way. She'll be invaluable in proclaiming the merits of Gorla's performance to all and sundry; that's why I invited her. She'll probably lunch to-day at the Hotel Cecil, and every one sitting within a hundred yards of her table will hear what an emotional education they can get by going to see Gorla dance at the Caravansery.'

'She seems to be like the Salvation Army,' said Yeovil; 'her noise reaches a class of people who wouldn't trouble to read Press notices.'

'Exactly,' said Cicely. 'Gorla gets quite good notices on the whole, doesn't she?'

'The one that took my fancy most was the one in the *Standard*,' said Yeovil, picking up that paper from a table by his side and searching its columns for the notice in question. '"The wolves which appeared earlier in the evening's entertainment are, the programme assures us, trained entirely by kindness. It would have been a further kindness, at any rate to the audience, if some of the training, which the wolves doubtless do not appreciate at its proper value, had been expended on Miss Mustelford's efforts at stage dancing. We are assured, again on the authority of the programme, that the much-talked-of Suggestion Dances are the last word in Posture dancing. The last word belongs by immemorial right to the sex which Miss Mustelford adorns, and it would be ungallant to seek to deprive her of her privilege. As far as the educational aspect of her performance is concerned we must admit that the life of the fern remains to us a private life still. Miss Mustelford has abandoned her own private life in an unavailing attempt to draw the fern into the gaze of publicity. And so it was with her other suggestions. They suggested many things, but nothing that was announced on the programme. Chiefly they suggested one outstanding reflection, that stage-dancing is not like those advertised breakfast foods that can be served up after three minutes' preparation. Half a lifetime, or rather half a youthtime is a much more satisfactory allowance." '

'The *Standard* is prejudiced,' said Cicely; 'some of the other papers are quite enthusiastic. The *Dawn* gives her a column and a quarter of notice, nearly all of it complimentary. It says the report of her fame as a dancer went before her, but that her performance last night caught it up and outstripped it.'

'I should not like to suggest that the *Dawn* is prejudiced,' said Yeovil, 'but Shalem is a managing director on it, and one of its biggest shareholders. Gorla's dancing is an event of the social season, and Shalem is one of those most interested in keeping up the appearance, at any rate, of a London social season. Besides, her début gave the opportunity for an Imperial visit to the theatre—the first appearance at a festive public function of the Conqueror among the conquered. Apparently the experiment passed off well; Shalem has every reason to feel pleased with himself and well-disposed towards Gorla. By the way,' added Yeovil, 'talking of Gorla, I'm going down to Torywood one day next week.'

'To Torywood?' exclaimed Cicely. The tone of her exclamation gave the impression that the announcement was not very acceptable to her.

'I promised the old lady that I would go and have a talk with her when I came back from my Siberian trip; she travelled in Eastern

Russia, you know, long before the Trans-Siberian railway was built, and she's enormously interested in those parts. In any case I should like to see her again.'

'She does not see many people nowadays,' said Cicely; 'I fancy she is breaking up rather. She was very fond of the son who went down, you know.'

'She has seen a great many of the things she cared for go down,' said Yeovil; 'it is a sad old life that is left to her, when one thinks of all that the past has been to her, of the part she used to play in the world, the work she used to get through. It used to seem as though she could never grow old, as if she would die standing up, with some unfinished command on her lips. And now I suppose her tragedy is that she has grown old, bitterly old, and cannot die.'

Cicely was silent for a moment, and seemed about to leave the room. Then she turned back and said:

'I don't think I would say anything about Gorla to her if I were you.'

'It would not have occurred to me to drag her name into our conversation,' said Yeovil coldly, 'but in any case the accounts of her dancing performance will have reached Torywood through the newspapers—also the record of your racially blended supper-party.'

Cicely said nothing. She knew that by last night's affair she had definitely identified herself in public opinion with the Shalem clique, and that many of her old friends would look on her with distrust and suspicion on that account. It was unfortunate, but she reckoned it a lesser evil than tearing herself away from her London life, its successes and pleasures and possibilities. These social dislocations and severing of friendships were to be looked for after any great and violent change in State affairs. It was Yeovil's attitude that really troubled her; she would not give way to his prejudices and accept his point of view, but she knew that a victory that involved estrangement from him would only bring a mockery of happiness. She still hoped that he would come round to an acceptance of established facts and deaden his political *malaise* in the absorbing distraction of field sports. The visit to Torywood was a misfortune; it might just turn the balance in the undesired direction. Only a few weeks of late summer and early autumn remained before the hunting season, and its preparations would be at hand, and Yeovil might be caught in the meshes of an old enthusiasm; in those few weeks, however, he might be fired by another sort of enthusiasm, an enthusiasm which would sooner or later mean voluntary or enforced exile for his part, and the probable breaking up of her own social plans and ambitions.

But Cicely knew something of the futility of improvising objections where no real obstacle exists. The visit to Torywood was a graceful attention on Yeovil's part to an old friend; there was no decent ground on which it could be opposed. If the influence of that visit came athwart Yeovil's life and hers with disastrous effect, that was 'Kismet'.

And once again the reek from her burned and smouldering boats mingled threateningly with the incense fumes of her *Te Deum* for victory. She left the room, and Yeovil turned once more to an item of news in the morning's papers that had already arrested his attention. The Imperial *Aufklärung* on the subject of military service was to be made public in the course of the day.

CHAPTER XI

The Tea Shop

Yeovil wandered down Piccadilly that afternoon in a spirit of restlessness and expectancy. The long awaited *Aufklärung* dealing with the new law of military service had not yet appeared; at any moment he might meet the hoarse-throated newsboys running along with their papers, announcing the special edition which would give the terms of the edict to the public. Every sound or movement that detached itself with isolated significance from the general whir and scurry of the streets seemed to Yeovil to herald the oncoming clamour and rush that he was looking for. But the long endless succession of motors and buses and vans went by, hooting and grunting, and such newsboys as were to be seen hung about listlessly, bearing no more attractive bait on their posters than the announcement of an 'earthquake shock in Hungary: feared loss of life'.

The Green Park end of Piccadilly was a changed, and in some respects a livelier thoroughfare to that which Yeovil remembered with affectionate regret. A great political club had migrated from its palatial home to a shrunken habitation in a less prosperous quarter; its place was filled by the flamboyant frontage of the Hotel Konstantinopel. Gorgeous Turkey carpets were spread over the wide entrance steps, and boys in Circassian and Anatolian costumes hung around the doors, or dashed forth in un-Oriental haste to carry such messages as the telephone was unable to transmit. Picturesque sellers of Turkish delight, attar-of-roses, and brass-work coffee services, squatted under the portico, on terms of obvious good understanding with the hotel management. A few doors farther down a service club that had long been a Piccadilly landmark was a landmark still, as the home of the Army Aeronaut Club, and there was a constant coming and going of gay-hued uniforms, Saxon, Prussian, Bavarian, Hessian, and so forth, through its portals. The mastering of the air and the creation of a scientific aerial war fleet, second to none in the world, was an achievement of which the conquering race was pardonably proud, and for which it had good reason to be duly thankful. Over the gateways was blazoned the badge of the club, an elephant, whale, and eagle, typifying the three armed forces of the State, by land and sea and air; the eagle bore in its beak a scroll with the proud legend: 'The last am I, but not the least.'

To the eastward of this gaily humming hive the long shuttered front of a deserted ducal mansion struck a note of protest and mourning amid the noise and whirl and colour of a seemingly uncaring city. On the other side of the roadway, on the gravelled paths of the Green Park, small ragged children from the back streets of Westminster looked wistfully at the smooth trim stretches of grass on which it was now forbidden, in two languages, to set foot. Only the pigeons, disregarding the changes of political geography, walked about as usual, wondering perhaps, if they ever wondered at anything, at the sudden change in the distribution of park humans.

Yeovil turned his steps out of the hot sunlight into the shade of the Burlington Arcade, familiarly known to many of its newer frequenters as the Passage. Here the change that new conditions and requirements had wrought was more immediately noticeable than anywhere else in the West End. Most of the shops on the western side had been cleared away, and in their place had been installed an 'open-air' café, converting the long alley into a sort of promenade tea-garden, flanked on one side by a line of haberdashers', perfumers', and jewellers' show windows. The patrons of the café could sit at the little round tables, drinking their coffee and syrups and *apéritifs*, and gazing, if they were so minded, at the pyjamas and cravats and Brazilian diamonds spread out for inspection before them. A string orchestra, hidden away somewhere in the gallery, was alternating grand opera with the *Gondola Girl* and the latest gems of Transatlantic melody. From around the tightly packed tables arose a babble of tongues, made up chiefly of German, a South American rendering of Spanish, and a North American rendering of English, with here and there the sharp shaken-out staccato of Japanese. A sleepy-looking boy, in a nondescript uniform, was wandering to and fro among the customers, offering for sale the *Matin*, *New York Herald*, *Berliner Tageblatt*, and a host of crudely coloured illustrated papers, embodying the hard-worked wit of a world-legion of comic artists. Yeovil hurried through the Arcade; it was not here, in this atmosphere of staring alien eyes and jangling tongues, that he wanted to read the news of the Imperial *Aufklärung*.

By a succession of by-ways he reached Hanover Square, and thence made his way into Oxford Street. There was no commotion of activity to be noticed yet among the newsboys; the posters still concerned themselves with the earthquake in Hungary, varied with references to the health of the King of Roumania, and a motor accident in South London. Yeovil wandered aimlessly along the street for a few dozen yards, and then turned down into the smoking-room of a cheap tea-shop, where he judged that the flourishing foreign element would be less conspicuously represented. Quiet-voiced, smooth-headed youths, from neighbouring shops and wholesale houses, sat drinking tea and munching pastry, some of them reading, others making a fitful rattle with dominoes on the marble-topped tables. A clean, wholesome smell of tea and coffee made itself felt through the clouds of cigarette smoke; cleanliness and listlessness seemed to be the dominant notes of the place, a cleanliness that was commendable, and a listlessness that seemed unnatural and undesirable where so much youth was gathered together for refreshment and recreation. Yeovil seated himself at a table already occupied by a young clergy-man who was smoking a cigarette over the remains of a plateful of buttered toast. He had a keen, clever, hard-lined face, the face of a man who, in an earlier stage of European history, might have been a warlike prior, awkward to tackle at the council-board, greatly to be avoided where blows were being exchanged. A pale, silent damsel drifted up to Yeovil and took his order with an air of being mentally some hundreds of miles away, and utterly indifferent to the require-ments of those whom she served; if she had brought calf's-foot jelly instead of the pot of China tea he had asked for, Yeovil would hardly have been surprised. However, the tea duly arrived on the table, and the pale damsel scribbled a figure on a slip of paper, put it silently by the side of the teapot, and drifted silently away. Yeovil had seen the same sort of thing done on the musical-comedy stage, and done rather differently.

'Can you tell me, sir, is the Imperial announcement out yet?' asked the young clergyman, after a brief scrutiny of his neighbour.

'No, I have been waiting about for the last half-hour on the look-out for it,' said Yeovil; 'the special editions ought to be out by now.' Then he added: 'I have only just lately come from abroad. I know scarcely anything of London as it is now. You may imagine that a good deal of it is very strange to me. Your profession must take you a good deal among all classes of people. I have seen something of what one may call the upper, or, at any rate, the richer classes, since I came back; do tell me something about the poorer classes of the community. How do they take the new order of things?'

'Badly,' said the young cleric, 'badly, in more senses than one. They are helpless and they are bitter—bitter in the useless kind of way that produces no great resolutions. They look round for some one to blame for what has happened; they blame the politicians, they blame the leisured classes; in an indirect way I believe they blame the Church. Certainly, the national disaster has not drawn them towards religion in any form. One thing you may be sure of, they do not blame themselves. No true Londoner ever admits that fault lies at his door. "No, I never!" is an exclamation that is on his lips from earliest childhood, whenever he is charged with anything blameworthy or punishable. That is why school discipline was ever a thing repugnant to the schoolboard child and its parents; no schoolboard scholar ever deserved punishment. However obvious the fault might seem to a disciplinarian, "No, I never" exonerated it as something that had not happened. Public schoolboys and private schoolboys of the upper and middle class had their fling and took their thrashings, when they were found out, as a piece of bad luck, but "our Bert" and "our Sid" were of those for whom there is no condemnation; if *they* were punished it was for faults that "no, they never" committed. Naturally the grown-up generation of Berts and Sids, the voters and householders, do not realize, still less admit, that it was they who called the tune to which the politicians danced. They had to choose between the vote-mongers and the so-called "scare-mongers", and their verdict was for the vote-mongers all the time. And now they are bitter; they are being punished, and punishment is not a thing that they have been schooled to bear. The taxes that are falling on them are a grievous source of discontent, and the military service that will be imposed on them, for the first time in their lives, will be another. There is a more lovable side to their character under misfortune, though,' added the young clergyman. 'Deep down in their hearts there was a very real affection for the old dynasty. Future historians will perhaps be able to explain how and why the Royal Family of Great Britain captured the imaginations of its subjects in so genuine and lasting a fashion. Among the poorest and the most matter-of-fact, for whom the name of no public man, politician or philanthropist, stands out with any especial significance, the old Queen, and the dead King, the dethroned monarch and the young prince live in a sort of domestic Pantheon, a recollection that is a proud and wistful personal possession when so little remains to be proud of or to possess. There is no favour that I am so often asked for among my poorer parishioners as the gift of the picture of this or that member of the old dynasty. "I have got all of them, only except Princess Mary," an old woman said to me last week, and she nearly cried with pleasure when I brought her an old *Bystander* portrait that filled the gap in her collection. And on Queen Alexandra's day they bring out and wear the faded wildrose favours that they bought with their pennies in days gone by.'

'The tragedy of the enactment that is about to enforce military service on these people is that it comes when they've no longer a country to fight for,' said Yeovil.

The young clergyman gave an exclamation of bitter impatience.

'That is the cruel mockery of the whole thing. Every now and then in the course of my work I have come across lads who were really drifting to the bad through the good qualities in them. A clean combative strain in their blood, and a natural turn for adventure, made the ordinary anæmic routine of shop or warehouse or factory almost unbearable for them. What splendid little soldiers they would have made, and how grandly the discipline of a military training would have steadied them in after-life when steadiness was wanted. The only adventure that their surroundings offered them has been the adventure of practising mildly criminal misdeeds without getting landed in reformatories and prisons; those of them that have not been successful in keeping clear of detection are walking round and round prison yards, experiencing the operation of a discipline that breaks and does not build. They were merry-hearted boys once, with nothing of the criminal or ne'er-do-well in their natures, and now—have you ever seen a prison yard, with that walk round and round and round between grey walls under a blue sky?'

Yeovil nodded.

'It's good enough for criminals and imbeciles,' said the parson, 'but think of it for those boys, who might have been marching along to the tap of the drum, with a laugh on their lips instead of Hell in their hearts. I have had Hell in my heart sometimes, when I have come in touch with cases like those. I suppose you are thinking that I am a strange sort of parson.'

'I was just defining you in my mind,' said Yeovil, 'as a man of God, with an infinite tenderness for little devils.'

The clergyman flushed.

'Rather a fine epitaph to have on one's tombstone,' he said, 'especially if the tombstone were in some crowded city graveyard. I suppose I am a man of God, but I don't think I could be called a man of peace.'

Looking at the strong young face, with its suggestion of a fighting prior of bygone days more marked than ever, Yeovil mentally agreed that he could not.

'I have learned one thing in life,' continued the young man, 'and that is that peace is not for this world. Peace is what God gives us when He takes us into His rest. Beat your sword into a ploughshare if you like, but beat your enemy into smithereens first.'

A long-drawn cry, repeated again and again, detached itself from the throb and hoot and whir of the street traffic.

'Speshul! Military service, spesh-ul!'

The young clergyman sprang from his seat and went up the staircase in a succession of bounds, causing the domino players and novelette readers to look up for a moment in mild astonishment. In a few seconds he was back again, with a copy of an afternoon paper. The Imperial Rescript was set forth in heavy type, in parallel columns of English and German. As the young man read a deep burning flush spread over his face, then ebbed away into a chalky whiteness. He read the announcement to the end, then handed the paper to Yeovil, and left without a word.

Beneath the courtly politeness and benignant phraseology of the document ran a trenchant searing irony. The British-born subjects of the Germanic Crown, inhabiting the islands of Great Britain and Ireland, had habituated themselves as a people to the disuse of arms, and resolutely excluded military service and national training from their political system and daily life. Their judgment that they were unsuited as a race to bear arms and conform to military discipline was not to be set aside. Their new Overlord did not propose to do violence to their feelings and customs by requiring from them the personal military sacrifices and services which were rendered by his subjects German-born. The British subjects of the Crown were to remain a people consecrated to peaceful pursuits, to commerce and trade and husbandry. The defence of their coasts and shipping and the maintenance of order and general safety would be guaranteed by a garrison of German troops, with the co-operation of the Imperial war fleet. German-born subjects residing temporarily or permanently in the British Isles would come under the same laws respecting compulsory military service as their fellow-subjects of German blood in the other parts of the Empire, and special enactments would be drawn up to ensure that their interests did not suffer from a periodical withdrawal on training or other military calls. Necessarily a heavily differentiated scale of war taxation would fall on British taxpayers, to provide for the upkeep of the garrison and to equalize the services and sacrifices rendered by the two branches of his Majesty's subjects. As military service was not henceforth open to any subject of British birth no further necessity for any training or exercise of a military nature existed, therefore all rifle clubs, drill associations, cadet corps and similar bodies were henceforth declared to be illegal. No weapons other than guns for specified sporting purposes, duly declared and registered and open to inspection when required, could be owned, purchased, or carried. The science of arms was to be eliminated altogether from the life of a people who had shown such marked repugnance to its study and practice.

The cold irony of the measure struck home with the greater force because its nature was so utterly unexpected. Public anticipation had guessed at various forms of military service, aggressively irksome or tactfully lightened as the case might be, in any event certain to be bitterly unpopular, and now there had come this contemptuous boon, which had removed, at one stroke, the bogey of compulsory military service from the troubled imaginings of the British people, and fastened on them the cruel distinction of being in actual fact what an enemy had called them in splenetic scorn long years ago—a nation of shopkeepers. Aye, something even below that level, a race of shopkeepers who were no longer a nation.

Yeovil crumpled the paper in his hand and went out into the sunlit street. A sudden roll of drums and crash of brass music filled the air. A company of Bavarian infantry went by, in all the pomp and circumstance of martial array and the joyous swing of rapid rhythmic movement. The street echoed and throbbed in the Englishman's ears with the exultant pulse of youth and mastery set to loud Pagan music. A group of lads from the tea-shop clustered on the pavement and watched the troops go by, staring at a phase of life in which they had no share. The martial trappings, the swaggering joy of life, the comradeship of camp and barracks, the hard discipline of drill yard and fatigue duty, the long sentry watches, the trench digging, forced marches, wounds, cold, hunger, makeshift hospitals, and the blood-wet laurels—these were not for them. Such things they might only guess at, or see on a cinema film, darkly; they belonged to the civilian nation.

The function of afternoon tea was still being languidly observed in the big drawing-room when Yeovil returned to Berkshire Street. Cicely was playing the part of hostess to a man of perhaps forty-one years of age, who looked slightly older from his palpable attempts to look very much younger. Percival Plarsey was a plump, pale-faced, short-legged individual, with puffy cheeks, over-prominent nose, and thin colourless hair. His mother, with nothing more than maternal prejudice to excuse her, had discovered some twenty odd years ago that he was a well-favoured young man, and had easily imbued her son with the same opinion. The slipping away of years and the natural transition of the unathletic boy into the podgy unhealthy-looking man did little to weaken the tradition; Plarsey had never been able to relinquish the idea that a youthful charm and comeliness still centred in his person, and laboured daily at his toilet with the devotion that a hopelessly lost cause is so often able to inspire. He babbled incessantly about himself and the accessory futilities of his life in short, neat, complacent sentences, and in a voice that Ronald Storre said reminded one of a fat bishop blessing a butter-making competition. While he babbled he kept his eyes fastened on his listeners to observe the impression which his important little announcements and pronouncements were making. On the present occasion he was peattering forth a detailed description of the upholstery and fittings of his new music-room.

'All the hangings, *violette de Parme*, all the furniture, rosewood. The only ornament in the room is a *replica* of the Mozart statue in Vienna. Nothing but Mozart is to be played in the room. Absolutely, nothing but Mozart.'

'You will get rather tired of that, won't you?' said Cicely, feeling that she was expected to comment on this tremendous announcement.

'One gets tired of everything,' said Plarsey, with a fat little sigh of resignation. 'I can't tell you *how* tired I am of Rubenstein, and one day

I suppose I shall be tired of Mozart, and *violette de Parme* and rosewood. I never thought it possible that I could ever tire of jonquils, and now I simply won't have one in the house. Oh, the scene the other day because some one brought some jonquils into the house! I'm afraid I was dreadfully rude, but I really couldn't help it.'

He could talk like this through a long summer day or a long winter evening.

Yeovil belonged to a race forbidden to bear arms. At the moment he would gladly have contented himself with the weapons with which nature had endowed him, if he might have kicked and pommelled the abhorrent specimen of male humanity whom he saw before him.

Instead he broke into the conversation with an inspired flash of malicious untruthfulness.

'It is wonderful,' he observed carelessly, 'how popular that Viennese statue of Mozart has become. A friend who inspects County Council Art Schools tells me you find a copy of it in every class-room you go into.'

It was a poor substitute for physical violence, but it was all that civilization allowed him in the way of relieving his feelings; it had, moreover, the effect of making Plarsey profoundly miserable.

CHAPTER XII

The Travelling Companions

The train bearing Yeovil on his visit to Torywood slid and rattled westward through the hazy dreamland of an English summer landscape. Seen from the train windows the stark bare ugliness of the metalled line was forgotten, and the eye rested only on the green solitude that unfolded itself as the miles went slipping by. Tall grasses and meadow-weeds stood in deep shocks, field after field, between the leafy boundaries of hedge or coppice, thrusting themselves higher and higher till they touched the low sweeping branches of the trees that here and there overshadowed them. Broad streams, bordered with a heavy fringe of reed and sedge, went winding away into a green distance where woodland and meadowland seemed indefinitely prolonged; narrow streamlets, lost to view in the growth that they fostered, disclosed their presence merely by the water-weed that showed in a riband of rank verdure threading the mellower green of the fields. On the stream banks moorhens walked with jerky confident steps, in the easy boldness of those who had a couple of other elements at their disposal in an emergency; more timorous partridges raced away from the apparition of the train, looking all leg and neck, like little forest elves fleeing from human encounter. And in the distance, over the tree line, a heron or two flapped with slow measured wing-beats and an air of being bent on an immeasurably longer journey than the train that hurtled so frantically along the rails. Now and then the meadowland changed itself suddenly into orchard, with close-growing trees already showing the measure of their coming harvest, and then strawyard and farm buildings would slide into view; heavy dairy cattle, roan and skewbald and dappled, stood near the gates, drowsily resentful of insect stings, and bunched-up companies of ducks halted in seeming irresolution between the charms of the horse-pond and the alluring neighbourhood of the farm kitchen. Away by the banks of some rushing mill-stream, in a setting of copse and cornfield, a village might be guessed at, just a hint of red roof, grey wreathed chimney and old church tower as seen from the windows of the passing train, and over it all brooded a happy, settled calm, like the dreaming murmur of a trout-stream and the far-away cawing of rooks.

It was a land where it seemed as if it must be always summer and generally afternoon, a land where bees hummed among the wild thyme and in the flower-beds of cottage gardens, where the harvest-mice rustled amid the corn and nettles, and the mill-race flowed cool and silent through water-weeds and dark tunnelled sluices, and made soft droning music with the wooden mill-wheel. And the music carried with it the wording of old undying rhymes, and sang of the jolly, uncaring, uncared-for miller, of the farmer who went riding upon his grey mare, of the mouse who lived beneath the merry mill-pin, of the sweet music on yonder green hill and the dancers all in yellow—the songs and fancies of a lingering olden time, when men took life as children take a long summer day, and went to bed at last with a simple trust in something they could not have explained.

Yeovil watched the passing landscape with the intent hungry eyes of a man who revisits a scene that holds high place in his affections. His imagination raced even quicker than the train, following winding roads and twisting valleys into unseen distances, picturing farms and hamlets, hills and hollows, clattering inn yards and sleepy woodlands.

'A beautiful country,' said his only fellow-traveller, who was also gazing at the fleeting landscape; 'surely a country worth fighting for.'

He spoke in fairly correct English, but he was unmistakably a foreigner; one could have allotted him with some certainty to the Eastern half of Europe.

'A beautiful country, as you say,' replied Yeovil; then he added the question, 'Are you German?'

'No, Hungarian,' said the other; 'and you, you are English?' he asked.

'I have been much in England, but I am from Russia,' said Yeovil, purposely misleading his companion on the subject of his nationality in order to induce him to talk with greater freedom on a delicate topic. While living among foreigners in a foreign land he had shrunk from hearing his country's disaster discussed, or even alluded to; now he was anxious to learn what unprejudiced foreigners thought of the catastrophe and the causes which had led up to it.

'It is a strange spectacle, a wonder, is it not so?' resumed the other, 'a great nation such as this was, one of the greatest nations in modern times, or of any time, carrying its flag and its language into all parts of the world, and now, after one short campaign, it is——'

And he shrugged his shoulders many times and made clucking noises at the roof of his voice, like a hen calling to a brood of roving chickens.

'They grew soft,' he resumed; 'great world-commerce brings great luxury, and luxury brings softness. They had everything to warn them, things happening in their own time and before their eyes, and they would not be warned. They had seen, in one generation, the rise of the military and naval power of the Japanese, a brown-skinned race living in some island rice-fields in a tropical sea, a people one thought of in connection with paper fans and flowers and pretty tea-gardens, who suddenly marched and sailed into the world's gaze as a Great Power; they had seen, too, the rise of the Bulgars, a poor herd of *zaptieh*-ridden peasants, with a few students scattered in exile in Bukarest and Odessa, who shot up in one generation to be an armed and aggressive nation with history in its hands. The English saw these things happening around them, and with a war-cloud growing blacker and bigger and always more threatening on their own threshold they sat down to grow soft and peaceful. They grew soft and accommodating in all things; in religion——'

'In religion?' said Yeovil.

'In religion, yes,' said his companion emphatically; 'they had come to look on the Christ as a sort of amiable elder Brother, whose letters from abroad were worth reading. Then, when they had emptied all the divine mystery and wonder out of their faith naturally they grew tired of it, oh, but dreadfully tired of it. I know many English of the country parts, and always they tell me they go to church once in each week to set the good example to the servants. They were tired of their faith, but they were not virile enough to become real Pagans; their dancing fauns were good young men who tripped Morris dances and ate health foods and believed in a sort of Socialism which made for the greatest dullness of the greatest number. You will find plenty of them still if you go into what remains of social London.'

Yeovil gave a grunt of acquiescence.

'They grew soft in their political ideas,' continued the unsparing critic; 'for the old insular belief that all foreigners were devils and rogues they substituted another belief, equally grounded on insular lack of knowledge, that most foreigners were amiable, good fellows, who only needed to be talked to and patted on the back to become your friends and benefactors. They began to believe that a foreign Minister would relinquish long-cherished schemes of national policy and hostile expansion if he came over on a holiday and was asked down to country houses and shown the tennis court and the rock-garden and the younger children. Listen. I once heard it solemnly stated at an after-dinner debate in some literary club that a certain very prominent German statesman had a daughter at school in England, and that future friendly relations between the two countries were improved in prospect, if not assured, by that circumstance. You think I am laughing; I am recording a fact, and the men present were politicians and statesmen as well as literary dilettanti. It was an insular lack of insight that worked the mischief, or some of the mischief. We, in Hungary, we live too much cheek by jowl with our racial neighbours to have many illusions about them. Austrians, Roumanians, Serbs, Italians, Czechs, we know what they think of us, and we know what to think of them, we know what we want in the world, and we know what they want; that knowledge does not send us flying at each other's throats, but it does keep us from growing soft. Ah, the British lion was in a hurry to inaugurate the Millennium and to lie down gracefully with the lamb. He made two mistakes, only two, but they were very bad ones; the Millennium hadn't arrived, and it was not a lamb that he was lying down with.'

'You do not like the English, I gather,' said Yeovil, as the Hungarian went off into a short burst of satirical laughter.

'I have always liked them,' he answered, 'but now I am angry with them for being soft. Here is my station,' he added, as the train slowed down, and he commenced to gather his belongings together. 'I am angry with them,' he continued, as a final word on the subject, 'because I *hate* the Germans.'

He raised his hat punctiliously in a parting salute and stepped out on to the platform. His place was taken by a large, loose-limbed man, with florid face and big staring eyes, and an immense array of fishing-basket, rod, fly-cases, and so forth. He was of the type that one could instinctively locate as a loud-voiced, self-constituted authority on whatever topic might happen to be discussed in the bars of small hotels.

'Are you English?' he asked, after a preliminary stare at Yeovil.

This time Yeovil did not trouble to disguise his nationality; he nodded curtly to his questioner.

'Glad of that,' said the fisherman; 'I don't like travelling with Germans.'

'Unfortunately,' said Yeovil, 'we have to travel with them, as partners in the same State concern, and not by any means the predominant partner either.'

'Oh, that will soon right itself,' said the other with loud assertiveness, 'that will right itself damn soon.'

'Nothing in politics rights itself,' said Yeovil; 'things have to be righted, which is a different matter.'

'What d'y'mean?' said the fisherman, who did not like to have his assertions taken up and shaken into shape.

'We have given a clever and domineering people a chance to plant themselves down as masters in our land; I don't imagine that they are going to give us an easy chance to push them out. To do that we shall have to be a little cleverer than they are, a little harder, a little fiercer, and a good deal more self-sacrificing than we have been in my lifetime or in yours.'

'We'll be that, right enough,' said the fisherman; 'we mean business this time. The last war wasn't a war, it was a snap. We weren't prepared and they were. That won't happen again, bless you. I know what I'm talking about. I go up and down the country, and I hear what people are saying.'

Yeovil privately doubted if he ever heard anything but his own opinions.

'It stands to reason,' continued the fisherman, 'that a highly civilized race like ours, with the record that we've had for leading the whole world, is not going to be held under for long by a lot of damned sausage-eating Germans. Don't you believe it! I know what I'm talking about. I've travelled about the world a bit.'

Yeovil shrewdly suspected that the world travels amounted to nothing more than a trip to the United States and perhaps the Channel Islands, with, possibly, a week or fortnight in Paris.

'It isn't the past we've got to think of, it's the future,' said Yeovil. 'Other maritime Powers had pasts to look back on; Spain and Holland, for instance. The past didn't help them when they let their sea-sovereignty slip from them. That is a matter of history and not very distant history either.'

'Ah, that's where you make a mistake,' said the other; 'our sea-sovereignty hasn't slipped from us, and won't do, neither. There's the British Empire beyond the seas; Canada, Australia, New Zealand, East Africa.'

He rolled the names round his tongue with obvious relish.

'If it was a list of first-class battleships, and armoured cruisers and destroyers and airships that you were reeling off, there would be some comfort and hope in the situation,' said Yeovil; 'the loyalty of the colonies is a splendid thing, but it is only pathetically splendid because it can do so little to recover for us what we've lost. Against the Zeppelin air fleet, and the Dreadnought sea squadrons and the new Gelberhaus cruisers, the last word in maritime mobility, of what avail is loyal devotion plus half-a-dozen warships, one keel to ten, scattered over one or two ocean coasts?'

'Ah, but they'll build,' said the fisherman confidently; 'they'll build. They're only waiting to enlarge their dockyard accommodation and get the right class of artificers and engineers and workmen together. The money will be forthcoming somehow, and they'll start in and build.'

'And do you suppose,' asked Yeovil in slow bitter contempt, 'that the victorious nation is going to sit and watch and wait till the defeated foe has created a new war fleet, big enough to drive it from the seas? Do you suppose it is going to watch keel added to keel, gun to gun, airship to airship, till its preponderance has been wiped out or even threatened? That sort of thing is done once in a generation, not twice. Who is going to protect Australia or New Zealand while they enlarge their dockyards and hangars and build their dreadnoughts and their airships?'

'Here's my station and I'm not sorry,' said the fisherman, gathering his tackle together and rising to depart; 'I've listened to you long enough. You and me wouldn't agree, not if we was to talk all day. Fact is, I'm an out-and-out patriot and you're only a half-hearted one. That's what you are, half-hearted.'

And with that parting shot he left the carriage and lounged heavily down the platform, a patriot who had never handled a rifle or mounted a horse or pulled an oar, but who had never flinched from demolishing his country's enemies with his tongue.

'England has never had any lack of patriots of that type,' thought Yeovil sadly; 'so many patriots and so little patriotism.'

CHAPTER XIII

Torywood

Yeovil got out of the train at a small, clean wayside station, and rapidly formed the conclusion that neatness, abundant leisure, and a devotion to the cultivation of wall flowers and wyandottes were the prevailing influences of the station-master's life. The train slid away into the hazy distance of trees and meadows, and left the traveller standing in a world that seemed to be made up in equal parts of rock-garden, chicken coops, and whisky advertisements. The station-master, who appeared also to act as emergency porter, took Yeovil's ticket with the gesture of a kind-hearted person brushing away a troublesome wasp, and returned to a study of the *Poultry Chronicle*, which was giving its readers sage counsel concerning the ailments of belated July chickens. Yeovil called to mind the station-master of a tiny railway town in Siberia, who had held him in long and rather intelligent converse on the poetical merits and demerits of Shelley, and he wondered what the result would be if he were to engage the English official in a discussion on Lermontoff—or for the matter of that, on Shelley. The temptation to experiment was, however, removed by the arrival of a young groom, with brown eyes and a friendly smile, who hurried into the station and took Yeovil once more into a world where he was of fleeting importance.

In the roadway outside was a four-wheeled dog-cart with a pair of the famous Torywood blue roans. It was an agreeable variation in modern locomotion to be met at a station with high-class horseflesh instead of the ubiquitous motor, and the landscape was not of such a nature that one wished to be whirled through it in a cloud of dust. After a quick spin of some ten or fifteen minutes through twisting hedge-girt country roads, the roans turned in at a wide gateway, and went with dancing, rhythmic step along the park drive. The screen of oak-crowned upland suddenly fell away and a grey sharp-cornered building came into view in a setting of low growing beeches and dark pines. Torywood was not a stately, reposeful-looking house; it lay amid the sleepy landscape like a couched watch-dog with pricked ears and wakeful eyes. Built somewhere about the last years of Dutch William's reign, it had been a centre, ever since, for the political life of the countryside; a storm centre of discontent or a rallying ground for the well affected, as the circumstances of the day might entail. On the stone-flagged terrace in front of the house, with its quaint leaden figures of Diana pursuing a hound-pressed stag, successive squires and lords of Torywood had walked to and fro with their friends, watching the thunder-clouds on the political horizon or the shifting shadows on the sundial of political favour, tapping the political barometer for indications of change, working out a party campaign or arranging for the support of some national movement. To and fro they had gone in their respective generations, men with the passion for statecraft and political combat strong in their veins, and many oft-recurring names had echoed under those wakeful-looking casements, names spoken in anger or exultation, or murmured in fear and anxiety: Bolingbroke, Charles Edward, Walpole, the Farmer King, Bonaparte, Pitt, Wellington, Peel, Gladstone—echo and Time might have graven those names on the stone flags and grey walls. And now one tired old woman walked there, with names on her lips that she never uttered.

A friendly riot of fox terriers and spaniels greeted the carriage, leaping and rolling and yelping in an exuberance of sociability, as though horses and coachman and groom were comrades who had been absent for long months instead of half an hour. An indiscriminately affectionate puppy lay flat and whimpering at Yeovil's feet, sending up little showers of gravel with its wildly thumping tail, while two of the terriers raced each other madly across lawn and shrubbery, as though to show the blue roans what speed really was. The laughing-eyed young groom disentangled the puppy from between Yeovil's legs, and then he was ushered into the grey silence of the entrance hall, leaving sunlight and noise and the stir of life behind him.

'Her ladyship will see you in her writing-room,' he was told, and he followed a servant along the dark passages to the well-remembered room.

There was something tragic in the sudden contrast between the vigour and youth and pride of life that Yeovil had seen crystallized in those dancing, high-stepping horses, scampering dogs, and alert, clean-limbed young men-servants, and the age-frail woman who came forward to meet him.

Eleanor, Dowager Lady Greymarten, had for more than half a century been the ruling spirit at Torywood. The affairs of the county had not sufficed for her untiring activities of mind and body; in the wider field of national and Imperial service she had worked and schemed and fought with an energy and a far-sightedness that came probably from the blend of caution and bold restlessness in her Scottish blood. For many educated minds the arena of politics and public life is a weariness of dust and disgust, to others it is a fascinating study, to be watched from the comfortable seat of a spectator. To her it was a home. In her town house or down at Torywood, with her writing-pad on her knee and the telephone at her elbow, or in personal counsel with some trusted colleague or persuasive argument with a halting adherent or half-convinced opponent, she had laboured on behalf of the poor and the ill-equipped, had fought for her idea of the Right, and above all, for the safety and sanity of her Fatherland. Spadework when necessary and leadership when called for, came alike within the scope of her activities, and not least of her achievements, though perhaps she hardly realized it, was the force of her example, a lone, indomitable fighter calling to the half-caring and the half-discouraged, to the laggard and the slow-moving.

And now she came across the room with 'the tired step of a tired king', and that look which the French so expressively called *l'air défait*. The charm which Heaven bestows on old ladies, reserving its highest gift to the end, had always seemed in her case to be lost sight of in the dignity and interest of a great dame who was still in the full prime of her fighting and ruling powers. Now, in Yeovil's eyes, she had suddenly come to be very old, stricken with the forlorn languor of one who knows that death will be weary to wait for. She had spared herself nothing in the long labour, the ceaseless building, the watch and ward, and in one short autumn week she had seen the overthrow of all that she had built, the falling asunder of the world in which she had laboured. Her life's end was like a harvest home when blight and storm have laid waste the fruit of long toil and unsparing outlay. Victory had been her goal, the death or victory of old heroic challenge, for she had always dreamed to die fighting to the last; death or victory—and the gods had given her neither, only the bitterness of a defeat that could not be measured in words, and the weariness of a life that had outlived happiness or hope. Such was Eleanor, Dowager Lady Greymarten, a shadow amid the young red-blooded life at Torywood, but a shadow that was too real to die, a shadow that was stronger than the substance that surrounded it.

Yeovil talked long and hurriedly of his late travels, of the vast Siberian forests and rivers, the desolate tundras, the lakes and marshes where the wild swans rear their broods, the flower carpet of the summer fields and the winter ice-mantle of Russia's northern sea. He talked as a man talks who avoids the subject that is uppermost in his mind, and in the mind of his hearer, as one who looks away from a wound or deformity that is too cruel to be taken notice of.

Tea was served in a long oak-panelled gallery, where generations of Mustelfords had romped and played as children, and remained yet in effigy, in a collection of more or less faithful portraits. After tea Yeovil was taken by his hostess to the aviaries, which constituted the sole claim which Torywood possessed to being considered a show place. The third Earl of Greymarten had collected rare and interesting birds, somewhere about the time when Gilbert White was penning the last of his deathless letters, and his successors in the title had perpetuated the hobby. Little lawns and ponds and shrubberies were partitioned off for the various ground-loving species, and higher cages with interlacing perches and rockwork shelves accommodated the birds whose natural expression of movement was on the wing. Quails and francolins scurried about under low-growing shrubs, peacock-pheasants strutted and sunned themselves, pugnacious ruffs engaged in perfunctory battles, from force of habit now that the rivalry of the mating season was over; choughs, ravens, and loud-throated gulls occupied sections of a vast rockery, and bright-hued Chinese pond-herons and delicately stepping egrets waded among the water-lilies of a marble-terraced tank. One or two dusky shapes seen dimly in the recesses of a large cage built round a hollow tree would be lively owls when evening came on.

In the course of his many wanderings Yeovil had himself contributed three or four inhabitants to this little feathered town, and he went round the enclosures, renewing old acquaintances and examining new additions.

'The falcon cage is empty,' said Lady Greymarten, pointing to a large wired dome that towered high above the other enclosures; 'I let the lanner fly free one day. The other birds may be reconciled to their comfortable quarters and abundant food and absence of dangers, but I don't think all those things could make up to a falcon for the wild range of cliff and desert. When one has lost one's own liberty one feels a quicker sympathy for other caged things, I suppose.'

There was silence for a moment, and then the Dowager went on, in a wistful, passionate voice:

'I am an old woman now, Murrey, I must die in my cage. I haven't the strength to fight. Age is a very real and very cruel thing, though we may shut our eyes to it and pretend it is not there. I thought at one time that I should never really know what it meant, what it brought to one. I thought of it as a messenger that one could keep waiting out in the yard till the very last moment. I know now what it means. . . . But you, Murrey, you are young, you can fight. Are you going to be a fighter, or the very humble servant of the *fait accompli?*'

'I shall never be the servant of the *fait accompli*,' said Yeovil. 'I loathe it. As to fighting, one must first find out what weapon to use, and how to use it effectively. One must watch and wait.'

'One must not wait too long,' said the old woman. 'Time is on their side, not ours. It is the young people we must fight for now, if they are ever to fight for us. A new generation will spring up, a weaker memory of old glories will survive, the *éclat* of the ruling race will capture young imaginations. If I had your youth, Murrey, and your sex, I would become a commercial traveller.'

'A commercial traveller!' exclaimed Yeovil.

'Yes, one whose business took him up and down the country, into contact with all classes, into homes and shops and inns and railway carriages. And as I travelled I would work, work on the minds of every boy and girl I came across, every young father and young mother too, every young couple that were going to be man and wife. I would awaken or keep alive in their memory the things that we have been, the grand, brave things that some of our race have done, and I would stir up a longing, a determination for the future that we must win back. I would be a counter-agent to the agents of the *fait accompli*. In course of time the Government would find out what I was doing, and I should be sent out of the country, but I should have accomplished something, and others would carry on the work. That is what I would do. Murrey, even if it is to be a losing battle, fight it, fight it!'

Yeovil knew that the old lady was fighting her last battle, rallying the discouraged, and spurring on the backward.

A footman came to announce that the carriage waited to take him back to the station. His hostess walked with him through the hall, and came out on to the stone-flagged terrace, the terrace from which a former Lady Greymarten had watched the twinkling bonfires that told of Waterloo.

Yeovil said good-bye to her as she stood there, a wan, shrunken shadow, yet with a greater strength and reality in her flickering life than those parrot men and women that fluttered and chattered through London drawing-rooms and theatre foyers.

As the carriage swung round a bend in the drive Yeovil looked back at Torywood, a lone, grey building, couched like a watch-dog with pricked ears and wakeful eyes in the midst of the sleeping landscape. An old pleading voice was still ringing in his ears:

> *Imperious and yet forlorn,*
> *Came through the silence of the trees,*
> *The echoes of a golden horn,*
> *Calling to distances.*

Somehow Yeovil knew that he would never hear that voice again, and he knew, too, that he would hear it always, with its message, 'Be a fighter.' And he knew now, with a shamefaced consciousness that sprang suddenly into existence, that the summons would sound for him in vain.

The weary brain-torturing months of fever had left their trail behind, a lassitude of spirit and a sluggishness of blood, a quenching of the desire to roam and court adventure and hardship. In the hours of waking and depression between the raging intervals of delirium he had speculated, with a sort of detached, listless indifference, on the chances of his getting back to life and strength and energy. The prospect of filling a corner of some lonely Siberian graveyard or Finnish cemetery had seemed near realization at times, and for a man who was already half dead the other half didn't particularly matter. But when he had allowed himself to dwell on the more hopeful side of the case it had always been a complete recovery that awaited him; the same Yeovil as of yore, a little thinner and more lined about the eyes perhaps, would go through life in the same way, alert, resolute, enterprising, ready to start off at short notice for some desert or upland where the eagles were circling and the wild-fowl were calling. He had not reckoned that Death, evaded and held off by the doctors' skill, might exact a compromise, and that only part of the man would go free to the West.

And now he began to realize how little of mental and physical energy he could count on. His own country had never seemed in his eyes so comfort-yielding and to-be-desired as it did now when it had passed into alien keeping and become a prison-land as much as a homeland. London with its thin mockery of a Season, and its chattering horde of empty-hearted self-seekers, held no attraction for him, but the spell of English country life was weaving itself round him, now that the charm of the desert was receding into a mist of memories. The waning of pleasant autumn days in an English woodland, the whir of game birds in the clean harvested fields, the grey moist mornings in the saddle, with the magical cry of hounds coming up from some misty hollow, and then the delicious abandon of physical weariness in bathroom and bedroom after a long run, and the heavenly snatched hour of luxurious sleep, before stirring back to life and hunger, the coming of the dinner hour and the jollity of a well-chosen house-party.

That was the call which was competing with that other trumpet-call, and Yeovil knew on which side his choice would incline.

CHAPTER XIV

'A Perfectly Glorious Afternoon'

It was one of the last days of July, cooled and freshened by a touch of rain and dropping back again to a languorous warmth. London looked at its summer best, rain-washed and sun-lit, with the maximum of coming and going in its more fashionable streets.

Cicely Yeovil sat in a screened alcove of the Anchorage Restaurant, a feeding-ground which had lately sprung into favour. Opposite her sat Ronnie, confronting the ruins of what had been a dish of prawns in aspic. Cool and clean and fresh-coloured, he was good to look on in the eyes of his companion, and yet, perhaps, there was a ruffle in her soul that called for some answering disturbance on the part of that superbly tranquil young man, and certainly called in vain. Cicely had set up for herself a fetish of onyx with eyes of jade, and doubtless hungered at times with an unreasonable but perfectly natural hunger for something of flesh and blood. It was the religion of her life to know exactly what she wanted and to see that she got it, but there was no possible guarantee against her occasionally experiencing a desire for something else. It is the golden rule of all religions that no one should really live up to their precepts; when a man observes the principles of his religion too exactly he is in immediate danger of founding a new sect.

'To-day is going to be your day of triumph,' said Cicely to the young man, who was wondering at the moment whether he would care to embark on an artichoke; 'I believe I'm more nervous than you are,' she added, 'and yet I rather hate the idea of you scoring a great success.'

'Why?' asked Ronnie, diverting his mind for a moment from the artichoke question and its ramifications of *sauce hollandaise* or *vinaigre*.

'I like you as you are,' said Cicely, 'just a nice-looking boy to flatter and spoil and pretend to be fond of. You've got a charming young body and you've no soul, and that's such a fascinating combination. If you had a soul you would either dislike or worship me, and I'd much rather have things as they are. And now you are going to go a step beyond that, and other people will applaud you and say that you are wonderful, and invite you to eat with them and motor with them and yacht with them. As soon as that begins to happen, Ronnie, a lot of other things will come to an end. Of course I've always known that you don't really care for me, but as soon as the world knows it you are irrevocably damaged as a plaything. That is the great secret that binds us together, the knowledge that we have no real affection for one another. And this afternoon every one will know that you are a great artist, and no great artist was ever a great lover.'

'I shan't be difficult to replace, anyway,' said Ronnie, with what he imagined was a becoming modesty; 'there are lots of boys standing round ready to be fed and flattered and put on an imaginary pedestal, most of them more or less good-looking and well turned out and amusing to talk to.'

'Oh, I dare say I could find a successor for your vacated niche,' said Cicely lightly; 'one thing I'm determined on though, he shan't be a musician. It's so unsatisfactory to have to share a grand passion with a grand piano. He shall be a delightful young barbarian who would think Saint-Saëns was a Derby winner or a claret.'

'Don't be in too much of a hurry to replace me,' said Ronnie, who did not care to have his successor too seriously discussed. 'I may not score the success you expect this afternoon.'

'My dear boy, a minor crowned head from across the sea is coming to hear you play, and that alone will count as a success with most of your listeners. Also, I've secured a real Duchess for you, which is rather an achievement in the London of to-day.'

'An English Duchess?' asked Ronnie, who had early in life learned to apply the Merchandise Marks Act to ducal titles.

'English, oh certainly, at least as far as the title goes; she was born under the constellation of the Star-spangled Banner. I don't suppose the Duke approves of her being here, lending her countenance to the *fait accompli*, but when you've got republican blood in your veins a Kaiser is quite as attractive a lodestar as a King, rather more so. And Canon Mousepace is coming,' continued Cicely, referring to a closely written list of guests; 'the excellent von Tolb has been attending his church lately, and the Canon is longing to meet her. She is just the sort of person he adores. I fancy he sincerely realizes how difficult it will be for the rich to enter the Kingdom of Heaven, and he tries to make up for it by being as nice as possible to them in this world.'

Ronnie held out his hand for the list.

'I think you know most of the others,' said Cicely, passing it to him.

'Leutnant von Gabelroth?' read out Ronnie; 'who is he?'

'In one of the hussar regiments quartered here; a friend of the Gräfin's. Ugly but amiable, and I'm told a good cross-country rider. I suppose Murrey will be disgusted at meeting the "outward and visible sign" under his roof, but these encounters are inevitable as long as he is in London.'

'I didn't know Murrey was coming,' said Ronnie.

'I believe he's going to look in on us,' said Cicely; 'it's just as well, you know, otherwise we should have Joan asking in her loudest voice when he was going to be back in England again. I haven't asked her, but she overheard the Gräfin arranging to come and hear you play, and I fancy that will be quite enough.'

'How about some Turkish coffee?' said Ronnie, who had decided against the artichoke.

'Turkish coffee, certainly, and a cigarette, and a moment's peace before the serious business of the afternoon claims us. Talking about peace, do you know, Ronnie, it has just occurred to me that we have left out one of the most important things in our *affaire*; we have never had a quarrel.'

'I hate quarrels,' said Ronnie, 'they are so domesticated.'

'That's the first time I've ever heard you talk about your home,' said Cicely.

'I fancy it would apply to most homes,' said Ronnie.

'The last boy-friend I had used to quarrel furiously with me at least once a week,' said Cicely reflectively; 'but then he had dark slumberous eyes that lit up magnificently when he was angry, so it would have been a sheer waste of God's good gifts not to have sent him into a passion now and then.'

'With your excursions into the past and the future you are making me feel dreadfully like an instalment of a serial novel,' protested Ronnie; 'we have now got to "synopsis of earlier chapters".'

'It shan't be teased,' said Cicely; 'we will live in the present and go no further into the future than to make arrangements for Tuesday's dinner-party. I've asked the Duchess; she would never have forgiven me if she'd found out that I had a crowned head dining with me and hadn't asked her to meet him.'

A sudden hush descended on the company gathered in the great drawing-room at Berkshire Street as Ronnie took his seat at the piano; the voice of Canon Mousepace outlasted the others for a moment or so, and then subsided into a regretful but gracious silence. For the next nine or ten minutes Ronnie held possession of the crowded room, a tense slender figure, with cold green eyes aflame in a sudden fire, and smooth burnished head bent low over the keyboard that yielded a disciplined riot of melody under his strong deft fingers. The world-weary Landgraf forgot for the moment the regrettable trend of his subjects towards Parliamentary Socialism, the excellent Gräfin von Tolb forgot all that the Canon had been saying to her for the last ten minutes, forgot the depressing certainty that he would have a great deal more that he wanted to say in the immediate future, over and above the thirty-five minutes or so of discourse that she would contract to listen to next Sunday. And Cicely listened with the wistful equivocal triumph of one whose goose has turned out to be a swan and who realizes with secret concern that she has only planned the rôle of goosegirl for herself.

The last chords died away, the fire faded out of the jade-coloured eyes, and Ronnie became once more a well-groomed youth in a drawing-room full of well-dressed people. But around him rose an explosive clamour of applause and congratulation, the sincere tribute of appreciation and the equally hearty expression of imitative homage.

'It is a great gift, a great gift,' chanted Canon Mousepace. 'You must put it to a great use. A talent is vouchsafed to us for a purpose; you must fulfil the purpose. Talent such as yours is a responsibility; you must meet that responsibility.'

The dictionary of the English language was an inexhaustible quarry, from which the Canon had hewn and fashioned for himself a great reputation.

'You must gom and blay to me at Schlachsenberg,' said the kindly-faced Landgraf, whom the world adored and thwarted in about equal proportions. 'At Christmas, yes, that will be a good time. We still keep the Christ-Fest at Schlachsenberg, though the "Sozi" keep telling our schoolchildren that it is only a Christ myth. Never mind, I will have the Vice-President of our Landtag to listen to you; he is "Sozi" but we are good friends outside the Parliament House; you shall blay to him, my young friendt, and gonfince him that there is a Got in Heaven. You will gom? Yes?'

'It was beautiful,' said the Gräfin simply; 'it made me cry. Go back to the piano again, please, at once.'

Perhaps the near neighbourhood of the Canon inspired this command, but the Gräfin had been genuinely charmed. She adored good music and she was unaffectedly fond of good-looking boys.

Ronnie went back to the piano and tasted the matured pleasure of a repeated success. Any measure of nervousness that he may have felt at first had completely passed away. He was sure of his audience and he played as though they did not exist. A renewed clamour of excited approval attended the conclusion of his performance.

'It is a triumph, a perfectly *glorious* triumph,' exclaimed the Duchess of Dreyshire, turning to Yeovil, who sat silent among his wife's guests; 'isn't it just *glorious?*' she demanded, with a heavy insistent intonation of the word.

'Is it?' said Yeovil.

'Well, isn't it?' she cried, with a rising inflection, 'isn't it just *perfectly* glorious?'

'I don't know,' confessed Yeovil; 'you see, glory hasn't come very much my way lately.' Then, before he exactly realized what he was doing, he raised his voice and quoted loudly for the benefit of half the room:

> ' "Other Romans shall arise,
> Heedless of a soldier's name,
> Sounds, not deeds, shall win the prize,
> Harmony the path to fame." '

There was a sort of shiver of surprised silence at Yeovil's end of the room.

'Hell!'

The word rang out in a strong young voice.

'Hell! And it's true, that's the worst of it. It's damned true!'

Yeovil turned, with some dozen others, to see who was responsible for this vigorously expressed statement.

Tony Luton confronted him, an angry scowl on his face, a blaze in his heavy-lidded eyes. The boy was without a conscience, almost without a soul, as priests and parsons reckon souls, but there was a slumbering devil-god within him, and Yeovil's taunting words had broken the slumber. Life had been for Tony a hard school, in which right and wrong, high endeavour and good resolve, were untaught subjects; but there was a sterling something in him, just that something that helped poor street-scavenged men to die brave-fronted deaths in the trenches of Salamanca, that fired a handful of apprentice boys to shut the gates of Derry and stare unflinchingly at grim leaguer and starvation. It was just that nameless something that was lacking in the young musician, who stood at the farther end of the room, bathed in a flood of compliment and congratulation, enjoying the honey-drops of his triumph.

Luton pushed his way through the crowd and left the room, without troubling to take leave of his hostess.

'What a strange young man,' exclaimed the Duchess; 'now do take me into the next room,' she went on almost in the same breath, 'I'm just dying for some iced coffee.'

Yeovil escorted her through the throng of Ronnie-worshippers to the desired haven of refreshment.

'Marvellous!' Mrs Menteith-Mendlesohnn was exclaiming in ringing trumpet tones; 'of course I always knew he could play, but this is not mere piano playing, it is tone-mastery, it is sound magic. Mrs Yeovil has introduced us to a new star in the musical firmament. Do you know, I feel this afternoon just like Cortez, in the poem, gazing at the newly discovered sea.'

' "Silent upon a peak in Darien," ' quoted a penetrating voice that could only belong to Joan Mardle; 'I say, can anyone picture Mrs Menteith-Mendlesohnn silent on any peak or under any circumstances?'

If anyone had that measure of imagination, no one acknowledged the fact.

'A great gift and a great responsibility,' Canon Mousepace was assuring the Gräfin; 'the power of evoking sublime melody is akin to the power of awakening thought; a musician can appeal to dormant consciousness as the preacher can appeal to dormant conscience. It is a responsibility, an instrument for good or evil. Our young friend here, we may be sure, will use it as an instrument for good. He has, I feel certain, a sense of his responsibility.'

'He is a nice boy,' said the Gräfin simply; 'he has such pretty hair.'

In one of the window recesses Rhapsodie Pantril was talking vaguely but beautifully to a small audience on the subject of chromatic chords; she had the advantage of knowing what she was talking about, an advantage that her listeners did not in the least share. 'All through his playing there ran a tone-note of malachite green,' she declared recklessly, feeling safe from immediate contradiction; 'malachite green, *my* colour—the colour of striving.'

Having satisfied the ruling passion that demanded gentle and dexterous self-advertisement, she realized that the Augusta Smith in her craved refreshment, and moved with one of her over-awed admirers towards the haven where peaches and iced coffee might be considered a certainty.

The refreshment alcove, which was really a good-sized room, a sort of chapel-of-ease to the larger drawing-room, was already packed with a crowd who felt that they could best discuss Ronnie's triumph between mouthfuls of fruit salad and iced draughts of hock-cup. So brief is human glory that two or three independent souls had even now drifted from the theme of the moment on to other more personally interesting topics.

'Iced mulberry salad, my dear, it's a *spécialité de la maison*, so to speak; they say the roving husband brought the recipe from Astrakhan, or Seville, or some such outlandish place.'

'I wish my husband would roam about a bit and bring back strange palatable dishes. No such luck, he's got asthma and has to keep on a gravel soil with a south aspect and all sorts of other restrictions.'

'I don't think you're to be pitied in the least; a husband with asthma is like a captive golf-ball, you can always put your hand on him when you want him.'

'All the hangings, *violette de Parme*, all the furniture, rosewood. Nothing is to be played in it except Mozart. Mozart only. Some of my friends wanted me to have a replica of the Mozart statue at Vienna put up in a corner of the room, with flowers always around it, but I really couldn't. I *couldn't*. One is *so* tired of it, one sees it everywhere. I couldn't do it. I'm like that, you know.'

'Yes, I've secured the hero of the hour, Ronnie Storre, oh yes, rather. He's going to join our yachting trip, third week of August. We're going as far afield as Fiume, in the Adriatic—or is it the

Ægean? Won't it be jolly. Oh no, we're not asking Mrs Yeovil; it's quite a small yacht, you know—at least, it's a small party.'

The excellent von Tolb took her departure, bearing off with her the Landgraf, who had already settled the date and duration of Ronnie's Christmas visit.

'It will be dull, you know,' he warned the prospective guest; 'our Landtag will not be sitting, and what is a bear-garden without the bears? However, we haf some wildt schwein in our woods, we can show you some sport in that way.'

Ronnie instantly saw himself in a well-fitting shooting costume, with a Tyrolese hat placed at a very careful angle on his head, but he confessed that the other details of boar-hunting were rather beyond him.

With the departure of the von Tolb party Canon Mousepace gravitated decently but persistently towards a corner where the Duchess, still at concert pitch, was alternatively praising Ronnie's performance and the mulberry salad. Joan Mardle, who formed one of the group, was not openly praising anyone, but she was paying a silent tribute to the salad.

'We were just talking about Ronnie Storre's music, Canon,' said the Duchess; 'I consider it just perfectly glorious.'

'It's a great talent, isn't it, Canon,' put in Joan briskly, 'and of course it's a responsibility as well, don't you think? Music can be such an influence, just as eloquence can; don't you agree with me?'

The quarry of the English language was of course a public property, but it was disconcerting to have one's own particular barrow-load of sentence-building material carried off before one's eyes. The Canon's impressive homily on Ronnie's gift and its possibilities had to be hastily whittled down to a weakly acquiescent, 'Quite so, quite so.'

'Have you tasted this iced mulberry salad, Canon?' asked the Duchess; 'it's perfectly luscious. Just hurry along and get some before it's all gone.'

And her Grace hurried along in an opposite direction, to thank Cicely for past favours and to express lively gratitude for the Tuesday to come.

The guests departed, with a rather irritating slowness, for which perhaps the excellence of Cicely's buffet arrangements was partly responsible. The great drawing-room seemed to grow larger and more oppressive as the human wave receded, and the hostess fled at last with some relief to the narrower limits of her writing-room and the sedative influences of a cigarette. She was inclined to be sorry for herself; the triumph of the afternoon had turned out much as she had predicted at lunch-time. Her idol of onyx had not been swept from its pedestal, but the pedestal itself had an air of being packed up ready for transport to some other temple. Ronnie would be flattered and spoiled by half a hundred people, just because he could conjure sounds out of a keyboard, and Cicely felt no great incentive to go on flattering and spoiling him herself. And Ronnie would acquiesce in his dismissal with the good grace born of indifference—the surest guarantor of perfect manners. Already he had social engagements for the coming months in which she had no share; the drifting apart would be mutual. He had been an intelligent and amusing companion, and he had played the game as she had wished it to be played, without the fatigue of keeping up pretences which neither of them could have believed in. 'Let us have a wonderfully good time together' had been the single stipulation in their unwritten treaty of comradeship, and they had had the good time. Their whole-hearted pursuit of material happiness would go on as keenly as before, but they would hunt in different company, that was all. Yes, that was all. . . .

Cicely found the effect of her cigarette less sedative than she was disposed to exact. It might be necessary to change the brand.

Some ten or eleven days later Yeovil read an announcement in the papers that, in spite of handsome offers of increased salary, Mr Tony Luton, the original singer of the popular ditty 'Eccleston Square', had terminated his engagement with Messrs Isaac Grosvenor and Leon Hebhardt of the Caravansery Theatre, and signed on as a deck hand in the Canadian Marine.

Perhaps, after all, there had been some shred of glory amid the trumpet triumph of that July afternoon.

CHAPTER XV

The Intelligent Anticipator of Wants

Two of Yeovil's London clubs, the two that he had been accustomed to frequent, had closed their doors after the catastrophe. One of them had perished from off the face of the earth, its fittings had been sold and its papers lay stored in some solicitor's office, a titbit of material for the pen of some future historian. The other had transplanted itself to Delhi, whither it had removed its early Georgian furniture and its traditions, and sought to reproduce its St James's Street atmosphere as nearly as the conditions of a tropical Asiatic city would permit. There remained the Cartwheel, a considerably newer institution, which had sprung into existence somewhere about the time of Yeovil's last sojourn in England; he had joined it on the solicitation of a friend who was interested in the venture, and his bankers had paid his subscription during his absence. As he had never been inside its doors there could be no depressing comparisons to make between its present state and aforetime glories, and Yeovil turned into its portals one afternoon with the adventurous detachment of a man who breaks new ground and challenges new experiences.

He entered with a diffident sense of intrusion, conscious that his standing as a member might not be recognized by the keepers of the doors; in a moment, however, he realized that a rajah's escort of elephants might almost have marched through the entrance hall and vestibule without challenge. The general atmosphere of the scene suggested a blend of the railway station at Cologne, the Hotel Bristol in any European capital, and the second act in most musical comedies. A score of brilliant and brilliantined pages decorated the foreground, while Hebraic-looking gentlemen, wearing tartan waistcoats of the clans of their adoption, flitted restlessly between the tape machines and telephone boxes. The army of occupation had obviously established a firm footing in the hospitable premises; a kaleidoscopic pattern of uniforms, sky-blue, indigo, and bottle-green, relieved the civilian attire of the groups that clustered in lounge and card-rooms and corridors. Yeovil rapidly came to the conclusion that the joys of membership were not for him. He had turned to go, after a very cursory inspection of the premises and their human occupants, when he was hailed by a young man, dressed with strenuous neatness, whom he remembered having met in past days at the houses of one or two common friends.

Hubert Herlton's parents had brought him into the world, and some twenty-one years later had put him into a motor business. Having taken these pardonable liberties they had completely exhausted their ideas of what to do with him, and Hubert seemed unlikely to develop any ideas of his own on the subject. The motor business elected to conduct itself without his connivance; journalism, the stage, tomato culture (without capital), and other professions that could be entered on at short notice were submitted to his consideration by nimble-minded relations and friends. He listened to their suggestions with polite indifference, being rude only to a cousin who demonstrated how he might achieve a settled income of from two hundred to a thousand pounds a year by the propagation of mushrooms in a London basement. While his walk in life was still an undetermined promenade his parents died, leaving him with a carefully invested income of thirty-seven pounds a year. At that point of his career Yeovil's knowledge of him stopped short; the journey to Siberia had taken him beyond the range of Herlton's domestic vicissitudes.

The young man greeted him in a decidedly friendly manner.

'I didn't know you were a member here,' he exclaimed.

'It's the first time I've ever been in the club,' said Yeovil, 'and I fancy it will be the last. There is rather too much of the fighting-machine in evidence here. One doesn't want a perpetual reminder of what has happened staring one in the face.'

'We tried at first to keep the alien element out,' said Herlton apologetically, 'but we couldn't have carried on the club if we'd stuck to that line. You see we'd lost more than two-thirds of our old members so we couldn't afford to be exclusive. As a matter of fact the whole thing was decided over our heads; a new syndicate took over the concern, and a new committee was installed, with a good many foreigners on it. I know it's horrid having these uniforms flaunting all over the place, but what is one to do?'

Yeovil said nothing, with the air of a man who could have said a great deal.

'I suppose you wonder, why remain a member under those conditions?' continued Herlton. 'Well, as far as I am concerned, a place like this is a necessity for me. In fact, it's my profession, my source of income.'

'Are you as good at bridge as all that?' asked Yeovil; 'I'm a fairly successful player myself, but I should be sorry to have to live on my winnings, year in, year out.'

'I don't play cards,' said Herlton, 'at least not for serious stakes. My winnings or losings wouldn't come to a tenner in an average year. No, I live by commissions, by introducing likely buyers to would-be sellers.'

'Sellers of what?' asked Yeovil.

'Anything, everything; horses, yachts, old masters, plate, shootings, poultry-farms, week-end cottages, motor-cars, almost anything you can think of. Look,' and he produced from his breast pocket a bulky notebook illusorily inscribed 'Engagements.'

'Here,' he explained, tapping the book, 'I've got a double entry of every likely client that I know, with a note of the things he may have to sell and the things he may want to buy. When it is something that he has for sale there are cross-references to likely purchasers of that particular line of article. I don't limit myself to things that I actually know people to be in want of, I go further than that and have theories, carefully indexed theories, as to the things that people might want to buy. At the right moment, if I can get the opportunity, I mention the article that is in my mind's eye to the possible purchaser who has also been in my mind's eye, and I frequently bring off a sale. I started a chance acquaintance on a career of print-buying the other day merely by telling him of a couple of good prints that I knew of, that were to be had at a quite reasonable price; he is a man with more money than he knows what to do with, and he has laid out quite a lot on old prints since his first purchase. Most of his collection he has got through me, and of course I net a commission on each transaction. So you see, old man, how useful, not to say necessary, a club with a large membership is to me. The more mixed and socially chaotic it is, the more serviceable it is.'

'Of course,' said Yeovil, 'and I suppose, as a matter of fact, a good many of your clients belong to the conquering race.'

'Well, you see, they are the people who have got the money,' said Herlton; 'I don't mean to say that the invading Germans are usually people of wealth, but while they live over here they escape the crushing taxation that falls on the British-born subject. They serve their country as soldiers, and we have to serve it in garrison money, ship money, and so forth, besides the ordinary taxes of the State. The German shoulders the rifle, the Englishman has to shoulder everything else. That is what will help more than anything towards the gradual Germanizing of our big towns; the comparatively lightly taxed German workman over here will have a much bigger spending power and purchasing power than his heavily taxed English neighbour. The public-houses, bars, eating-houses, places of amusement, and so forth, will come to cater more and more for money-yielding German patronage. The stream of British emigration will swell rather than diminish, and the stream of Teuton immigration will be equally persistent and progressive. Yes, the military-service ordinance was a cunning stroke on the part of that old fox, von Kwarl. As a civilian statesman he is far and away cleverer than Bismarck was; he smothers with a feather-bed where Bismarck would have tried to smash with a sledge-hammer.'

'Have you got me down on your list of noteworthy people?' asked Yeovil, turning the drift of the conversation back to the personal topic.

'Certainly I have,' said Herlton, turning the pages of his pocket directory to the letter Y. 'As soon as I knew you were back in England I made several entries concerning you. In the first place it was possible that you might have a volume on Siberian travel and natural history notes to publish, and I've cross-referenced you to a publisher I know who rather wants books of that sort on his list.'

'I may tell you at once that I've no intentions in that direction,' said Yeovil, in some amusement.

'Just as well,' said Herlton cheerfully, scribbling a hieroglyphic in his book; 'that branch of business is rather outside my line—too little in it, and the gratitude of author and publisher for being introduced to one another is usually short-lived. A more serious entry was the item that if you were wintering in England you would be looking out for a hunter or two. You used to hunt with the East Wessex, I remember; I've got just the very animal that will suit that country, ready waiting for you. A beautiful clean jumper. I've put it over a fence or two myself, and you and I ride much the same weight. A stiffish price is being asked for it, but I've got the letters D.O. after your name.'

'In Heaven's name,' said Yeovil, now openly grinning, 'before I die of curiosity tell me what D. O. stands for.'

'It means some one who doesn't object to pay a good price for anything that really suits him. There are some people of course who won't consider a thing unless they can get it for about a third of what they imagine to be its market value. I've got another suggestion down against you in my book; you may not be staying in the country at all, you may be clearing out in disgust at existing conditions. In that case you would be selling a lot of things that you wouldn't want to cart away with you. That involves another set of entries and a whole lot of cross-references.'

'I'm afraid I've given you a lot of trouble,' said Yeovil drily.

'Not at all,' said Herlton, 'but it would simplify matters if we take it for granted that you are going to stay here, for this winter anyhow, and are looking out for hunters. Can you lunch with me here on Wednesday, and come and look at the animal afterwards? It's only thirty-five minutes by train. It will take us longer if we motor. There is a two-fifty-three from Charing Cross that we could catch comfortably.'

'If you are going to persuade me to hunt in the East Wessex country this season,' said Yeovil, 'you must find me a convenient hunting-box somewhere down there.'

'I *have* found it,' said Herlton, whipping out a stylograph, and hastily scribbling an 'order to view' on a card; 'central as possible for all the meets, grand stabling accommodation, excellent water-supply, big bathroom, game larder, cellarage, a bakehouse if you want to bake your own bread——'

'Any land with it?'

'Not enough to be a nuisance. An acre or two of paddock and about the same of garden. You are fond of wild things; a wood comes down to the edge of the garden, a wood that harbours owls and buzzards and kestrels.'

'Have you got all those details in your book?' asked Yeovil; '"wood adjoining property, O. B. K".'

'I keep those details in my head,' said Herlton, 'but they are quite reliable.'

'I shall insist on something substantial off the rent if there are no buzzards,' said Yeovil; 'now that you have mentioned them they seem an indispensable accessory to any decent hunting-box. Look,' he exclaimed, catching sight of a plump middle-aged individual crossing the vestibule with an air of restrained importance, 'there goes the delectable Pitherby. Does he come on your books at all?'

'I should say!' exclaimed Herlton fervently. 'The delectable P. nourishes expectations of a barony or viscounty at an early date. Most of his life has been spent in streets and squares, with occasional migrations to the esplanades of fashionable watering-places or the gravelled walks of country house gardens. Now that *noblesse* is about to impose its obligations on him, quite a new catalogue of wants has sprung into his mind. There are things that a plain esquire may leave undone without causing scandalized remark, but a fiercer light beats on a baron. Trigger-pulling is one of the obligations. Up to the present Pitherby has never hit a partridge in anger, but this year he has commissioned me to rent him a deer forest. Some pedigree Herefords for his "home farm" was another commission, and a dozen and a half swans for a swannery. The swannery, I may say, was my idea; I said once in his hearing that it gave a baronial air to an estate; you see, I knew a man who had got a lot of surplus swan stock for sale. Now Pitherby wants a heronry as well. I've put him in communication with a client of mine who suffers from superfluous herons, but of course I can't guarantee that the birds' nesting arrangements will fall in with his territorial requirements. I'm getting him some carp, too, of quite respectable age, for a carp pond; I thought it would look so well for his lady-wife to be discovered by interviewers feeding the carp with her own fair hands, and I put the same idea into Pitherby's mind.'

'I had no idea that so many things were necessary to endorse a patent of nobility,' said Yeovil. 'If there should be any miscarriage in the bestowal of the honour at least Pitherby will have absolved himself from any charge of contributory negligence.'

'Shall we say Wednesday, here, one o'clock, lunch first, and go down and look at the horse afterwards?' said Herlton, returning to the matter in hand.

Yeovil hesitated, then he nodded his head.

'There is no harm in going to look at the animal,' he said.

CHAPTER XVI

Sunrise

Mrs Kerrick sat at a little teakwood table in the verandah of a low-pitched teak-built house that stood on the steep slope of a brown hill-side. Her youngest child, with the grave natural dignity of nine-year-old girlhood, maintained a correct but observant silence, looking carefully yet unobtrusively after the wants of the one guest, and checking from time to time the incursions of ubiquitous ants that were obstinately disposed to treat the table-cloth as a foraging ground. The wayfaring visitor, who was experiencing a British blend of Eastern hospitality, was a French naturalist, travelling thus far afield in quest of feathered specimens to enrich the aviaries of a bird-collecting Balkan King. On the previous evening, while shrugging his shoulders and unloosing his vocabulary over the meagre accommodation afforded by the native rest-house, he had been enchanted by receiving an invitation to transfer his quarters to the house on the hillside, where he found not only a pleasant-voiced hostess and some drinkable wine, but three brown-skinned English youngsters who were able to give him a mass of intelligent first-hand information about the bird life of the region. And now, at the early morning breakfast, ere yet the sun was showing over the rim of the brown-baked hills, he was learning something of the life of the little community he had chanced on.

'I was in these parts many years ago,' explained the hostess, 'when my husband was alive and had an appointment out here. It is a healthy hill district and I had pleasant memories of the place, so when it became necessary, well, desirable let us say, to leave our English home and find a new one, it occurred to me to bring my boys and my little girl here—my eldest girl is at school in Paris. Labour is cheap here and I try my hand at farming in a small way. Of course it is very different work to just superintending the dairy and poultry-yard arrangements of an English country estate. There are so many things, insect ravages, bird depredations, and so on, that one only knows on a small scale in England, that happen here in wholesale fashion, not to mention droughts and torrential rains and other tropical visitations. And then the domestic animals are so disconcertingly different from the ones one has been used to; humped cattle never seem to behave in the way that straight-backed cattle would, and goats and geese and chickens are not a bit the same here that they are in Europe—and of course the farm servants are utterly unlike the same class in England. One has to unlearn a good deal of what one thought one knew about stock-keeping and agriculture, and take note of the native ways of doing things; they are primitive and unenterprising of course, but they have an accumulated store of experience behind them, and one has to tread warily in initiating improvements.'

The Frenchman looked round at the brown sun-scorched hills, with the dusty empty road showing here and there in the middle distance and other brown sun-scorched hills rounding off the scene; he looked at the lizards on the verandah walls, at the jars for keeping the water cool, at the numberless little insect-bored holes in the furniture, at the heat-drawn lines on his hostess's comely face. Notwithstanding his present wanderings he had a Frenchman's strong homing instinct, and he marvelled to hear this lady, who should have been a lively and popular figure in the social circle of some English county town, talking serenely of the ways of humped cattle and native servants.

'And your children, how do they like the change?' he asked.

'It is healthy up here among the hills,' said the mother, also looking round at the landscape and thinking doubtless of a very different scene; 'they have an outdoor life and plenty of liberty. They have their ponies to ride, and there is a lake up above us that is a fine place for them to bathe and boat in; the three boys are there now, having their morning swim. The eldest is sixteen and he is allowed to have a gun, and there is some good wild-fowl shooting to be had in the reed beds at the farther end of the lake. I think that part of the joy of his shooting expeditions lies in the fact that many of the duck and plover that he comes across belong to the same species that frequent our English moors and rivers.'

It was the first hint that she had given of a wistful sense of exile, the yearning for other skies, the message that a dead bird's plumage could bring across rolling seas and scorching plains.

'And the education of your boys, how do you manage for that?' asked the visitor.

'There is a young tutor living out in these wilds,' said Mrs Kerrick; 'he was assistant master at a private school in Scotland, but it had to be given up when—when things changed; so many of the boys left the country. He came out to an uncle who has a small estate eight miles from here, and three days in the week he rides over to teach my boys, and three days he goes to another family living in the opposite direction. To-day he is due to come here. It is a great boon to have such an opportunity for getting the boys educated, and of course it helps him to earn a living.'

'And the society of the place?' asked the Frenchman.

His hostess laughed.

'I must admit it has to be looked for with a strong pair of field-glasses,' she said; 'it is almost as difficult to get a good bridge four together as it would have been to get up a tennis tournament or a subscription dance in our particular corner of England. One has to ignore distances and forget fatigue if one wants to be gregarious even on a limited scale. There are one or two officials who are our chief social mainstays, but the difficulty is to muster the few available souls under the same roof at the same moment. A road will be impassable in one quarter, a pony will be lame in another, a stress of work will prevent some one else from coming, and another may be down with a touch of fever. When my little girl gave a birthday party here her only little girl guest had come twelve miles to attend it. The Forest officer happened to drop in on us that evening, so we felt quite festive.'

The Frenchman's eyes grew round in wonder. He had once thought that the capital city of a Balkan kingdom was the uttermost limit of social desolation, viewed from a Parisian standpoint, and there at any rate one could get *café chantant*, tennis, picnic parties, an occasional theatre performance by a foreign troupe, now and then a travelling circus, not to speak of Court and diplomatic functions of a more or less sociable character. Here, it seemed, one went a day's journey to reach an evening's entertainment, and the chance arrival of a tired official took on the nature of a festivity. He looked round again at the rolling stretches of brown hills; before he had regarded them merely as the background to this little shut-away world, now he saw that they were foreground as well. They were everything, there was nothing else. And again his glance travelled to the face of his hostess, with its bright, pleasant eyes and smiling mouth.

'And you live here with your children,' he said, 'here in this wilderness? You leave England, you leave everything, for this?'

His hostess rose and took him over to the far side of the verandah. The beginnings of a garden were spread out before them, with young fruit trees and flowering shrubs, and bushes of pale pink roses. Exuberant tropical growths were interspersed with carefully tended vestiges of plants that had evidently been brought from a more temperate climate, and had not borne the transition well. Bushes and trees and shrubs spread away for some distance, to where the ground rose in a small hillock and then fell away abruptly into bare hill-side.

'In all this garden that you see,' said the Englishwoman, 'there is one tree that is sacred.'

'A tree?' said the Frenchman.

'A tree that we could not grow in England.'

The Frenchman followed the direction of her eyes and saw a tall, bare pole at the summit of the hillock. At the same moment the sun came over the hill-tops in a deep, orange glow, and a new light stole like magic over the brown landscape. And, as if they had timed their arrival to that exact moment of sunburst, three brown-faced boys appeared under the straight, bare pole. A cord shivered and flapped, and something ran swiftly up into the air, and swung out in the breeze that blew across the hills—a blue flag with red and white crosses. The three boys bared their heads and the small girl on the verandah steps stood rigidly to attention. Far away down the hill, a young man, cantering into view round a corner of the dusty road, removed his hat in loyal salutation.

'That is why we live out here,' said the Englishwoman quietly.

CHAPTER XVII

The Event of the Season

In the first swelter room of the new Osmanli Baths in Cork Street four or five recumbent individuals, in a state of moist nudity and self-respecting inertia, were smoking cigarettes or making occasional pretence of reading damp newspapers. A glass wall with a glass door shut them off from the yet more torrid regions of the further swelter chambers; another glass partition disclosed the dimly lit vault where other patrons of the establishment had arrived at the stage of being pounded and kneaded and sluiced by Oriental-looking attendants. The splashing and trickling of taps, the flip-flap of wet slippers on a wet floor, and the low murmur of conversation, filtered through glass doors, made an appropriately drowsy accompaniment to the scene.

A new-comer fluttered into the room, beamed at one of the occupants, and settled himself with an air of elaborate languor in a long canvas chair. Cornelian Valpy was a fair young man, with perpetual surprise impinged on his countenance, and a chin that seemed to have retired from competition with the rest of his features. The beam of recognition that he had given to his friend or acquaintance subsided into a subdued but lingering simper.

'What is the matter?' drawled his neighbour lazily, dropping the end of a cigarette into a small bowl of water, and helping himself from a silver case on the table at his side.

'Matter?' said Cornelian, opening wide a pair of eyes in which unhealthy intelligence seemed to struggle in undetermined battle with utter vacuity; 'why should you suppose that anything is the matter?'

'When you wear a look of idiotic complacency in a Turkish bath,' said the other, 'it is the more noticeable from the fact that you are wearing nothing else.'

'Were you at the Shalem House dance last night?' asked Cornelian, by way of explaining his air of complacent retrospection.

'No,' said the other, 'but I feel as if I had been; I've been reading columns about it in the *Dawn*.'

'The last event of the season,' said Cornelian, 'and quite one of the most amusing and lively functions that there have been.'

'So the *Dawn* said; but then, as Shalem practically owns and controls that paper, its favourable opinion might be taken for granted.'

'The whole idea of the Revel was quite original,' said Cornelian, who was not going to have his personal narrative of the event forestalled by anything that a newspaper reporter might have given to the public; 'a certain number of guests went as famous personages in the world's history, and each one was accompanied by another guest typifying the prevailing characteristic of that personage. One man went as Julius Cæsar, for instance, and had a girl typifying Ambition as his shadow, another went as Louis the Eleventh, and his companion personified Superstition. Your shadow had to be some one of the opposite sex, you see, and every alternate dance throughout the evening you danced with your shadow-partner. Quite a clever idea; young Graf von Schnatelstein is supposed to have invented it.'

'New York will be deeply beholden to him,' said the other; 'shadow-dances, with all manner of eccentric variations, will be the rage there for the next eighteen months.'

'Some of the costumes were really sumptuous,' continued Cornelian; 'the Duchess of Dreyshire was magnificent as Aholibah, you never saw so many jewels on one person, only of course she didn't look dark enough for the character; she had Billy Carnset for her shadow, representing Unspeakable Depravity.'

'How on earth did he manage that?'

'Oh, a blend of Beardsley and Bakst as far as get-up and costume, and of course his own personality counted for a good deal. Quite one of the successes of the evening was Leutnant von Gabelroth, as George Washington, with Joan Mardle as his shadow, typifying Inconvenient Candour. He put her down officially as Truthfulness, but every one had heard the other version.'

'Good for the Gabelroth, though he does belong to the invading Horde; it's not often that anyone scores off Joan.'

'Another blaze of magnificence was the loud-voiced Bessimer woman, as the Goddess Juno, with peacock tails and opals all over her; she had Ronnie Storre to represent Green-eyed Jealousy. Talking of Ronnie Storre *and* of jealousy, you will naturally wonder whom

Mrs Yeovil went with. I forget what her costume was, but she'd got that dark-headed youth with her that she's been trotting round everywhere the last few days.'

Cornelian's neighbour kicked him furtively on the shin, and frowned in the direction of a dark-haired youth reclining in an adjacent chair. The youth in question rose from his seat and stalked into the farther swelter room.

'So clever of him to go into the furnace room,' said the unabashed Cornelian; 'now if he turns scarlet all over we shall never know how much is embarrassment and how much is due to the process of being boiled. La Yeovil hasn't done badly by the exchange; he's better looking than Ronnie.'

'I see that Pitherby went as Frederick the Great,' said Cornelian's neighbour, fingering a sheet of the *Dawn*.

'Isn't that exactly what one would have expected Pitherby to do?' said Cornelian. 'He's so desperately anxious to announce to all whom it may concern that he has written a life of that hero. He had an uninspiring-looking woman with him, supposed to represent Military Genius.'

'The Spirit of Advertisement would have been more appropriate,' said the other.

'The opening scene of the Revel was rather effective,' continued Cornelian; 'all the Shadow people reclined in the dimly lit centre of the ballroom in an indistinguishable mass, and the human characters marched round the illuminated sides of the room to solemn processional music. Every now and then a shadow would detach itself from the mass, hail its partner by name, and glide out to join him or her in the procession. Then, when the last shadows had found their mates and every one was partnered, the lights were turned up in a blaze, the orchestra crashed out a whirl of nondescript dance music, and people just let themselves go. It was Pandemonium. Afterwards every one strutted about for half an hour or so, showing themselves off, and then the legitimate programme of dances began. There were some rather amusing incidents throughout the evening. One set of lancers was danced entirely by the Seven Deadly Sins and their human exemplars; of course seven couples were not sufficient to make up the set, so they had to bring in an eighth sin, I forget what it was.'

'The sin of Patriotism would have been rather appropriate, considering who were giving the dance,' said the other.

'Hush!' exclaimed Cornelian nervously. 'You don't know who may overhear you in a place like this. You'll get yourself into trouble.'

'Wasn't there some rather daring new dance of the "bunny-hug" variety?' asked the indiscreet one.

'The "Cubby-Cuddle",' said Cornelian; 'three or four adventurous couples danced it towards the end of the evening.'

'The *Dawn* says that without being strikingly new it was strikingly modern.'

'The best description I can give of it,' said Cornelian, 'is summed up in the comment of the Gräfin von Tolb when she saw it being danced: "if they *really* love each other I suppose it doesn't matter". By the way,' he added with apparent indifference, 'is there any detailed account of my costume in the *Dawn*?'

His companion laughed cynically.

'As if you hadn't read everything that the *Dawn* and the other morning papers have to say about the ball hours ago.'

'The naked truth should be avoided in a Turkish bath,' said Cornelian; 'kindly assume that I've only had time to glance at the weather forecast and the news from China.'

'On, very well,' said the other; 'your costume isn't described; you simply come amid a host of others as "Mr Cornelian Valpy, resplendent as the Emperor Nero; with him Miss Kate Lerra, typifying Insensate Vanity." Many hard things have been said of Nero, but his unkindest critics have never accused him of resembling you in feature. Until some very clear evidence is produced I shall refuse to believe it.'

Cornelian was proof against these shafts; leaning back gracefully in his chair he launched forth into that detailed description of his last night's attire which the *Dawn* had so unaccountably failed to supply.

'I wore a tunic of white Nepaulese silk, with a collar of pearls, real pearls. Round my waist I had a girdle of twisted serpents in beaten gold, studded all over with amethysts. My sandals were of gold, laced with scarlet thread, and I had seven bracelets of gold on each arm. Round my head I had a wreath of golden laurel leaves set with scarlet berries, and hanging over my left shoulder was a silk robe of mulberry purple, broidered with the signs of the zodiac in gold and scarlet; I had it made specially for the occasion. At my side I had an ivory-sheathed dagger, with a green jade handle, hung in a green Cordova leather——'

At this point of the recital his companion rose softly, flung his cigarette end into the little water-bowl, and passed into the farther swelter room. Cornelian Valpy was left, still clothed in a look of ineffable complacency, still engaged, in all probability, in reclothing himself in the finery of the previous evening.

CHAPTER XVIII

The Dead who do not Understand

The pale light of a November afternoon faded rapidly into the dusk of a November evening. Far over the countryside housewives put up their cottage shutters, lit their lamps, and made the customary remark that the days were drawing in. In barnyards and poultry-runs the greediest pullets made a final tour of inspection, picking up the stray remaining morsels of the evening meal, and then, with much scrambling and squawking, sought the places on the roosting-pole that they thought should belong to them. Labourers working in yard and field began to turn their thoughts homeward or tavernward as the case might be. And through the cold squelching slush of a water-logged meadow a weary, bedraggled, but unbeaten fox stiffly picked his way, climbed a high bramble-grown bank, and flung himself into the sheltering labyrinth of a stretching tangle of woods. The pack of fierce-mouthed things that had rattled him from copse and gorse-cover, along fallow and plough, hedgerow and wooded lane, for nigh on an hour, and had pressed hard on his life for the last few minutes, receded suddenly into the background of his experiences. The cold, wet meadow, the thick mask of woods, and the on-coming dusk had stayed the chase—and the fox had outstayed it. In a short time he would fall mechanically to licking off some of the mud that caked on his weary pads; in a shorter time horsemen and hounds would have drawn off kennelward and homeward.

Yeovil rode through the deepening twilight, relying chiefly on his horse to find its way in the network of hedge-bordered lanes that presumably led to a high road or to some human habitation. He was desperately tired after his day's hunting, a legacy of weakness that the fever had bequeathed to him, but even though he could scarcely sit upright in his saddle his mind dwelt complacently on the day's sport and looked forward to the snug cheery comfort that awaited him at his hunting-box. There was a charm, too, even for a tired man, in the eerie stillness of the lone twilight land through which he was passing, a grey shadow-hung land which seemed to have been emptied of all things that belonged to the daytime, and filled with a lurking, moving life of which one knew nothing beyond the sense that it was there. There, and very near. If there had been wood-gods and wicked-eyed fauns in the sunlit groves and hill-sides of old Hellas, surely there were watchful, living things of kindred mould in this dusk-hidden wilderness of field and hedge and coppice.

It was Yeovil's third or fourth day with the hounds, without taking into account a couple of mornings' cub-hunting. Already he felt that he had been doing nothing different from this all his life. His foreign travels, his illness, his recent weeks in London, they were part of a tapestried background that had very slight and distant connection with his present existence. Of the future he tried to think with greater energy and determination. For this winter, at any rate, he would hunt and do a little shooting, entertain a few of his neighbours and make friends with any congenial fellow-sportsmen who might be within reach. Next year things would be different; he would have had time to look round him, to regain something of his aforetime vigour of mind and body. Next year, when the hunting season was over, he would set about finding out whether there was any nobler game for him to take a hand in. He would enter into correspondence with old friends who had gone out into the tropics and the backwoods—he would do something.

So he told himself, but he knew thoroughly well that he had found his level. He had ceased to struggle against the fascination of his present surroundings. The slow, quiet comfort and interest of country life appealed with enervating force to the man whom death had half conquered. The pleasures of the chase, well-provided for in every detail, and dovetailed in with the assured luxury of a well-ordered, well-staffed establishment, were exactly what he wanted and exactly what his life down here afforded him. He was experiencing, too, that passionate recurring devotion to an old loved scene that comes at times to men who have travelled far and willingly up and down the world. He was very much at home. The alien standard floating over Buckingham Palace, the Crown of Charlemagne on public buildings and official documents, the grey ships of war riding in Plymouth Bay and Southampton Water with a flag at their stern that older genera-tions of Britons had never looked on, these things seemed far away and inconsequent amid the hedgerows and woods and fallows of the East Wessex country. Horse and hound-craft, harvest, game broods, the planting and felling of timber, the rearing and selling of stock, the letting of grasslands, the care of fisheries, the upkeep of markets and fairs, they were the things that immediately mattered. And Yeovil saw himself, in moments of disgust and self-accusation, settling down into this life of rustic littleness, concerned over the late nesting of a partridge or the defective draining of a loose-box, hugely busy over affairs that a gardener's boy might grapple with, ignoring the struggle-cry that went up, low and bitter and wistful, from a dethroned dispossessed race, in whose glories he had gloried, in whose struggle he lent no hand. In what way, he asked himself in such moments, would his life be better than the life of that parody of manhood who upholstered his rooms with art hangings and rosewood furniture and babbled over the effect?

The lanes seemed interminable and without aim or object except to bisect one another; gates and gaps disclosed nothing in the way of a landmark, and the night began to draw down in increasing shades of darkness. Presently, however, the tired horse quickened its pace, swung round a sharp corner into a broader roadway, and stopped with an air of thankful expectancy at the low doorway of a wayside inn. A cheerful glow of light streamed from the windows and door, and a brighter glare came from the other side of the road, where a large motor-car was being got ready for an immediate start. Yeovil tumbled stiffly out of his saddle, and in answer to the loud rattle of his hunting crop on the open door the innkeeper and two or three hangers-on hurried out to attend to the wants of man and beast. Flour and water for the horse and something hot for himself were Yeovil's first concern, and then he began to clamour for geographical information. He was rather dismayed to find that the cumulative opinions of those whom he consulted, and of several others who joined unbidden in the discussion, placed his destination at nothing nearer than nine miles. Nine miles of dark and hilly country road for a tired man on a tired horse assumed enormous, far-stretching proportions, and although he dimly remembered that he had asked a guest to dinner for that evening he began to wonder whether the wayside inn possessed anything endurable in the way of a bedroom. The landlord interrupted his desperate speculations with a really brilliant effort of suggestion. There was a gentleman in the bar, he said, who was going in a motor-car in the direction for which Yeovil was bound, and who would no doubt be willing to drop him at his destination; the gentleman had also been out with the hounds. Yeovil's horse could be stabled at the inn and fetched home by a groom the next morning. A hurried embassy to the bar parlour resulted in the news that the motorist would be delighted to be of assistance to a fellow-sportsman. Yeovil gratefully accepted the chance that had so obligingly come his way, and hastened to superintend the housing of his horse in its night's quarters. When he had duly seen to the tired animal's comfort and foddering he returned to the roadway, where a young man in hunting garb and a liveried chauffeur were standing by the side of the waiting car.

'I am so very pleased to be of some use to you, Mr Yeovil,' said the car-owner, with a polite bow, and Yeovil recognized the young Leutnant von Gabelroth, who had been present at the musical after-noon at Berkshire Street. He had doubtless seen him at the meet that morning, but in his hunting kit he had escaped his observation.

'I, too, have been out with the hounds,' the young man continued; 'I have left my horse at the "Crow and Sceptre" at Dolford. You are living at Black Dene, are you not? I can take you right past your door, it is all on my way.'

Yeovil hung back for a moment, overwhelmed with vexation and embarrassment, but it was too late to cancel the arrangement he had unwittingly entered into, and he was constrained to put himself under obligation to the young officer with the best grace he could muster. After all, he reflected, he had met him under his own roof as his wife's guest. He paid his reckoning to mine host, tipped the stable lad who had helped him with his horse, and took his place beside von Gabelroth in the car.

As they glided along the dark roadway and the young German reeled off a string of comments on the incidents of the day's sport, Yeovil lay back amid his comfortable wraps and weighed the measure of his humiliation. It was Cicely's gospel that one should know what one wanted in life and take good care that one got what one wanted. Could he apply that test of achievement to his own life? Was this what he really wanted to be doing, pursuing his uneventful way as a country squire, sharing even his sports and pastimes with men of the nation that had conquered and enslaved his Fatherland?

The car slackened its pace somewhat as they went through a small hamlet, past a schoolhouse, past a rural police-station with the new monogram over its notice-board, past a church with a little tree-grown graveyard. There, in a corner, among wild-rose bushes and tall yews, lay some of Yeovil's own kinsfolk, who had lived in these parts and hunted and found life pleasant in the days that were not so very long ago. Whenever he went past that quiet little gathering-place of the dead Yeovil was wont to raise his hat in mute affectionate salutation to those who were now only memories in his family; to-night he somehow omitted the salute and turned his head the other way. It was as though the dead of his race saw and wondered.

Three or four months ago the thing he was doing would have seemed an impossibility, now it was actually happening; he was listening to the gay, courteous, tactful chatter of his young companion, laughing now and then at some joking remark, answering some question of interest, learning something of hunting ways and traditions in von Gabelroth's own country. And when the car turned in at the gate of the hunting lodge and drew up at the steps the laws of hospitality demanded that Yeovil should ask his benefactor of the road to come in for a few minutes and drink something a little better than the wayside inn had been able to supply. The young officer spent the best part of a half-hour in Yeovil's snuggery, examining and discussing the trophies of rifle and collecting gun that covered the walls. He had a good knowledge of woodcraft, and the beasts and birds of Siberian forests and North African deserts were to him new pages in a familiar book. Yeovil found himself discoursing eagerly with his chance guest on the European distribution and local variation of such and such a species, recounting peculiarities in its habits and incidents of its pursuit and capture. If the cold observant eyes of Lady Shalem could have rested on the scene she would have hailed it as another root-fibre thrown out by the *fait accompli*.

Yeovil closed the hall door on his departing visitor, and closed his mind on the crowd of angry and accusing thoughts that were waiting to intrude themselves. His valet had already got his bath in readiness and in a few minutes the tired huntsman was forgetting weariness and the consciousness of outside things in the languorous abandonment that steam and hot water induce. Brain and limbs seemed to lay themselves down in a contented waking sleep, the world that was beyond the bathroom walls dropped away into a far unreal distance; only somewhere through the steam clouds pierced a hazy consciousness that a dinner, well chosen, was being well cooked, and would presently be well served—and right well appreciated. That was the lure to drag the bather away from the Nirvana land of warmth and steam. The stimulating after-effect of the bath took its due effect, and Yeovil felt that he was now much less tired and enormously hungry. A cheery fire burned in his dressing-room and a lively black kitten helped him to dress, and incidentally helped him to require a new tassel to the cord of his dressing-gown. As he finished his toilet and the kitten finished its sixth and most notable attack on the tassel a ring was heard at the front door, and a moment later a loud, hearty, and unmistakably hungry voice resounded in the hall. It belonged to the local doctor, who had also taken part in the day's run and had been bidden to enliven the evening meal with the entertainment of his inexhaustible store of sporting and social reminiscences. He knew the countryside and the countryfolk inside out, and he was a living unwritten chronicle of the East Wessex hunt. His conversation seemed exactly the right accompaniment to the meal; his stories brought glimpses of wet hedgerows, stiff ploughlands, leafy spinneys, and muddy brooks in among the rich old Worcester and Georgian silver of the dinner service, the glow and crackle of the wood fire, the pleasant succession of well-cooked dishes and mellow wines. The world narrowed itself down again to a warm, drowsy-scented dining-room, with a productive hinterland of kitchen and cellar beyond it, and beyond that an important outer world of loose-box and harness-room and stable-yard; farther again a dark hushed region where pheasants roosted and owls flitted and foxes prowled.

Yeovil sat and listened to story after story of the men and women and horses of the neighbourhood; even the foxes seemed to have a personality, some of them, and a personal history. It was a little like Hans Andersen, he decided, and a little like the *Reminiscences of an Irish R.M.*, and perhaps just a little like some of the more probable adventures of Baron Munchausen. The newer stories were evidently true to the smallest detail, the earlier ones had altered somewhat in repetition, as plants and animals vary under domestication.

And all the time there was one topic that was never touched on. Of half the families mentioned it was necessary to add the qualifying information that they 'used to live' at such and such a place; the countryside knew them no longer. Their properties were for sale or had already passed into the hands of strangers. But neither man cared to allude to the grinning shadow that sat at the feast and sent an icy chill now and again through the cheeriest jest and most jovial story.

The brisk run with the hounds that day had stirred and warmed their pulses; it was an evening for comfortable forgetting.

Later that night, in the stillness of his bedroom, with the dwindling noises of a retiring household dropping off one by one into ordered silence, a door shutting here, a fire being raked out there, the thoughts that had been held away came crowding in. The body was tired, but the brain was not, and Yeovil lay awake with his thoughts for company. The world grew suddenly wide again, filled with the significance of things that mattered, held by the actions of men that mattered. Hunting-box and stable and gun-room dwindled to a mere pinpoint in the universe, there were other larger, more absorbing things on which the mind dwelt. There was the grey cold sea outside Dover and Portsmouth and Cork, where the great grey ships of war rocked and swung with the tides, where the sailors sang, in doggerel English, that bitter-sounding adaptation, 'Germania rules t'e waves,' where the flag of a World-Power floated for the world to see. And in oven-like cities of India there were men who looked out at the white sun-glare, the heat-baked dust, the welter of crowded streets, who listened to the unceasing chorus of harsh-throated crows, the strident creaking of cart-wheels, the buzz and drone of insect swarms, and the rattle call of the tree lizards; men whose thoughts went hungrily to the cool grey skies and wet turf and moist ploughlands of an English hunting country, men whose memories listened yearningly to the music of a deep-throated hound and the call of a game-bird in the stubble. Yeovil had secured for himself the enjoyment of the things for which these men hungered; he had known what he wanted in life, slowly and with hesitation, yet nevertheless surely, he had arrived at the achievement of his unconfessed desires. Here, installed under his own roof-tree, with as good horse-flesh in his stable as man could desire, with sport lying almost at his door, with his wife ready to come down and help him to entertain his neighbours, Murrey Yeovil had found the life that he wanted—and was accursed in his own eyes. He argued with himself, and palliated and explained, but he knew why he had turned his eyes away that evening from the little graveyard under the trees; one cannot explain things to the dead.

CHAPTER XIX

The Little Foxes

'Take us the foxes, the little foxes, that spoil the vines'

On a warm and sunny May afternoon, some ten months since Yeovil's return from his Siberian wanderings and sickness, Cicely sat at a small table in the open-air restaurant in Hyde Park, finishing her after-luncheon coffee and listening to the meritorious performance of the orchestra. Opposite her sat Larry Meadowfield, absorbed for the moment in the slow enjoyment of a cigarette, which also was not without its short-lived merits. Larry was a well-dressed youngster, who was, in Cicely's opinion, distinctly good to look on—an opinion which the boy himself obviously shared. He had the healthy, well-cared-for appearance of a country-dweller who has been turned into a town dandy without suffering in the process. His blue-black hair, growing very low down on a broad forehead, was brushed back in a smoothness that gave his head the appearance of a rain-polished sloe; his eyebrows were two dark smudges and his large violet-grey eyes expressed the restful good temper of an animal whose immediate requirements have been satisfied. The lunch had been an excellent one, and it was jolly to feed out of doors in the warm spring air—the only drawback to the arrangement being the absence of mirrors. However, if he could not look at himself a great many people could look at him.

Cicely listened to the orchestra as it jerked and strutted through a fantastic dance measure, and as she listened she looked appreciatively at the boy on the other side of the table, whose soul for the moment seemed to be in his cigarette. Her scheme of life, knowing just what you wanted and taking good care that you got it, was justifying itself by results. Ronnie, grown tiresome with success, had not been difficult to replace, and no one in her world had had the satisfaction of being able to condole with her on the undesirable experience of a long interregnum. To feminine acquaintances with fewer advantages of purse and brains and looks she might figure as 'that Yeovil woman', but never had she given them justification to allude to her as 'poor Cicely Yeovil'. And Murrey, dear old soul, had cooled down, as she had hoped and wished, from his white heat of disgust at the things that she had prepared herself to accept philosophically. A new chapter of their married life and man-and-woman friendship had opened; many a rare gallop they had had together that winter, many a cheery dinner gathering and long bridge evening in the cosy hunting-lodge. Though he still hated the new London and held himself aloof from most of her Town set, yet he had not shown himself rigidly intolerant of the sprinkling of Teuton sportsmen who hunted and shot down in his part of the country.

The orchestra finished its clicking and caracoling and was accorded a short clatter of applause.

'The *Danse Macabre*,' said Cicely to her companion; 'one of Saint-Saëns' best known pieces.'

'Is it?' said Larry indifferently; 'I'll take your word for it. 'Fraid I don't know much about music.'

'You dear boy, that's just what I like in you,' said Cicely; 'you're such a delicious young barbarian.'

'Am I?' said Larry. 'I dare say. I suppose you know.'

Larry's father had been a brilliantly clever man who had married a brilliantly handsome woman; the Fates had not had the least intention that Larry should take after both parents.

'The fashion of having one's lunch in the open air has quite caught on this season,' said Cicely; 'one sees everybody here on a fine day. There is Lady Bailquist over there. She used to be Lady Shalem, you know, before her husband got the earldom—to be more correct, before she got it for him. I suppose she is all agog to see the great review.'

It was in fact precisely the absorbing topic of the forthcoming Boy-Scout march-past that was engaging the Countess of Bailquist's earnest attention at the moment.

'It is going to be an historical occasion,' she was saying to Sir Leonard Pitherby (whose services to literature had up to the present received only a half-measure of recognition); 'if it miscarries it will be a serious set-back for the *fait accompli*. If it is a success it will be the biggest step forward in the path of reconciliation between the two races that has yet been taken. It will mean that the younger generation is on our side—not all, of course, but some, that is all we can expect at present, and that will be enough to work on.'

'Supposing the Scouts hang back and don't turn up in any numbers,' said Sir Leonard anxiously.

'That of course is the danger,' said Lady Bailquist quietly; 'probably two-thirds of the available strength will hold back, but a third or even a sixth would be enough; it would redeem the parade from the calamity of fiasco, and it would be a nucleus to work on for the future. That is what we want, a good start, a preliminary rally. It is the first step that counts, that is why to-day's event is of such importance.'

'Of course, of course, the first step on the road,' assented Sir Leonard.

'I can assure you,' continued Lady Bailquist, 'that nothing has been left undone to rally the Scouts to the new order of things. Special privileges have been showered on them, alone among all the cadet corps they have been allowed to retain their organization, a decoration of merit has been instituted for them, a large hostelry and gymnasium has been provided for them in Westminster, His Majesty's youngest son is to be their Scoutmaster-in-Chief, a great athletic meeting is to be held for them each year, with valuable prizes, three or four hundred of them are to be taken every summer, free of charge, for a holiday in the Bavarian Highlands and the Baltic Seaboard; besides this the parent of every scout who obtains the medal for efficiency is to be exempted from part of the new war taxation that the people are finding so burdensome.'

'One certainly cannot say that they have not had attractions held out to them,' said Sir Leonard.

'It is a special effort,' said Lady Bailquist; 'it is worth making an effort for. They are going to be the Janissaries of the Empire; the younger generation knocking at the doors of progress, and thrusting back the bars and bolts of old racial prejudices. I tell you, Sir Leonard, it will be an historic moment when the first corps of those little khaki-clad boys swings through the gates of the Park.'

'When do they come?' asked the baronet, catching something of his companion's zeal.

'The first detachment is due to arrive at three,' said Lady Bailquist, referring to a small time-table of the afternoon's proceedings; 'three, punctually, and the others will follow in rapid succession. The Emperor and Suite will arrive at two-fifty and take up their positions at the saluting base—over there, where the big flag-staff has been set up. The boys will come in by Hyde Park Corner, the Marble Arch, and the Albert Gate, according to their districts, and form in one big column over there, where the little flags are pegged out. Then the young Prince will inspect them and lead them past His Majesty.'

'Who will be with the Imperial party?' asked Sir Leonard.

'Oh, it is to be an important affair; everything will be done to emphasize the significance of the occasion,' said Lady Bailquist, again consulting her programme. 'The King of Würtemberg, and two of the Bavarian royal Princes, an Abyssinian Envoy who is over here—he will lend a touch of picturesque barbarism to the scene—the general commanding the London district and a whole lot of other military bigwigs, and the Austrian, Italian, and Roumanian military attachés.'

She reeled off the imposing list of notables with an air of quiet satisfaction. Sir Leonard made mental notes of personages to whom he might send presentation copies of his new work 'Frederick-William, the Great Elector, a Popular Biography', as a souvenir of to-day's auspicious event.

'It is nearly a quarter to three now,' he said; 'let us get a good position before the crowd gets thicker.'

'Come along to my car, it is just opposite to the saluting base,' said her ladyship; 'I have a police pass that will let us through. We'll ask Mrs Yeovil and her young friend to join us.'

Larry excused himself from joining the party; he had a barbarian's reluctance to assisting at an Imperial triumph.

'I think I'll push off to the swimming-bath,' he said to Cicely; 'see you again about tea-time.'

Cicely walked with Lady Bailquist and the literary baronet towards the crowd of spectators, which was steadily growing in dimensions. A newsboy ran in front of them displaying a poster with the intelligence 'Essex wickets fall rapidly'—a semblance of county cricket still survived under the new order of things. Near the saluting base some thirty or forty motor-cars were drawn up in line, and Cicely and her companions exchanged greetings with many of the occupants.

'A lovely day for the review, isn't it?' cried the Gräfin von Tolb, breaking off her conversation with Herr Rebinok, the little Pomeranian banker, who was sitting by her side. 'Why haven't you brought young Mr Meadowfield? Such a nice boy. I wanted him to come and sit in my carriage and talk to me.'

'He doesn't talk, you know,' said Cicely; 'he's only brilliant to look at.'

'Well, I could have looked at him,' said the Gräfin.

'There'll be thousands of other boys to look at presently,' said Cicely, laughing at the old woman's frankness.

'Do you think there will be thousands?' asked the Gräfin, with an anxious lowering of the voice; 'really, thousands? Hundreds, perhaps; there is some uncertainty. Every one is not sanguine.'

'Hundreds, anyway,' said Cicely.

The Gräfin turned to the little banker and spoke to him rapidly and earnestly in German.

'It is most important that we should consolidate our position in this country; we must coax the younger generation over by degrees, we must disarm their hostility. We cannot afford to be always on the watch in this quarter; it is a source of weakness, and we cannot afford to be weak. This Slav upheaval in south-eastern Europe is becoming a serious menace. Have you seen to-day's telegrams from Agram? They are bad reading. There is no computing the extent of this movement.'

'It is directed against us,' said the banker.

'Agreed,' said the Gräfin; 'it is in the nature of things that it must be against us. Let us have no illusions. Within the next ten years, sooner perhaps, we shall be faced with a crisis which will be only a beginning. We shall need all our strength; that is why we cannot afford to be weak over here. To-day is an important day; I confess I am anxious.'

'Hark! The kettledrums!' exclaimed the commanding voice of Lady Bailquist. 'His Majesty is coming. Quick, bundle into the car.'

The crowd behind the police-kept lines surged expectantly into closer formation; spectators hurried up from side-walks and stood craning their necks above the shoulders of earlier arrivals.

Through the archway at Hyde Park Corner came a resplendent cavalcade with a swirl of colour and rhythmic movement and a crash of exultant music; life-guards with gleaming helmets, a detachment of Würtemberg lancers with a flutter of black and yellow pennons, a rich medley of staff uniforms, a prancing array of princely horsemen, the Imperial Standard, and the King of Prussia, Great Britain, and Ireland, Emperor of the West. It was the most imposing display that Londoners had seen since the catastrophe.

Slowly, grandly, with thunder of music and beat of hoofs, the procession passed through the crowd, across the sward towards the saluting base, slowly the eagle standard, charged with the leopards, lion and harp of the conquered kingdoms, rose mast-high on the flag-staff and fluttered in the breeze, slowly and with military precision the troops and suite took up their position round the central figure of the great pageant. Trumpets and kettledrums suddenly ceased their music, and in a moment there rose in their stead an eager buzz of comment from the nearest spectators.

'How well the young Prince looks in his scout uniform. . . .' 'The King of Würtemberg is a much younger man than I thought he was. . . .' 'Is that a Prussian or Bavarian uniform, there on the right, the man on a black horse? . . .' 'Neither, it's Austrian, the Austrian military attaché. . . .' 'That is von Stoppel talking to His Majesty; he organized the Boy Scouts in Germany, you know. . . .' 'His Majesty is looking very pleased.' 'He has reason to look pleased; this is a great event in the history of the two countries. It marks a new epoch. . . .' 'Oh, do you see the Abyssinian Envoy? What a picturesque figure he makes. How well he sits his horse. . . .' 'That is the Grand Duke of Baden's nephew, talking to the King of Würtemberg now.'

On the buzz and chatter of the spectators fell suddenly three sound strokes, distant, measured, sinister; the clang of a clock striking three.

'Three o'clock and not a boy scout within sight or hearing!' exclaimed the loud ringing voice of Joan Mardle; 'one can usually hear their drums and trumpets a couple of miles away.'

'There is the traffic to get through,' said Sir Leonard Pitherby in an equally high-pitched voice; 'and of course,' he added vaguely, 'it takes some time to get the various units together. One must give them a few minutes' grace.'

Lady Bailquist said nothing, but her restless watchful eyes were turned first to Hyde Park Corner and then in the direction of the Marble Arch, back again to Hyde Park Corner. Only the dark lines of the waiting crowd met her view, with the yellow newspaper placards flitting in and out, announcing to an indifferent public the fate of Essex wickets. As far as her searching eyes could travel the green stretch of tree and sward remained unbroken, save by casual loiterers. No small brown columns appeared, no drum-beat came throbbing up from the distance. The little flags pegged out to mark the positions of the awaited scout-corps fluttered in meaningless isolation on the empty parade ground.

His Majesty was talking unconcernedly with one of his officers, the foreign attachés looked steadily between their chargers' ears, as though nothing in particular was hanging in the balance, the Abyssinian Envoy displayed an untroubled serenity which was probably genuine. Elsewhere among the Suite was a perceptible fidget, the more obvious because it was elaborately cloaked. Among the privileged onlookers drawn up near the saluting point the fidgeting was more unrestrained.

'Six minutes past three, and not a sign of them!' exclaimed Joan Mardle, with the explosive articulation of one who cannot any longer hold back a truth.

'Hark!' said some one; 'I hear trumpets!'

There was an instant concentration of listening, a straining of eyes. It was only the toot of a passing motor-car. Even Sir Leonard Pitherby, with the eye of faith, could not locate as much as a cloud of dust on the Park horizon.

And now another sound was heard, a sound difficult to define, without beginning, without dimension; the growing murmur of a crowd waking to a slowly dawning sensation.

'I wish the band would strike up an air,' said the Gräfin von Tolb fretfully; 'it is stupid waiting here in silence.'

Joan fingered her watch, but she made no further remark; she realized that no amount of malicious comment could be so dramatically effective now as the slow slipping away of the intolerable seconds.

The murmur from the crowd grew in volume. Some satirical wit started whistling an imitation of an advancing fife and drum band; others took it up and the air resounded with the shrill music of a phantom army on the march. The mock throbbing of drum and squealing of fife rose and fell above the packed masses of spectators, but no answering echo came from beyond the distant trees. Like mushrooms in the night a muster of uniformed police and plain clothes detectives sprang into evidence on all sides; whatever happened there must be no disloyal demonstration. The whistlers and mockers were pointedly invited to keep silence, and one or two addresses were taken.

Under the trees, well at the back of the crowd, a young man stood watching the long stretch of road along which the Scouts should come. Something had drawn him there, against his will, to witness the Imperial Triumph, to watch the writing of yet another chapter in the history of his country's submission to an accepted fact. And now a dull flush crept into his grey face; a look that was partly new-born hope and resurrected pride, partly remorse and shame, burned in his eyes. Shame, the choking, searing shame of self-reproach that cannot be reasoned away, was dominant in his heart. *He* had laid down his arms—there were others who had never hoisted the flag of surrender. He had given up the fight and joined the ranks of the hopelessly subservient; in thousands of English homes throughout the land there were young hearts that had not forgotten, had not compounded, would not yield.

The younger generation had barred the door.

And in the pleasant May sunshine the Eagle standard floated and flapped, the black and yellow pennons shifted restlessly, Emperor and Princes, Generals and guards, sat stiffly in their saddles, and waited.

And waited. . . .

OXFORD

MORE OXFORD PAPERBACKS

This book is just one of nearly 1000 Oxford Paperbacks currently in print. If you would like details of other Oxford Paperbacks, including titles in the World's Classics, Oxford Reference, Oxford Books, OPUS, Past Masters, Oxford Authors, and Oxford Shakespeare series, please write to:

UK and Europe: Oxford Paperbacks Publicity Manager, Arts and Reference Publicity Department, Oxford University Press, Walton Street, Oxford OX2 6DP.

Customers in UK and Europe will find Oxford Paperbacks available in all good bookshops. But in case of difficulty please send orders to the Cash-with-Order Department, Oxford University Press Distribution Services, Saxon Way West, Corby, Northants NN18 9ES. Tel: 01536 741519; Fax: 01536 746337. Please send a cheque for the total cost of the books, plus £1.75 postage and packing for orders under £20; £2.75 for orders over £20. Customers outside the UK should add 10% of the cost of the books for postage and packing.

USA: Oxford Paperbacks Marketing Manager, Oxford University Press, Inc., 200 Madison Avenue, New York, N.Y. 10016.

Canada: Trade Department, Oxford University Press, 70 Wynford Drive, Don Mills, Ontario M3C 1J9.

Australia: Trade Marketing Manager, Oxford University Press, G.P.O. Box 2784Y, Melbourne 3001, Victoria.

South Africa: Oxford University Press, P.O. Box 1141, Cape Town 8000.

OXFORD POPULAR FICTION

THE ORIGINAL MILLION SELLERS!

This series boasts some of the most talked-about works of British and US fiction of the last 150 years—books that helped define the literary styles and genres of crime, historical fiction, romance, adventure, and social comedy, which modern readers enjoy.

Riders of the Purple Sage	Zane Grey
The Four Just Men	Edgar Wallace
Trilby	George Du Maurier
Trent's Last Case	E C Bentley
The Riddle of the Sands	Erskine Childers
Under Two Flags	Ouida
The Lost World	Arthur Conan Doyle
The Woman Who Did	Grant Allen

Forthcoming in October:

Olive	Dinah Craik
The Diary of a Nobody	George and Weedon Grossmith
The Lodger	Belloc Lowndes
The Wrong Box	Robert Louis Stevenson

OXFORD REFERENCE

THE CONCISE OXFORD COMPANION TO ENGLISH LITERATURE

Edited by Margaret Drabble and Jenny Stringer

Based on the immensely popular fifth edition of the *Oxford Companion to English Literature* this is an indispensable, compact guide to the central matter of English literature.

There are more than 5,000 entries on the lives and works of authors, poets, playwrights, essayists, philosophers, and historians; plot summaries of novels and plays; literary movements; fictional characters; legends; theatres; periodicals; and much more.

The book's sharpened focus on the English literature of the British Isles makes it especially convenient to use, but there is still generous coverage of the literature of other countries and of other disciplines which have influenced or been influenced by English literature.

From reviews of *The Oxford Companion to English Literature*:

'a book which one turns to with constant pleasure . . . a book with much style and little prejudice' Iain Gilchrist, *TLS*

'it is quite difficult to imagine, in this genre, a more useful publication' Frank Kermode, *London Review of Books*

'incarnates a living sense of tradition . . . sensitive not to fashion merely but to the spirit of the age' Christopher Ricks, *Sunday Times*

THE OXFORD AUTHORS

General Editor: Frank Kermode

THE OXFORD AUTHORS is a series of authoritative editions of major English writers. Aimed at both students and general readers, each volume contains a generous selection of the best writings—poetry, prose, and letters—to give the essence of a writer's work and thinking. All the texts are complemented by essential notes, an introduction, chronology, and suggestions for further reading.

Matthew Arnold
William Blake
Lord Byron
John Clare
Samuel Taylor Coleridge
John Donne
John Dryden
Ralph Waldo Emerson
Thomas Hardy
George Herbert and Henry Vaughan
Gerard Manley Hopkins
Samuel Johnson
Ben Jonson
John Keats
Andrew Marvell
John Milton
Alexander Pope
Sir Philip Sidney
Oscar Wilde
William Wordsworth